U0085545

全民英檢 聽力測驗 SO EASY

中級篇

三民英語編輯小組　彙編

最新穎！符合全新改版英檢題型
最逼真！模擬試題提升應試能力
最精闢！範例分析傾授高分技巧

 附　解答本
　　電子朗讀音檔

三民書局

為反映 108 新課綱「素養」精神及「2030 雙語國家政策」，財團法人語言訓練測驗中心 (LTTC) 推出全民英檢 (GEPT) 新題型。期待考生可以透過標準參照 (criterion-referenced) 測驗、選擇適合自己的級數、精準評量英語能力。

新題型內容更加生活化，同時亦融入多元體裁和文本，藉此評量英語溝通及解決問題的能力。因此，我們分析 LTTC 所公告之考試資訊，為本書打造全新內容，以期考生能得到全面、充分的練習。

英語文學習之道無它，唯勤而已。事前準備和練習有助於考試的過關；所謂「臨陣磨槍，不快也光」亦即如此。而日常實力的累積，語言四技的均衡使用及持之有恆的態度和做法更是成功的不二法門！在我們開始進一步解析全民英檢聽力測驗（中級篇）之前，希望這番「老生常談」能對正要參加或準備參加全民英檢的考生有所啟發。

全民英檢中級聽力測驗簡介

全民英檢中級聽力測驗題型介紹：共分為四個部份，總作答時間約 30 分鐘。

第一部份：看圖辨義

共 5 題。每一圖畫搭配 1～3 個描述該圖的題目，需要仔細聆聽題目以及四個英語敘述後，選出與所看到的圖畫最相符的答案。每題只播出一遍。

第二部份：問答

共 10 題。每題音檔會播出一英語問句或直述句，考生需從試題冊上 A、B、C、D 四個回答（或回應）中，選出一個最適合者作答。每題只播出一遍。

第三部份：簡短對話

共 10 題。每題音檔會播出一段對話及一個相關的問題，考生需從試題冊上 A、B、C、D 中選出最適合的選項作答。每段對話及問題只播出一遍。

第四部份：簡短談話

共 10 題。每題音檔會播出一段談話及一個相關的問題後，考生需從試題冊上 A、B、C、D 中選出最適合的選項作答。每段談話及問題只播出一遍。

全民英檢中級成績計算：

測驗項目	聽力	閱讀	加考項目	寫作	口說
通過標準	兩項測驗成績總和達 160 分，且其中任一項成績不低於 72 分。			80 分	80 分
滿分	120 分	120 分		100 分	100 分

現在我們已經了解中級聽力測驗的題型和通過標準了！
讓我們從「範例分析」開始攻破各大題後，進入「實戰練習」吧。

＊詳細資訊請至全民英檢官方網站查詢。

電子朗讀音檔下載

請先輸入網址或掃描 QR code 進入「三民・東大音檔網」
https://elearning.sanmin.com.tw/Voice/

① 輸入本書書名即可找到音檔。請再依提示下載音檔。

② 也可點擊「英文」進入英文專區查找音檔後下載。

③ 若無法順利下載音檔，可至「常見問題」查看相關問題。

④ 若有音檔相關問題，請點擊「聯絡我們」，將盡快為你處理。

⑤ 更多英文新知都在臉書粉絲專頁。

All pictures in this publication are authorized for use by Shutterstock & 谷佩純 & 李吳宏 .

CONTENTS

全民英檢聽力測驗
SO EASY（中級篇）

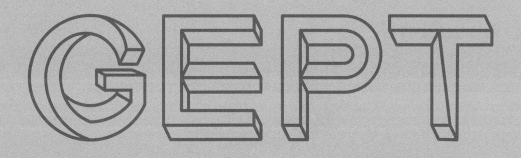

聽力測驗試題範例分析

第一部份：看圖辨義

　　此部份的聽力題目圍繞在一張情境圖片上，每張圖片具備一定程度的線索，供答題者作答。試題融入素養精神，題目取材更貼近日常生活，因此只要熟悉日常生活用語與常用句型，便能理解文意、輕鬆應試。題目通常會針對情境圖片的概述和整體印象 (overview, general impression)、特定的資訊和細節 (specific information, details) 或從已知事實推論 (inference) 提問；而問題形式不外乎為 "What"、"Where"、"When"、"Who"、"Why"、"How"、"How + adj." 等疑問詞。

　　請特別注意：問題與選項完全以「聽力」的方式呈現，不會有文字在試卷上。因此，在作答前先快速瀏覽圖片的細節，掌握圖片中的情境，就能預測試題方向。

　　以下我們就以五個範例來介紹各種題型與答題技巧吧！

A. Question 1

TRACK 0-1

For question number 1, please look at picture A.

Question number 1: Where are these people?

A. In a library.

B. In a circus.

C. In a hospital.

D. In a museum.

翻 譯

第一題,請看圖片 A。

第一題:這些人在哪裡?

選項:A. 在圖書館。

　　　B. 在馬戲團。

　　　C. 在醫院。

　　　D. 在博物館。

解 析

這題的第一個字是疑問詞 "Where",詢問「地點」。根據圖片資訊所示,觀眾正在看小丑雜耍和大象特技等表演。因此可以判斷這裡是在馬戲團,故答案選 B。

答 案　　B

B. Question 2

For question number 2, please look at picture B.

Question number 2: What might Ben be saying?

A. What's up?

B. Get over it!

C. Make up your mind!

D. That's enough.

翻 譯

第二題，請看圖片 B。

第二題：Ben 可能正在說什麼？

選項：A. 近來如何？

B. 克服它！

C. 下定決心吧！

D. 不要這樣，夠了。

解 析

這題的關鍵字是 "What might" 和 "saying"，由此可以得知要考的題目是 Ben 可能正在說什麼。根據圖片資訊所示，可以看出教室一團糟的現象，有學生在玩紙飛機，有學生舉起椅子，地板上有紙屑；觀察圖片中 Ben 的表情和動作，可以得知他不高興，選項 A、B、C 和本題情境不符，故答案選 D。

答 案　D

C. Question 3

RECEIPT	
1. Sugar	$90
2. Milk	$150
3. Rice	$130
4. Tissue	$120
5. Cheese	$100
*****************************	
TOTAL	$590

For question number 3, please look at picture C.

Question number 3: How much is it for dairy?

A. $100.

B. $150.

C. $250.

D. $590.

翻 譯

第三題，請看圖片 C。

第三題：乳製品要花多少錢？

選項：A. 100 美元。

B. 150 美元。

C. 250 美元。

D. 590 美元。

解 析

這題的第一個字是疑問詞 "How much"，詢問乳製品「多少錢」。根據圖片資訊所示，購買的乳製品分別為牛奶 ($150) 和起司 ($100)，合計為 250 美元，故答案選 C。

答 案　　C

D. Questions 4 and 5

For questions number 4 and 5, please look at picture D.

Question number 4: Why is this poster being displayed?

A. The store is going out of business.

B. These shoes are no longer fashionable.

C. The store is competing with other shoe stores.

D. The store owner is promoting some new products.

翻 譯

第四題及第五題,請看圖片 D。

第四題:這張海報為何會被貼出?

選項:A. 這家店將要歇業。

　　　B. 這些鞋子不再流行。

　　　C. 這家店與其他鞋店競爭。

　　　D. 老闆在推廣一些新產品。

解 析

接下來的第四題及第五題是從一張圖片考兩個問題。根據圖片資訊所示,可以馬上判斷這是一家鞋店的櫥窗;櫥窗上貼著海報,上面寫著歇業大拍賣 (Closing down sale!)、商品全面五折等特價訊息。這題的第一個字是疑問詞 "Why",詢問這張海報「為什麼」會被貼出,從圖片中可以得知本店正在進行歇業大拍賣,故答案選 A。

答 案　　**A**

Question number 5: Please look at picture D again. When will the special offer end?

A. Before stocks are low.

B. After the store owner comes to the store.

C. When the store is bought by someone.

D. When everything has been sold.

翻 譯

第五題：請再看一次圖片 D。

這特惠價將何時結束？

選項：A. 在庫存低之前。

B. 在老闆來店家之後。

C. 當店面被某人買走的時候。

D. 當所有東西都賣完時。

解 析

這題的第一個字是疑問詞 "When"，詢問這特惠價「什麼時候」結束。根據圖片資訊所示，當有庫存時 (while stocks last) 商品全面五折，也就是當所有東西都賣完時，特惠價就結束，故答案選 D。

答 案　　D

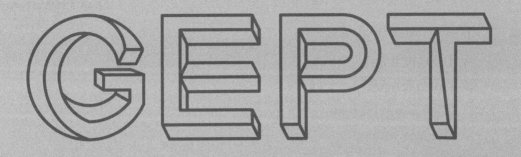

聽力測驗試題範例分析

第二部份：問答

　　此部份的聽力題目只有「一句話」。聽完題目後，答題者須在試卷上列出的四個選項中，選出一個最適當的回應。

　　問答題主要是評量答題者能否理解題目中的問句或直述句以及說話者的語氣及態度，情境多與日常生活相關，我們可以將這部份的題目分為三種：直述句、Wh- 問句和非 Wh- 問句，並且針對該句的情境，去思考最適當的回應以選出正確的答案。

　　請特別注意：這部份所有的選項會呈現在試卷上。因此，音檔播放前可以先快速瀏覽選項細節來判斷及預測問題屬性，但同時也要留意選項間的關聯並小心容易造成誤判的選項。

　　以下我們就以五個範例來介紹各種題型與答題技巧吧！

1 This room is in a mess!

A. I'll tidy it up!
B. Don't let go!
C. Take a quick break.
D. Behave yourself.

翻 譯

這房間真是一團亂！
A. 我會整理乾淨的！
B. 別放手！
C. 休息一下。
D. 規矩點。

解 析

這題可以判斷出是一個直述句，而非疑問句。由這一句可以看出說話者表達房間很髒亂而感到不滿。選項 A 直接回應題目，表示會整理乾淨的，而其他選項與題目完全不相關，故答案選 A。

答 案　**A**

2 Do you have any change for the locker?

A. Yes, I need a break!
B. I only have a ten-dollar bill.
C. No, I'm just the same as before.
D. I'm taller than I was last month.

翻 譯

你有零錢投置物櫃嗎？
A. 是的，我需要休息！
B. 我只有一張 10 元鈔票。
C. 不，我還是一如往昔。
D. 我的身高比上個月還高。

說話者詢問是否有零錢。選項 B 直接回應題目，表示「我只有一張 10 元鈔票。」，而其他選項與題目完全不相關，故答案選 B。

答案 **B**

3 What's the matter between you two?

    A. You can count on me!

    B. Let's get something to eat.

    C. Today's my birthday.

    D. Tom and I just broke up.

翻譯

你們兩人間發生什麼事了？

A. 你可以依賴我！

B. 我們找點東西吃。

C. 今天是我的生日。

D. Tom 和我剛分手了。

解析

這題的關鍵字是 "What" 和 "matter"，如果有聽到這兩個字，就知道這題想問發生什麼事。選項 D 直接回答到問題，表示他們兩人分手，而選項 C 雖有提到今天是他的生日，但並不是針對這個問句所做的回應，而其他選項也與題目完全不相關，故答案選 D。

答案 **D**

4 Why are you going to the doctor?

    A. I'm getting my hair cut.

    B. I'm on my way to the hospital.

    C. I want to get a flu shot.

    D. I don't think I'll have time.

翻 譯

你為什麼去看醫生？

A. 我要剪頭髮。

B. 我正在前往醫院的路上。

C. 我要打流感疫苗。

D. 我不認為我會有空閒時間。

解 析

這題為 "Why" 開頭的 Wh- 問句，詢問原因。因此在回答問題時，要針對問題本身回答為什麼，故答案選 C，去看醫生的原因是要去打流感疫苗。

答 案　　**C**

5　　How have you been lately?

A. Pretty good, thanks.

B. No, I was right on time.

C. I need a new alarm clock!

D. I only just got here.

翻 譯

你最近過得好嗎？

A. 很好，謝謝你。

B. 不，我剛好準時抵達。

C. 我需要一個新鬧鐘！

D. 我才剛到這裡。

解 析

這題為 "How" 開頭的問句，通常是問感覺或對人、事、物的喜好或厭惡程度。例如：本題詢問「你最近過得好嗎？」，是一個典型的問候語，因此在回答問題時，要告知對方的是好或不好或問候對方，才算是一個得體的回答。問候他人和回答社交用語時，通常不會告知對方自己過得不好，而會禮貌性地表示很好，因此選項 A 為正確答案。

答 案　　**A**

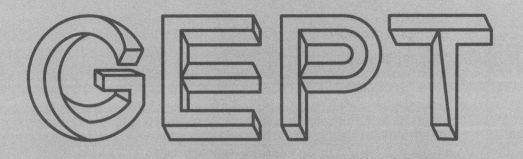

聽力測驗試題範例分析

第三部份：簡短對話

此部份的聽力題目是一段簡短的兩人對話。除了聆聽對話外，全民英檢新增「圖表題」，答題者必須具備整合聽與讀資訊的能力。

答題者聆聽一段四到八句的對話內容後，從四個選項中選出一個最適當的答案。對話包含各式各樣的情境，以日常生活對話為主，例如：與家人、朋友、同事、老闆或同學間的對話，因此平常就可培養日常生活的口語對話能力。

請特別注意：這部份所有的選項會呈現在試卷上。簡短對話的內容較長、複雜，說話者也可能會以暗示的語句表達意思，因此答題者要能分析訊息之間的關聯。圖表題看似困難，但把握題目播放前的時間，快速瀏覽圖表和選項，就能掌握先機。

題目通常以疑問詞為主，包含 "What"、"Where"、"When"、"Who"、"Why"、"How"、"How + adj." 等不同的 Wh- 問句和非 Wh- 問句，必須了解對話細節及理解對話者之間的關係，才能選出最適合的答案。

以下我們就以五個範例來介紹各種題型與答題技巧吧！

1

W: Are you sure you've checked everywhere, including the bathroom? Why not take another look?

M: Yes! I've searched the whole room, closets, curtains, and everywhere several times, including our suitcases and the pockets of our clothes.

W: Try dialing the number. We may be able to hear it ringing.

M: That was the first thing I tried. It just rings and goes to voicemail.

W: Oh, no.

Q: Where do the man and woman seem to be?

A. At a train station.

B. In a hotel room.

C. In an airport lounge.

D. At an electronics store.

翻 譯

女：你確定你每個地方都找過了，連浴室裡都看過了？為何不再多找一次？

男：有！整個房間、壁櫥櫃、窗簾、到處我都已經查找過好幾次了，包含我們的行李箱和我們衣服的口袋。

女：試著撥打電話。我們或許能聽到它的鈴聲。

男：那是我第一個試圖做的事。它響鈴後就進語音信箱了。

女：喔，不。

問題：男子和女子可能在何處？

選項：A. 在火車車站。

　　　B. 在飯店房間。

　　　C. 在機場候機室。

　　　D. 在電子器材商店。

解 析

這題的第一個字是疑問詞 "Where"，用來詢問「地點」。從對話的本身類推尋找線索，對話內容在尋找手機，而當我們聽到 "bathroom"、"the whole room"、"closets"、"suitcase" 這幾個關鍵字時，可以判斷對話場景是飯店房間，故答案選 B。

答 案　　**B**

2

M: Have you filled out that job application form yet?

W: It's on my desk. I'll do it on the weekend.

M: But today's only Tuesday. Is there any special reason you want to delay applying for that position?

W: I will get around to finishing it, I promise. I just have a bunch of other stuff that needs to get done first.

M: You mean like binge-watching Korean dramas?

W: Yeah, that and other things as well.

Q: What does the man want the woman to do first?

A. Watching latest TV dramas.

B. Explaining the reason for being late.

C. Helping around the house.

D. Applying for a job.

翻 譯

男：你填好工作申請的表格了嗎？

女：在我桌上。我會在週末填好它。

男：但今天才週二。有什麼特殊原因讓你想要延遲申請這份工作嗎？

女：我會找時間完成它，我保證。我只是還有其他很多事要先完成。

男：你是說追韓劇嗎？

女：是啊，這件事還有其他事也一樣。

問題：男子希望女子先做什麼事？

選項：A. 看最新的電視劇。

B. 解釋遲到的理由。

C. 幫忙整理家務。

D. 申請一份工作。

解 析

這題的第一個字是疑問詞 "What"，用來詢問「什麼」。在一段對話之後問這樣的問題，可以判斷想問對話主旨，並需要從整段對話內容去判斷答案。綜觀對話可知男子希望女子盡快申請工作。選項 A 則是誘答選項，選項 A 中出現了 "dramas"，是在對話中出現的字；而其他選項與題目不相關，故答案選 D。

答 案　　D

13

3

W: Have you ever thought about settling down?

M: How do you mean? Get married and have kids?

W: That's right. But I guess your answer is "no" then.

M: Actually, I have considered it, but I'm only 29. I think I'd like to get married in my mid-thirties.

W: I see.

Q: When does the man say he will get married?

A. In his forties.

B. At the age of 29.

C. When his girlfriend is thirty.

D. Maybe in about ten years.

翻 譯

女：你有想過要定下來嗎？

男：什麼意思？結婚和生小孩？

女：對啊。但我猜你的答案是「不」。

男：事實上，我曾想過，但我才二十九歲。我想我會在三十幾歲的時候結婚。

女：了解。

問題：男子說他什麼時候會結婚？

選項：A. 在他四十幾歲的時候。

B. 二十九歲的時候。

C. 當他女友三十歲的時候。

D. 或許在十年內。

解 析

這題的第一個字是疑問詞 "When"，用來詢問「時間」。必須從對話的本身去尋找線索。這題的對話內容是在討論何時要定下來結婚生子。根據對話內容男子現在二十九歲，並且會在三十幾歲的時候結婚，由此可以推估出十年內或許會結婚，故答案選 D。

答 案   D

4

M: What is that on your arm?

W: I don't know. I have several on my back, too.

M: I'm not a doctor, but that doesn't look right to me. I think you ought to have a medical examination.

W: Well, it has been quite itchy for the past few weeks.

M: That's not a good sign. It may need to be removed.

W: I'll make an appointment tomorrow.

Q: Why is the man concerned?

A. He doesn't trust the woman.

B. He kept scratching his arm.

C. He thinks the woman is not looking after herself.

D. He noticed something wrong with the woman's skin.

翻 譯

男：你的手臂上的是什麼？

女：我不知道。我背上也有好幾個。

男：我不是醫生，但那在我看來不太正常。我覺得你應該去做醫療檢查。

女：嗯，它已經癢了好幾週了。

男：那不是個好現象。它可能需要被移除。

女：我明天會去預約。

問題：男子為何會擔心？

選項：A. 他不信任女子。

　　　B. 他一直在抓他的手臂。

　　　C. 他認為女子沒有照顧她自己。

　　　D. 他注意到女子的皮膚有問題。

解 析

這題的第一個字是疑問詞 "Why"，用來詢問「為什麼」，為何男子會擔心。對話內容是在討論女子的皮膚問題，而且已經持續好幾週了，故答案選 D。

答 案　　D

5 For question number 5, please look at the railway timetable.

W: Excuse me. Is the next train on time?

M: Yes, it will leave at 2 p.m.

W: 2 p.m.? Is this the right platform for Taichung?

M: No, this is the platform for Taipei.

Q: Which train will the woman travel by?

Time	No.	Destination	Status
13:30	609	Tainan	Delayed
13:45	503	Taichung	On Time
14:00	271	Taipei	On Time
14:15	308	Hualien	On Time

A. Train No. 609.
B. Train No. 503.
C. Train No. 271.
D. Train No. 308.

翻譯

第五題，請看火車時刻表。

女：不好意思。請問下一班火車準點嗎？

男：是的，下午兩點會出發。

女：下午兩點？這是往臺中的月臺嗎？

男：不是，這是往臺北的月臺。

問題：女子會搭乘哪一班火車？

選項：A. 609 車次列車。

B. 503 車次列車。

C. 271 車次列車。

D. 308 車次列車。

時間	車次	目的地	狀態
13:30	609	臺南	誤點
13:45	503	臺中	準點
14:00	271	臺北	準點
14:15	308	花蓮	準點

解析

這題的第一個字是疑問詞 "which"，用來詢問「哪一個」，詢問女子要搭乘哪輛火車。由對話可知女子是要去開往臺中的月臺；根據火車時刻表，開往臺中的火車應該是 13:45 的 503 車次列車，故答案選 B。

答案　　B

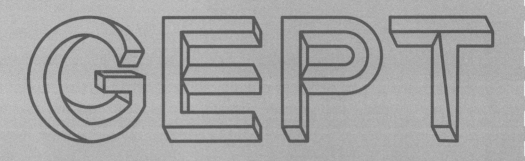

聽力測驗試題範例分析

第四部份：簡短談話

　　此部份的聽力題目為一段短文。全民英檢官方最新題型亦新增「圖表題」，需整合理解聽、讀的資訊作答。其情境多元，包含電話留言、演講、報導、公共場所廣播、宣布事項、廣播節目和廣告等。短文內容皆以聽力的方式呈現，在試卷上不會有文字敘述。

　　請特別注意：簡短談話的聽力內容雖然較長，但和「第三部份：簡短對話」相比，「第四部份：簡短談話」敘述單一情境，所以仔細聆聽並理解內容，就能掌握內容的重點，選出正確答案。在題目開始播放前，可以先快速瀏覽四個選項，來預測試題方向。音檔播放簡短談話後，就會播出問題。聽完內容後，必須根據問題與內容的關鍵字來找出最適合的選項作答。

　　以下我們就以五個範例來介紹各種題型與答題技巧吧！

🎧 TRACK 0-4

1

I used to be very afraid of flying. During the flight, I would always imagine that something would go wrong with the plane. However, without flying, I wouldn't have been able to visit so many wonderful countries. What I really needed was a way to overcome my fear of flying, but I had no idea how to do it. I took a pill to calm me down before flights, but I did not want to depend on drugs. In the end, the solution was something I never would have believed—I signed up for flying lessons. That was ten years ago. Now, I'm a pilot, and I absolutely love flying. Problem solved!

Q: Which of the following is true about the speaker?

A. She used to be a crazy passenger.

B. She is still afraid of flying.

C. She flies planes for a living now.

D. She has never been overseas.

翻譯

我以前很怕搭飛機。在飛行途中，我會一直想像飛機出了問題。然而，如果不搭飛機，我就沒辦法去很多很棒的國家了。我真正需要的是一種能讓我克服飛行恐懼的方法，但我想不到該怎麼做。我會在飛行前吞顆藥讓自己鎮定下來，但我不想依賴藥物。最後，解決方式是我當時絕不會相信的——我報名了飛行課程。那是十年前的事了。現在，我是一名飛行員，而且我超愛飛行。問題解決！

問題：下列有關說話者的描述，何者正確？

選項：A. 她以前是個瘋狂的乘客。

　　　B. 她現在還害怕搭飛機。

　　　C. 她現在以開飛機為生。

　　　D. 她從未出過國。

解析

這題問 "Which of the following is true about the speaker?"。必須要聽懂整段談話內容去判斷答案。選項 C 符合談話內容，說話者現在是一名飛行員。至於選項 B 則是誘答選項，選項 B 中出現了 "afraid"，是談話中出現的字，但她現在已不害怕搭飛機；而其他選項與題目不符合，故答案選 C。

答案　　C

2 People used to rely on typewriters to type letters or documents. However, in the digital age, people use computers to do all the paperwork, and typewriters are rarely seen. Therefore, it is very rare to find a typewriter in good condition, and typewriters have become quite valuable. Some collectors even search websites and markets for typewriters and pay hundreds or thousands of dollars for them.

Q: Why are typewriters treasured by collectors?

A. They are worthless.

B. They are rare and valuable.

C. It is easy to find one on the Internet.

D. They are more popular than computers.

翻譯

以前人們都依賴打字機打信件或文件。然而，到了數位時代，人們用電腦處理所有的文書工作，打字機便難得一見了。因此，要找到一部操作狀況良好的打字機非常難得，而這也使得打字機變得非常珍貴。有一些收藏家甚至會在網站和市場中搜尋打字機，並以數百或數千元的代價收購。

問題：為什麼收藏家認為打字機值得珍藏？

選項：A. 它們毫無價值。

B. 它們稀有又珍貴。

C. 在網路上很容易就能找到它們。

D. 它們比電腦更受歡迎。

解析

這題的第一個字是疑問詞 "Why"，「為什麼」收藏家認為打字機值得珍藏？由談話中的 "rare to find" 以及 "become quite valuable" 可以得知因為它們稀有又珍貴，收藏家才願意花錢購買，故答案選 B。

答案 **B**

3 Good morning, parents! What are you doing with the children this weekend? Why not come to our farm? We have a lot of fun stuff to keep your kids happy all day. The children can feed the goats, watch the cows being milked, ride a horse, help to make our special goat cheese, and learn about nature on our twice daily hikes around the farm. For more information, check out our website or give us a call!

Q: Which of the following activities is not offered by the farm?

A. Hiking.
B. Riding horses.
C. Fruit picking.
D. Making goat cheese.

翻譯

早安,各位父母!這個週末跟孩子有什麼活動呢?何不來我們的農場一遊?我們有很多有趣的東西可以讓你們的孩子快樂一整天。孩子可以餵山羊、觀看擠牛奶、騎馬、幫忙製作我們特別的山羊起司,和藉由我們一天兩次、環繞農場的健行活動認識大自然。如果需要更多資訊,就到我們的官網或打電話給我們!

問題:下列哪項活動農場並未提供?

選項:A. 健行。
　　　B. 騎馬。
　　　C. 採水果。
　　　D. 製作山羊起司。

解析

這題的關鍵字是 "Which" 和 "not",如果有聽到這兩個字,就可以了解這題想問是哪一項沒有。這題在詢問哪項活動農場並未提供,而談話內容並未提及選項 C,故答案選 C。

答案 C

4 Did you know you can make pizza in a frying pan in a short time? All the ingredients are easy to find in a supermarket. Here's how you make it. For the pizza base, add a little baking powder to the flour and then slowly mix the butter into the flour with your fingers. Next, make the dough a ball and roll it into a flat circle. Once that's done, fry the pizza base in a little oil until it turns brown on the bottom. Finally, add tomato sauce and cheese on top, put a lid on the frying pan and wait about 3 minutes until all the cheese has melted. Bon appétit!

Q: What is the best name for this pizza?

A. Three-minute Pizza.

B. Traditional Pizza.

C. Quick and Easy Pizza.

D. Fast Food Pizza.

翻 譯

你知道你可以用平底鍋在短時間內製作披薩嗎?所有的食材在超市都可輕易找到。這裡告訴你如何製作。製作披薩餅皮時,加入些許泡打粉至麵粉裡,然後慢慢地用手指將奶油和麵粉混合。接下來,將麵團揉成球狀,再擀成扁平的圓形。完成後,用少許的油煎披薩餅皮,直到底部變棕色為止。最後,在餅皮上加上番茄醬和起司,用蓋子蓋住平底鍋,等三分鐘左右,直到起司都融化為止。用餐愉快!

問題:這個披薩的最佳名稱是什麼?

選項:A. 三分鐘的披薩。

　　　B. 傳統的披薩。

　　　C. 快速簡單的披薩。

　　　D. 速食披薩。

解 析

這題的第一個字是疑問詞 "What",詢問這個披薩的最佳名稱「是什麼」?由談話中的 "in a short time" 以及 "ingredients are easy to find" 可知披薩的製作可以在短時間內完成且過程中也相當簡單,故答案選 C。至於選項 A 則是誘答選項,選項 A 中出現了 "Three-minute",是談話中出現的內容,但內容是說要等三分鐘讓起司融化,而非三分鐘就可以將披薩製作完成。

答案 C

5 For question number 5, please look at the flight schedule.

This is the final boarding call for passengers Emma Spenser and Bob Williams booked on Flight PA208 to London. Please proceed to Gate A5 immediately. The final checks are being completed, and the doors of the aircraft will be closed in about fifteen minutes. I repeat. This is the final boarding call for Emma Spenser and Bob Williams. Thank you.

Q: When will Emma Spenser and Bob Williams' flight take off?

A. At 12:30.
B. At 13:30.
C. At 14:00.
D. At 14:30.

Departures

Time	Destination	Gate	Flight
12:30	New York	A4	PE820
13:30	Paris	C2	JX536
14:00	London	A5	PA208
14:30	Sidney	D3	AK487

翻譯

第五題，請看航班時刻表。

這是對飛往倫敦 PA208 航班的乘客 Emma Spenser 和 Bob Williams 的最後登機廣播。請立刻前往 A5 登機門。最後檢查正要完成，飛機艙門將在大約十五分鐘內關閉。重複。這是對 Emma Spenser 和 Bob Williams 的最後登機廣播。謝謝你。

問題：Emma Spenser 和 Bob Williams 的航班將於何時起飛？

選項：A. 12:30。
B. 13:30。
C. 14:00。
D. 14:30。

起飛

時間	目的地	登機門	航班
12:30	紐約	A4	PE820
13:30	巴黎	C2	JX536
14:00	倫敦	A5	PA208
14:30	雪梨	D3	AK487

解析

這題的第一個字是疑問詞 "When"，詢問航班起飛「時間」。由廣播內容可知 Emma Spenser 和 Bob Williams 是搭乘飛往倫敦、登機門在 A5 的 PA208 航班；而根據航班時刻表，此航班將在 14:00 起飛，故答案選 C。

答案 C

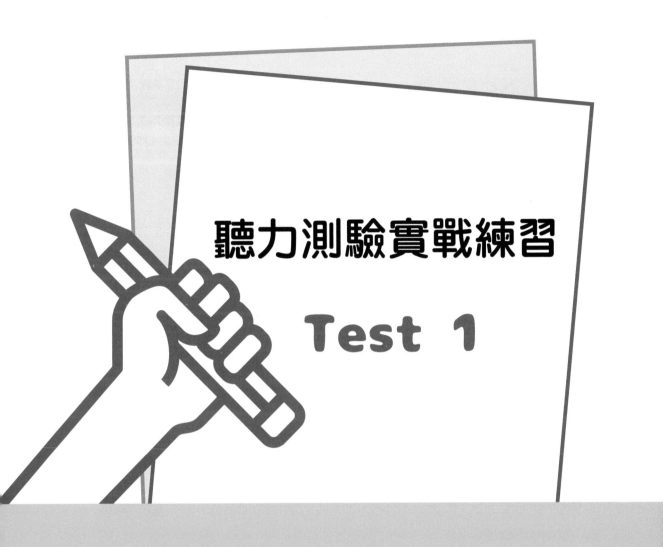

聽力測驗實戰練習

Test 1

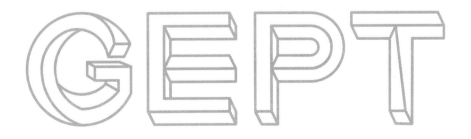

本測驗分四部份，全為四選一之選擇題，共 35 題，作答時間約 30 分鐘。

GEPT

🎧 TRACK 1-1

第一部份：看圖辨義

共 5 題，試題冊上有數幅圖畫，每一圖畫有 1～3 個描述該圖的題目，每題請聽音檔播出題目以及四個英語敘述之後，選出與所看到的圖畫最相符的答案，每題只播出一遍。

A. Question 1

1. _____

B. Question 2

2. _____

C. Questions 3 and 4

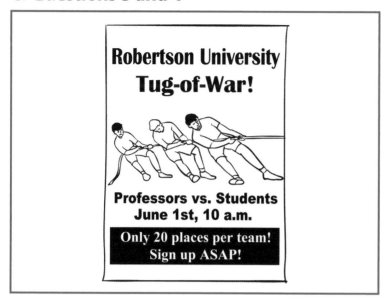

3. _____

4. _____

D. Question 5

5. _____

🎧 TRACK 1-2

第二部份：問答

共 10 題，每題請聽音檔播出一英語問句或直述句之後，從試題冊上 A、B、C、D 四個回答或回應中，選出一個最適合者作答。每題只播出一遍。

_____ 6. A. No way. I haven't been to Italy.

B. Why not? Sushi is always the best.

C. Cool. I'll call and make a reservation.

D. Sure! I would love to travel there one day.

_____ 7. A. Thank you.

B. You bet!

C. Do I have to call him?

D. I think so.

_____ 8. A. The one is the latest version.

B. My parents like to play games.

C. I played games last weekend.

D. It's the best game I have ever seen.

_____ 9. A. I am learning to cook.

B. I run a toy company.

C. I'm very well, thanks.

D. I finally found my smartphone.

_____ 10. A. I'm available now.

B. I don't have the slightest idea.

C. My watch says 1 p.m.

D. I am late for work.

_____ 11. A. It's all Greek to me.

B. Sorry, I missed your phone.

C. Yeah, you deserve a medal.

D. Thank you. That's my birthday present.

_____ 12. A. I'll call the technician.

   B. I'll see if I can get some.

   C. The machine doesn't work.

   D. The battery needs to be charged.

_____ 13. A. It is a suitable place to live.

   B. I can't wait to go to the new school.

   C. I decide to transfer to a new office.

   D. I am not happy with the environment here.

_____ 14. A. I'm jealous!

   B. We've had enough.

   C. Stop lying to me!

   D. I'm not making it up!

_____ 15. A. Watch your step.

   B. What's the matter?

   C. No way! I'm on a diet.

   D. All right. Just one sip.

第三部份：簡短對話   🎧 TRACK 1-3

   共 10 題，每題請聽音檔播出一段對話及一個相關的問題後，從試題冊上 A、B、C、D 四個選項中選出一個最適合者作答。每段對話及問題只播出一遍。

_____ 16. A. Organic food is healthier.

   B. Chemicals help plants grow better.

   C. Chemicals are necessary in vegetable gardens.

   D. Not all vegetables are good for you.

_____ 17. A. Mary didn't provide a clear statement.

   B. Mary will work in an office straight down the road.

   C. He doesn't know what type of job Mary was offered.

   D. He owes Mary a lunch for giving him a lift.

_____ 18. A. She worked as a nurse.

　　B. She chopped off one of her fingers.

　　C. She burned her hand while cooking.

　　D. She injured herself accidentally.

_____ 19. A. At a tea shop.

　　B. At a coffee shop.

　　C. In a convenience store.

　　D. In a supermarket.

_____ 20. A. Take nothing.

　　B. Take some special herbs.

　　C. Go to see the Chinese medical physician.

　　D. Get some medicine from the pharmacy.

_____ 21. A. He doesn't know what else to do.

　　B. He wants to make a fortune.

　　C. He agrees with the woman's suggestion.

　　D. He is interested in doing business.

_____ 22. A. At the electronics store.

　　B. On his desk.

　　C. In the trash can.

　　D. In the blender.

_____ 23. A. She wants to try a new diet.

　　B. Her jeans are now too tight.

　　C. The man teased her about her figure.

　　D. She bought a pair of large-sized jeans.

_____ 24.

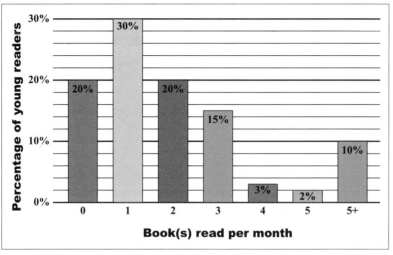

A. Reading 1 book every day.

B. Reading less than 1 book a month.

C. Reading more than 1 book a month.

D. Reading more than 5 books a month.

_____ 25.

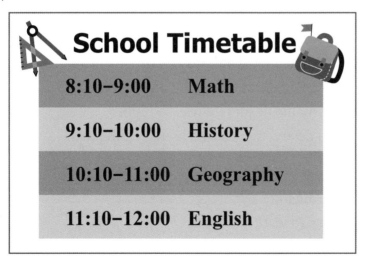

A. The math class.

B. The history class.

C. The geography class.

D. The English class.

🎧TRACK 1-4

第四部份：簡短談話

共 10 題，每題請聽音檔播出一段談話及一個相關的問題後，從試題冊上 A、B、C、D 四個選項中選出一個最適合者作答。每段談話及問題只播出一遍。

_____ 26. A. It is nonsense.

B. It is a weird theory.

C. It has countless stars.

D. It has not been proven yet.

_____ 27. A. Paying more attention to advertisements.

B. Paying a lot of money for mobile games.

C. Losing the ability to hold a conversation.

D. Losing temper with close friends.

_____ 28. A. To pay attention to the ingredients.

B. To eat animal products carefully.

C. To mix together the meat, onion, and garlic.

D. To enjoy cheese and eggs from Taiwan.

_____ 29. A. The influence on the local culture.

B. The difficult rescues after the earthquake.

C. The reasons why the death rate was so high.

D. The death and destruction caused by the earthquake.

_____ 30. A. He tries to avoid it.

B. He enjoys learning it.

C. He finds it easy to learn.

D. He improves his English.

_____ 31. A. They are dirty.

B. They lick your face.

C. They are always hungry.

D. They follow you everywhere.

_____ 32. A. Flying helicopters will cost much.

B. More people will use selfie sticks.

C. Selfie drones will become cheaper.

D. People will be good at photography.

_____ 33. A. Smartphones.

B. Education.

C. Homework.

D. PE classes.

_____ 34.

A. 1 egg.

B. Flour.

C. White sugar.

D. Unsalted butter.

_____ 35.

> **You are invited to**
> **a party honoring**
> **Jerry White**
> **as the new president**
> **of Sanmin University**
>
> Saturday, January 26th
> 6:30 p.m.–9:30 p.m.
> MCA Center

A. The time of the party.
B. The location of the party.
C. The entrance fee to the party.
D. The purpose of the party.

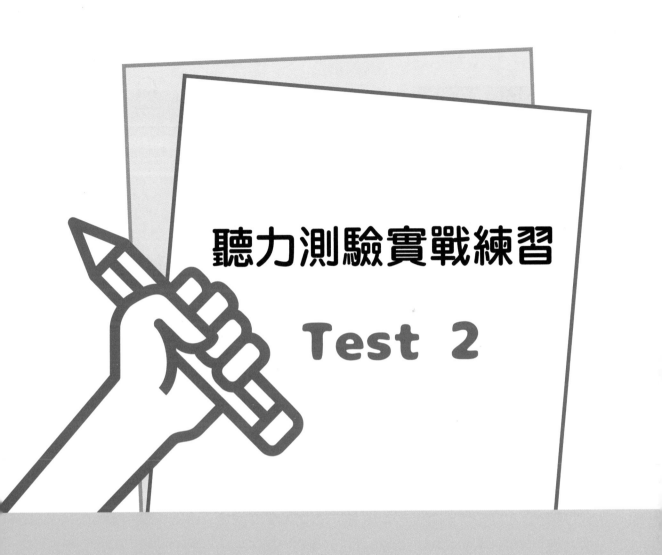

聽力測驗實戰練習

Test 2

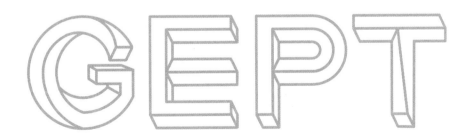

本測驗分四部份，全為四選一之選擇題，共 35 題，作答時間約 30 分鐘。

GEPT

🎧 TRACK 2-1

第一部份：看圖辨義

　　共 5 題，試題冊上有數幅圖畫，每一圖畫有 1～3 個描述該圖的題目，每題請聽音檔播出題目以及四個英語敘述之後，選出與所看到的圖畫最相符的答案，每題只播出一遍。

A. Questions 1 and 2

1. _____

2. _____

B. Question 3

3. _____

C. Question 4

4. _____

D. Question 5

5. _____

第二部份：問答

共 10 題，每題請聽音檔播出一英語問句或直述句之後，從試題冊上 A、B、C、D 四個回答或回應中，選出一個最適合者作答。每題只播出一遍。

_____ 6. A. I will put it on.

　　　 B. OK. I am freezing.

　　　 C. Do you feel cold?

　　　 D. Sure. No problem.

_____ 7. A. It's a piece of cake.

　　　 B. Sorry, life is too short.

　　　 C. What about tomorrow?

　　　 D. Sure. What do you have in mind?

_____ 8. A. What time on Saturday?

　　　 B. How about another cup of coffee?

　　　 C. I won't be available that day.

　　　 D. Something suddenly came up at home.

_____ 9. A. Sorry, but I'll be 10 minutes late.

　　　 B. It starts at seven o'clock.

　　　 C. What's the name of the movie?

　　　 D. The theater is around the corner.

_____ 10. A. The food there is great.

　　　 B. Please show me the way.

　　　 C. I had a good time last weekend.

　　　 D. Did you talk to your parents first?

_____ 11. A. Get lost!

　　　 B. Hang on!

　　　 C. Beats me!

　　　 D. Get down!

_____ 12. A. To go, please.

B. Here's your change.

C. I'm afraid we've sold out.

D. Do you take credit cards?

_____ 13. A. My goodness!

B. We had a blast.

C. You're welcome.

D. Apology accepted.

_____ 14. A. I've lost my place in the book.

B. Check your route on this online map.

C. It's on the top shelf in the storeroom.

D. He called to say he's stuck in traffic.

_____ 15. A. Put this mask on.

B. Try this cream.

C. Go to the dentist now!

D. There are germs everywhere!

🎧 TRACK 2-3

第三部份：簡短對話

　　共 10 題，每題請聽音檔播出一段對話及一個相關的問題後，從試題冊上 A、B、C、D 四個選項中選出一個最適合者作答。每段對話及問題只播出一遍。

_____ 16. A. She was born deaf.

B. The volume is too loud.

C. She has terrible taste in music.

D. He can't tell what she's saying.

_____ 17. A. Keep driving at the same speed.

B. Catch up with the other driver.

C. Ask the man to drive instead.

D. Take medicine to calm down.

_____ 18. A. It is illegal.

B. It is dangerous.

C. It is quite cruel.

D. It is environmentally friendly.

_____ 19. A. He has been to Tibet.

B. He doesn't have his own travel plans.

C. He'd like to go with the woman.

D. He is not interested in the woman's idea.

_____ 20. A. He had a stroke.

B. He's got sunburn.

C. He's got a skin disease.

D. He pulled a muscle in his back.

_____ 21. A. She is unwell.

B. She is in grave danger.

C. She got divorced.

D. She will come this weekend.

_____ 22. A. The woman's ex-husband.

B. The woman's supervisor.

C. The woman's bank manager.

D. The woman's landlord.

_____ 23. A. He will tell him to move.

B. He will take away his drums.

C. He will communicate with him.

D. He will teach him how to bake.

_____ 24.

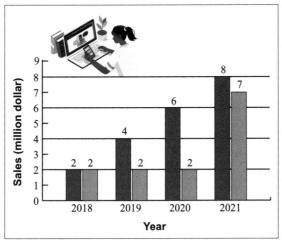

A. 2 million.

B. 4 million.

C. 6 million.

D. 7 million.

_____ 25.

A. At 8 a.m.

B. At 12 p.m.

C. At 1:30 p.m.

D. At 3:30 p.m.

TRACK 2-4

第四部份：簡短談話

共 10 題，每題請聽音檔播出一段談話及一個相關的問題後，從試題冊上 A、B、C、D 四個選項中選出一個最適合者作答。每段談話及問題只播出一遍。

_____ 26. A. We rely on them for power.

B. They are replacing solar energy.

C. A new type of fuel has been invented.

D. New technology removes carbon dioxide from them.

_____ 27. A. They were to be expected.

B. They were unprofessional.

C. They pleased the customers.

D. They did not surprise the manager.

_____ 28. A. They cost little to make.

B. It is not difficult to make them.

C. It is an activity you can do alone.

D. He can try his own cookie recipes.

_____ 29. A. It's not as hard as you think.

B. It brings bugs and weeds.

C. Hens can give you artificial fertilizers.

D. Hens get along well with your other pets.

_____ 30. A. He forgives him for what he did.

B. He thinks he deserved what he got.

C. He feels confused about his emotions.

D. He deeply regrets how he treated him.

_____ 31. A. Don't trust the advice of so-called experts.

B. Don't have too much sugar in your diet.

C. Foods containing salt and pepper are still risky.

D. Sugar is a major cause of stroke and heart disease.

_____ 32. A. Residents of Chicago.

     B. Captain and his crew.

     C. Residents of San Francisco.

     D. Passengers heading to San Francisco.

_____ 33. A. Sea fog.

     B. Wind power.

     C. Coastal clouds.

     D. Mountain streams.

_____ 34.

Competitor: Abbie Lin _Singing Contest_	
Judge	Score
Simon Smith	82
David Mitchell	80
Thomas Dave	96
Bob Tyler	79

A. Simon Smith.

B. David Mitchell.

C. Thomas Dave.

D. Bob Tyler.

_____ 35.

Tour A	Tour B
* A 3-day tour * Viewing splendid cherry blossoms	* A 4-day tour * Enjoying the tropical climate and water sports
Tour C	Tour D
* A 4-day tour * W Spa Resort * Enjoying a relaxing time	* A 3-day tour * Great hiking trails * Having forest bathing and relax

A. Tour A.
B. Tour B.
C. Tour C.
D. Tour D.

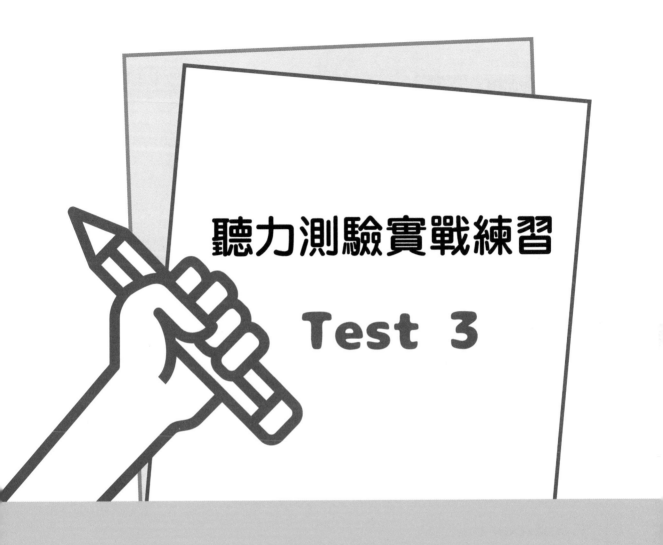

聽力測驗實戰練習

Test 3

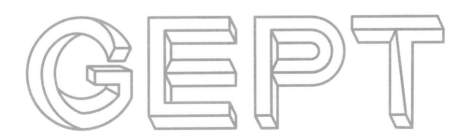

本測驗分四部份，全為四選一之選擇題，共 35 題，作答時間約 30 分鐘。

GEPT

TRACK 3-1

第一部份：看圖辨義

共 5 題，試題冊上有數幅圖畫，每一圖畫有 1～3 個描述該圖的題目，每題請聽音檔播出題目以及四個英語敘述之後，選出與所看到的圖畫最相符的答案，每題只播出一遍。

A. Question 1

1. _____

B. Question 2

2. _____

C. Question 3

3. _____

D. Questions 4 and 5

4. _____

5. _____

第二部份：問答

共 10 題，每題請聽音檔播出一英語問句或直述句之後，從試題冊上 A、B、C、D 四個回答或回應中，選出一個最適合者作答。每題只播出一遍。

_____ 6. A. No dessert. Just black tea.

B. Can I have the check, please?

C. All right. Let's go Dutch this time.

D. Actually, the steak was a bit tough.

_____ 7. A. I'd like two spoons of sugar.

B. Sorry. I'm seeing someone.

C. Yes, I've collected ten coupons.

D. No. I usually have milk for breakfast.

_____ 8. A. Sure! Let's grab a bite to eat.

B. No! Don't even think about it.

C. Not really. It's not my cup of tea.

D. Yes. Someone just stole my bicycle!

_____ 9. A. Please enter your password.

B. I have been busy these days.

C. You can't cut in line like that.

D. How about the 12th at 10 a.m.?

_____ 10. A. No way. I don't have time.

B. Cut it out. I'm in a bad mood.

C. Never mind! I'll try again tomorrow.

D. It sure has been. I'm completely exhausted.

_____ 11. A. I took it yesterday.

B. I wrote a great essay.

C. My mind just went blank.

D. I think the answer was either C or D.

_____ 12. A. I'm from Texas.

　　B. The train station.

　　C. Here's my bus pass.

　　D. A return ticket to Boston.

_____ 13. A. Medium, please.

　　B. A glass of red wine.

　　C. Just a little bit. Thank you.

　　D. Tea with one sugar, please.

_____ 14. A. I appreciate it.

　　B. My darling!

　　C. Thank you for coming.

　　D. It's my pleasure!

_____ 15. A. Sign here, please. Have a good journey.

　　B. I'm afraid not. The restaurant closes at 10 p.m.

　　C. I'm sorry. We don't have any rooms available.

　　D. Let me see. There's a seat available in business class.

第三部份：簡短對話　　　　　　　　🎧 TRACK 3-3

　　共 10 題，每題請聽音檔播出一段對話及一個相關的問題後，從試題冊上 A、B、C、D 四個選項中選出一個最適合者作答。每段對話及問題只播出一遍。

_____ 16. A. The restaurant manager helped her get a table.

　　B. The restaurant manager refused to let them eat there.

　　C. The restaurant manager didn't get along with her.

　　D. The restaurant manager invited them for dinner on Valentine's Day.

_____ 17. A. To seek help.

　　B. To ask for sick leave.

　　C. To ask for a promotion.

　　D. To let him know she's busy.

_____ 18. A. She's being dishonest.

B. She always gets confused.

C. She is using the phone too much.

D. She can't use the phone properly.

_____ 19. A. They are mother and son.

B. They are doctor and patient.

C. They are teacher and student.

D. They are clerk and customer.

_____ 20. A. Recycle some parts.

B. Fix his laptop on his own.

C. Purchase a brand-new laptop.

D. Have his laptop repaired.

_____ 21. A. Their house was broken into.

B. The door of their house is missing.

C. They have been locked out of their house.

D. They were threatened by a gang of burglars.

_____ 22. A. He has quit drinking.

B. He has had health issues.

C. He has taken up jogging.

D. He has an alcohol problem.

_____ 23. A. She is going to South Africa.

B. She speaks Spanish very well.

C. She will travel to Brazil with her boyfriend.

D. She doesn't know what the official language of Brazil is.

24.

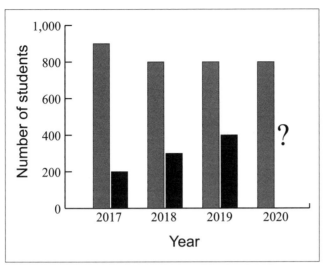

A. 500.

B. 800.

C. 1,100.

D. 1,200.

25.

Customer	*Complaint*
Lillian Wang	Wrong dish
Emily Lin	Smelly soup
Helen Liu	Overcooked steak
Cathy Chang	Dirty table

A. Lillian Wang.

B. Emily Lin.

C. Helen Liu.

D. Cathy Chang.

第四部份：簡短談話

共 10 題，每題請聽音檔播出一段談話及一個相關的問題後，從試題冊上 A、B、C、D 四個選項中選出一個最適合者作答。每段談話及問題只播出一遍。

_____ 26. A. They will be stuck in a traffic jam.
　　　　B. Andrew will be on the scene.
　　　　C. The police will ask them to pull over.
　　　　D. The traffic will be light.

_____ 27. A. To fire an employee.
　　　　B. To offer medical benefits.
　　　　C. To cancel English lessons.
　　　　D. To give tips on learning English.

_____ 28. A. The government.
　　　　B. The hotel guests.
　　　　C. The lawmaker.
　　　　D. Their parents.

_____ 29. A. Their working conditions were very poor.
　　　　B. The city government has heard their complaints.
　　　　C. The group was forced by their leader to protest.
　　　　D. They have not received a raise for a long time.

_____ 30. A. Jobs and money.
　　　　B. Water and food.
　　　　C. Roads and railroads.
　　　　D. Soldiers and weapons.

_____ 31. A. Soldier.
　　　　B. Coach.
　　　　C. Firefighter.
　　　　D. Physician.

_____ 32. A. No one broke the window.

B. A window was broken in the principal's office.

C. Students need permission to play basketball at the school.

D. Students are forbidden to play dodgeball near the school buildings.

_____ 33. A. An English listening workshop.

B. A working holiday visa.

C. A one-month study program in Boston.

D. A chance to be a language instructor.

_____ 34.

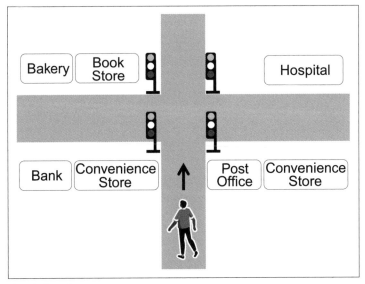

A. A bank.

B. A bakery.

C. A park.

D. A post office.

_____ 35.

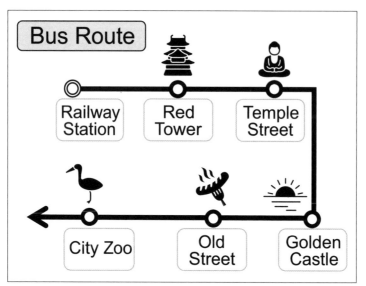

A. Red Tower.

B. Temple Street.

C. Golden Castle.

D. Old Street.

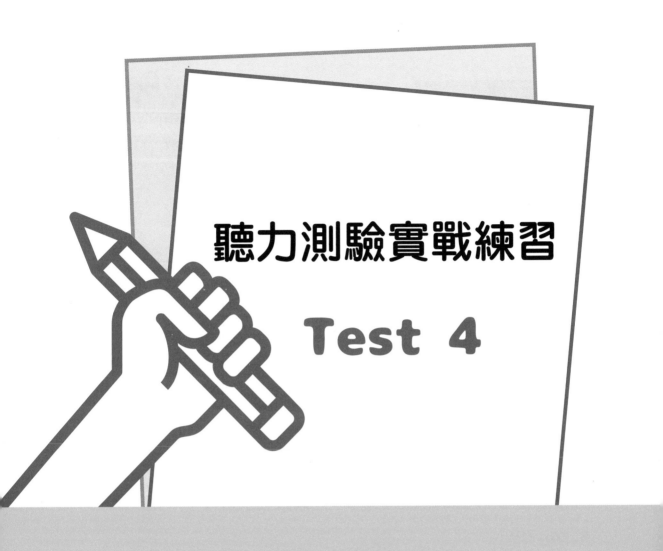

聽力測驗實戰練習

Test 4

本測驗分四部份，全為四選一之選擇題，共 35 題，作答
時間約 30 分鐘。

GEPT

🎧 TRACK 4-1

第一部份：看圖辨義

共 5 題，試題冊上有數幅圖畫，每一圖畫有 1～3 個描述該圖的題目，每題請聽音檔播出題目以及四個英語敘述之後，選出與所看到的圖畫最相符的答案，每題只播出一遍。

A. Question 1

1. _____

B. Question 2

2. _____

C. Question 3

3. _____

D. Questions 4 and 5

4. _____
5. _____

第二部份：問答

共 10 題，每題請聽音檔播出一英語問句或直述句之後，從試題冊上 A、B、C、D 四個回答或回應中，選出一個最適合者作答。每題只播出一遍。

_____ 6. A. Physics.
　　　　 B. Essay.
　　　　 C. Engineer.
　　　　 D. Passion.

_____ 7. A. Stay here!
　　　　 B. Get off!
　　　　 C. Wake up!
　　　　 D. Calm down!

_____ 8. A. Put this sunscreen on.
　　　　 B. You will feel better.
　　　　 C. What kind of excuse is that?
　　　　 D. Do you have any other symptoms?

_____ 9. A. It looks good on me.
　　　　 B. They really suit you.
　　　　 C. They were on sale.
　　　　 D. It's a lovely dress.

_____ 10. A. Our special today is roast duck.
　　　　 B. Are you ready to order?
　　　　 C. Oh dear. I'll get you another one.
　　　　 D. I'll bring you the wine menu.

_____ 11. A. Nicely done.
　　　　 B. Here you go.
　　　　 C. That's it.
　　　　 D. Take it easy.

_____ 12. A. There's one every half hour.

B. We'll arrive there in an hour.

C. You need to be on platform 3.

D. I booked a seat in business class.

_____ 13. A. Don't believe that rumor.

B. He proposed to me on the beach.

C. I am sure it was a touching moment.

D. The wedding will be held in the summer.

_____ 14. A. Thank you for your compliment!

B. No, thanks. I'm cutting back on snacks.

C. Yes! I used my grandmother's recipe.

D. Oh! Check the expiration date on the package.

_____ 15. A. I'm not a movie fan.

B. I can do some magic tricks.

C. I wish I could be invisible.

D. The new movie is awesome.

🎧 TRACK 4-3

第三部份：簡短對話

　　共 10 題，每題請聽音檔播出一段對話及一個相關的問題後，從試題冊上 A、B、C、D 四個選項中選出一個最適合者作答。每段對話及問題只播出一遍。

_____ 16. A. Imported fruit.

B. Being cheated.

C. Paying too much.

D. Eating chemicals.

_____ 17. A. He used a teaspoon.

B. He made a mild curry.

C. He bought the wrong kind of spice.

D. He didn't follow the recipe exactly.

_____ 18. A. She's put on a lot of weight lately.

B. He will make all the travel arrangements.

C. She won't be able to put her bag on the plane.

D. There's a weight limit for luggage.

_____ 19. A. The gift would have been rejected.

B. Dana would have been jealous.

C. The woman would have felt embarrassed.

D. Dana would have invited her to join her party.

_____ 20. A. Stress.

B. His job.

C. City life.

D. Air pollution.

_____ 21. A. Wine.

B. Chilies.

C. Red pepper.

D. Chicken breast.

_____ 22. A. She also has a job.

B. She has trouble saving money.

C. She wants the man to work less.

D. She can't pay her bills on time.

_____ 23. A. In a jewelry store.

B. In a liquor store.

C. In a cosmetic store.

D. In a furniture store.

24.

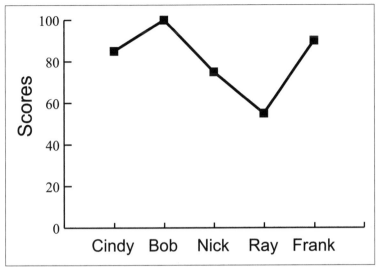

A. Bob.

B. Nick.

C. Ray.

D. Frank.

25.

Floor Guide

3F Men's Wear

2F Women's Wear

1F Cosmetics

B1 Supermarket

A. B1.

B. 1F.

C. 2F.

D. 3F.

第四部份：簡短談話

共 10 題，每題請聽音檔播出一段談話及一個相關的問題後，從試題冊上 A、B、C、D 四個選項中選出一個最適合者作答。每段談話及問題只播出一遍。

_____ 26. A. A busy holiday weekend.

B. The Central Weather Bureau.

C. An approaching typhoon.

D. The official's outdoor activities.

_____ 27. A. The chocolate gift can be more personalized.

B. A chocolate gift is certain to make everyone happy.

C. The customized notebooks will have your name on it.

D. Switzerland produces the best chocolate in the world.

_____ 28. A. How to reach your sales targets.

B. The importance of business cards.

C. The difference between two products.

D. Effective methods to serve customers.

_____ 29. A. In a zoo.

B. In a library.

C. In a pet shop.

D. In a laboratory.

_____ 30. A. A local police chief.

B. A bomb disposal team.

C. A British commander.

D. A pupil.

_____ 31. A. Ingredients for brownies are hard to find.

B. You can learn how to make brownies today.

C. It is easy to carry brownies wherever you go.

D. Brownies are more expensive than cakes and cookies.

_____ 32. A. Provide nutrition for your body.

   B. A discount on traveling to Germany.

   C. Wash your clothes without harmful chemicals.

   D. Naturally make your skin clean and healthy.

_____ 33. A. To help increase tourism in Japan.

   B. To attend a conference in the foreign country.

   C. To share her experiences of traveling in Japan.

   D. To study Japan's successful methods of tourism marketing.

_____ 34.

A. Pizza Papa.

B. Sunny Café.

C. Big Burgers.

D. Jason's Mart.

_____ 35.

A. $40.

B. $54.

C. $60.

D. $150.

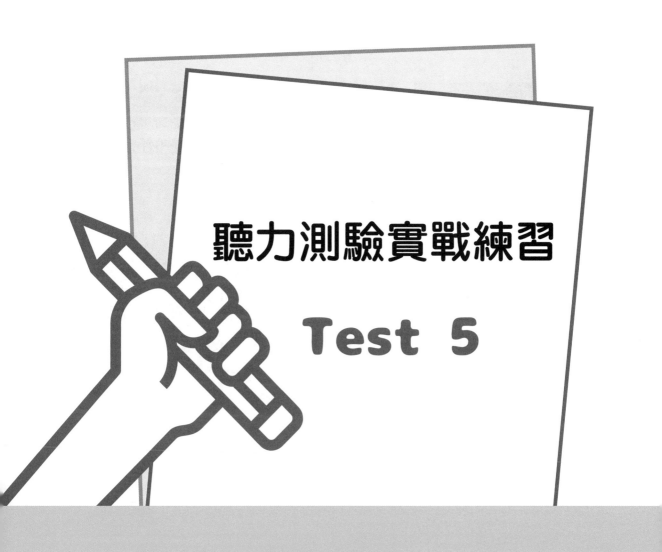

聽力測驗實戰練習

Test 5

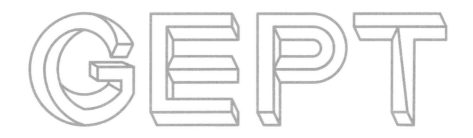

本測驗分四部份，全為四選一之選擇題，共 35 題，作答
時間約 30 分鐘。

GEPT

TRACK 5-1

第一部份：看圖辨義

共 5 題，試題冊上有數幅圖畫，每一圖畫有 1～3 個描述該圖的題目，每題請聽音檔播出題目以及四個英語敘述之後，選出與所看到的圖畫最相符的答案，每題只播出一遍。

A. Question 1

1. _____

B. Question 2

Receipt

Toothbrush x10	NT$300
Queen organic eggs x12	NT$100
Subtotal:	NT$400
TOTAL	NT$400
Cash:	NT$500
Change:	NT$100

2. _____

C. Question 3

3. _____

D. Questions 4 and 5

4. _____
5. _____

第二部份：問答

　　共 10 題，每題請聽音檔播出一英語問句或直述句之後，從試題冊上 A、B、C、D 四個回答或回應中，選出一個最適合者作答。每題只播出一遍。

_____ 6. A. I don't think so. It's a little too casual.

B. Well, it's certainly fashionable.

C. I've never worn a suit before.

D. 50% off all neckties. Not a bad deal!

_____ 7. A. The ship is approaching the port.

B. We close on Saturdays.

C. Please print an extra copy for me.

D. Just fill out this form and sign at the bottom.

_____ 8. A. I usually prepare my own lunch.

B. I much prefer iced coffee to iced tea.

C. No wonder she has to visit the dentist.

D. No doubt she'll expect me to pay the bill.

_____ 9. A. What have I ever done to you?

B. How on earth should I know?

C. Where have you been recently?

D. Why not take a long hot bath?

_____ 10. A. Yes, we caught the train just in time.

B. No, we missed the deadline by one day.

C. Well, the final decision is not up to me.

D. If we hurry, I think we can catch up.

_____ 11. A. The piano concert.

B. The modern art museum.

C. A sculpture of an ant.

D. Digital photography.

_____ 12. A. Pay at the end of the meal.

　　　 B. 15% of the total bill.

　　　 C. My advice is to book early.

　　　 D. The service was wonderful, thanks.

_____ 13. A. Why didn't you let me know sooner?

　　　 B. Oh, sure! I'm a huge jazz fan.

　　　 C. Don't forget to return my CD!

　　　 D. I watch videos on YouTube.

_____ 14. A. I must have dropped my map.

　　　 B. I joined a tour group.

　　　 C. Let's ask at the information desk.

　　　 D. There may be a bank along this street.

_____ 15. A. The interest rate is set at 5%.

　　　 B. Thanks a million. I owe you big time.

　　　 C. There's no need. It was the very least I could do.

　　　 D. I make it a rule never to borrow money from friends.

🎧 TRACK 5-3

第三部份：簡短對話

　　共 10 題，每題請聽音檔播出一段對話及一個相關的問題後，從試題冊上 A、B、C、D 四個選項中選出一個最適合者作答。每段對話及問題只播出一遍。

_____ 16. A. On a bus.

　　　 B. At a train station.

　　　 C. In a post office.

　　　 D. In a travel agency.

_____ 17. A. Susan is Bob's manager.

　　　 B. Bob and Susan are going to get divorced.

　　　 C. Bob and Susan work together.

　　　 D. Susan had never seen Bob before.

_____ 18. A. At home.

B. In the health center.

C. In the classroom.

D. In the school playground.

_____ 19. A. His smartphone was ringing.

B. He almost had a car accident.

C. He kept in touch with his friends all the time.

D. The truck driver was staring at his smartphone.

_____ 20. A. The ice cream is too big to eat.

B. The woman promises to give him two spoons.

C. He likes to eat ice cream with two spoons.

D. His friend will eat the ice cream together with him.

_____ 21. A. She wants to kill time.

B. Her parents never give her an allowance.

C. She wants to save up for her trip to Australia.

D. Ask her parents to increase her allowance.

_____ 22. A. He is only a beginner.

B. He doesn't ask her politely.

C. He is a professional pianist.

D. She is not a good piano teacher.

_____ 23. A. Book a table for two.

B. Break the rule for her friend.

C. Tell the man today is her birthday.

D. Ask the man to apologize to her.

24.

Train 125

Taipei 11:20 → Taichung 13:05

5car 2C

NT$375

A. At 11:20.
B. At 11:50.
C. At 13:05.
D. At 13:35.

25.

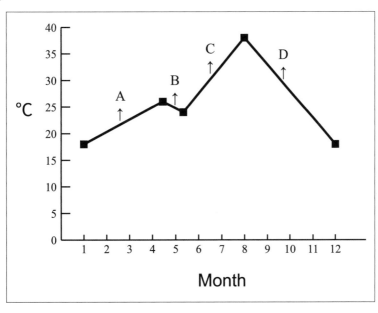

第四部份：簡短談話

共 10 題，每題請聽音檔播出一段談話及一個相關的問題後，從試題冊上 A、B、C、D 四個選項中選出一個最適合者作答。每段談話及問題只播出一遍。

_____ 26. A. The company is seeking a vice president.

B. Applicants can't send their résumés by email.

C. The starting pay is at least NT$400 per hour.

D. The applicant should be good at English.

_____ 27. A. Outstanding views of the city.

B. Several outdoor activities.

C. Tall mountains and great skiing.

D. An Italian restaurant famous for its pasta.

_____ 28. A. On a bus.

B. In an emergency room.

C. On an airplane.

D. At a train station.

_____ 29. A. Turn in her history report.

B. Send her an email.

C. Stop by her house.

D. Tell her Mr. Lin's phone number.

_____ 30. A. The theme of the college ball.

B. How to dress properly for a ball.

C. Directions to find the college ball.

D. The class schedule for the new semester.

_____ 31. A. There has been plenty of rain in the past year.

B. People are happy with the new prices for electricity.

C. The cost of electricity has increased last year.

D. The company uses only wind power to produce electricity.

_____ 32. A. Fresh air.

B. High pay.

C. Free milk.

D. Living close to the city.

_____ 33. A. The woman taught her Chinese.

B. The woman was willing to visit Germany.

C. The woman made her feel at home in Taiwan.

D. The woman visited Heidi at the hospital when she was sick.

_____ 34.

A. He boarded Flight CY909 to New York at Gate D3.

B. His home is in New York, but he studies in Boston.

C. His flight will land in New York on schedule.

D. He left the message to his mother after 6:30 p.m.

_____ 35.

A. Pizza Margherita.

B. Greek Roast Chicken.

C. Pan-Fried Duck Breast.

D. T-Bone Steak.

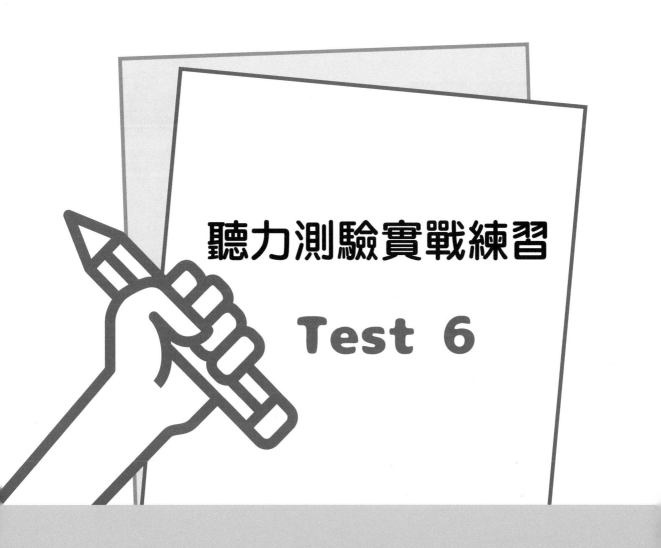

聽力測驗實戰練習

Test 6

本測驗分四部份，全為四選一之選擇題，共 35 題，作答
時間約 30 分鐘。

第一部份：看圖辨義

　　共 5 題，試題冊上有數幅圖畫，每一圖畫有 1～3 個描述該圖的題目，每題請聽音檔播出題目以及四個英語敘述之後，選出與所看到的圖畫最相符的答案，每題只播出一遍。

A. Question 1

1. _____

B. Question 2

2. _____

C. Question 3

3. _____

D. Questions 4 and 5

4. _____
5. _____

TRACK 6-2

第二部份：問答

共 10 題，每題請聽音檔播出一英語問句或直述句之後，從試題冊上 A、B、C、D 四個回答或回應中，選出一個最適合者作答。每題只播出一遍。

_____ 6. A. I'll bring one up to your room right away.

B. There's one on the bottom shelf over there.

C. We don't have any available rooms at the moment.

D. Go down to the end of the hall and you'll see them on the left.

_____ 7. A. The schedule has been changed.

B. Check your answers online.

C. That's not the right attitude.

D. Spend your allowance more wisely.

_____ 8. A. March 1st.

B. I'm a mechanic.

C. I have two sons.

D. I live in an apartment.

_____ 9. A. Great! I'm looking forward to it.

B. Certainly! I'd be honored.

C. Never mind. It's no big deal.

D. Thanks. I've been working out.

_____ 10. A. It was canceled.

B. I'm the head of sales.

C. The line is busy.

D. You'll get a promotion!

_____ 11. A. I'd like a chicken salad.

B. I think buffets are my favorite.

C. I had a lunch box and a piece of fruit.

D. I'll have the chocolate pudding, please.

_____ 12. A. To tidy up my bedroom and wash my socks.

        B. To make dinner and get an early night.

        C. To get a PhD and buy an apartment.

        D. To have a beer and surf the Internet.

_____ 13. A. This skin cream should help.

        B. Take one of these pills every four hours.

        C. I need to clean the wound first.

        D. I've scheduled a meeting for next month.

_____ 14. A. I'm afraid we don't take checks anymore.

        B. I'm sorry. I'll send some up right away.

        C. Good morning! How may I help you?

        D. All right. So that's a single room for April 14th.

_____ 15. A. For goodness' sake!

        B. Amen!

        C. Good heavens!

        D. Bless you!

🎧 TRACK 6-3

第三部份：簡短對話

    共 10 題，每題請聽音檔播出一段對話及一個相關的問題後，從試題冊上 A、B、C、D 四個選項中選出一個最適合者作答。每段對話及問題只播出一遍。

_____ 16. A. In a hotel.

        B. In Room 612.

        C. In an elevator.

        D. In a hospital.

_____ 17. A. 7 to 9 a.m.

        B. 5 to 8 p.m.

        C. 11 a.m. to 1 p.m.

        D. 11 p.m. to 2 a.m.

_____ 18. A. He has taken a group photo.

B. He has rejected the woman's request.

C. He has lied to others about the woman.

D. He has forgotten to bring his selfie stick.

_____ 19. A. Some spoiled food.

B. Some spicy food.

C. Some greasy food.

D. Some plain food.

_____ 20. A. She stamps it.

B. She inspects it.

C. She checks its weight.

D. She measures its volume.

_____ 21. A. He is receiving treatment.

B. He is having a routine check-up.

C. He is working at home.

D. He is devoting himself to his business.

_____ 22. A. Go shopping.

B. Rush to airport lounge.

C. Make a phone call.

D. Take off her make-up.

_____ 23. A. It's her favorite comedy.

B. She wants to watch it later.

C. The man had watched it before.

D. The man will buy a DVD of the film online.

24.

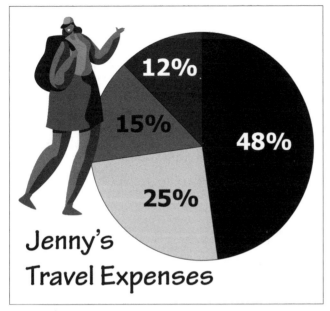

A. NT$4,800.

B. NT$6,000.

C. NT$10,000.

D. NT$19,000.

25.

L Hotel	S Hotel
Location: ★★★	Location: ★
Price: ★	Price: ★★★
Facilities: ★★	Facilities: ★
Reviews: ★	Reviews: ★★

A. Location.

B. Price.

C. Facilities.

D. Reviews.

第四部份：簡短談話

共 10 題，每題請聽音檔播出一段談話及一個相關的問題後，從試題冊上 A、B、C、D 四個選項中選出一個最適合者作答。每段談話及問題只播出一遍。

_____ 26. A. Students will have to miss the PE class.
B. Teachers will have to eat in the cafeteria.
C. Students will be required to have lunch indoors.
D. People who litter will pay a fine.

_____ 27. A. Moving away from them.
B. Competing against them.
C. Accusing them of laziness.
D. Spreading rumors about them.

_____ 28. A. He was coaching a basketball team.
B. He was honored with a medal for being a hero.
C. He died while trying to fight bank robbers.
D. He was considered the most devoted father.

_____ 29. A. To save money.
B. To follow the trend.
C. To give the grandmother a rest.
D. To have more time to chat with each other.

_____ 30. A. Some people were treated in the hospital.
B. People were moved out in the afternoon.
C. The fire has claimed over 20 lives.
D. The fire was started by someone who was smoking in bed.

_____ 31. A. A campground.
B. A hotel.
C. A resort.
D. A training camp.

_____ 32. A. A hairdryer.

    B. An electric fan.

    C. A air fryer.

    D. An electric toaster.

_____ 33. A. A purse that contained $2,000.

    B. A bronze bell that weighs five tons.

    C. The oldest tree in the province.

    D. A large bronze statue of the first President.

_____ 34.

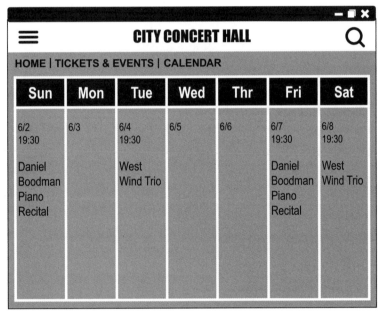

A. 6/2, Daniel Boodman Piano Recital.

B. 6/4, West Wind Trio.

C. 6/7, Daniel Boodman Piano Recital.

D. 6/8, West Wind Trio.

_____ 35.

Marry Me

Scarlet Jefferson Tony Davis
Produced by Allan Willser
Directed by Steve Hopson

A. The male lead.
B. The female lead.
C. The producer.
D. The director.

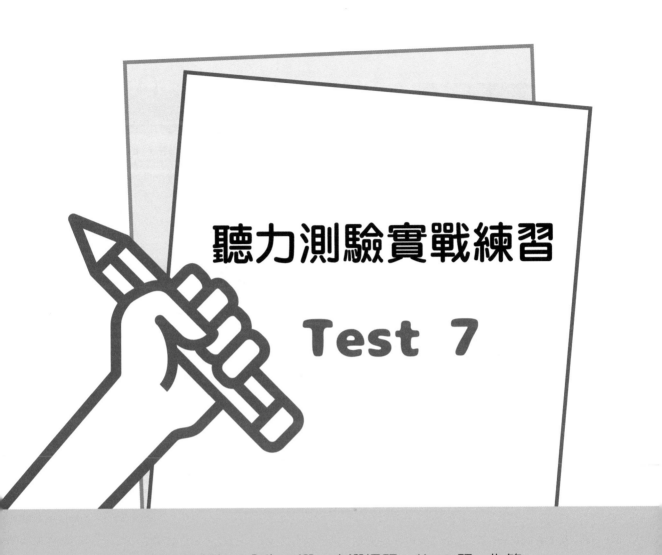

聽力測驗實戰練習

Test 7

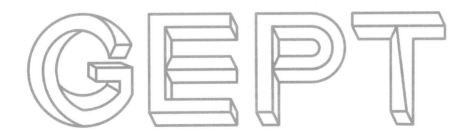

本測驗分四部份，全為四選一之選擇題，共 35 題，作答
時間約 30 分鐘。

GEPT

第一部份：看圖辨義

　　共 5 題，試題冊上有數幅圖畫，每一圖畫有 1～3 個描述該圖的題目，每題請聽音檔播出題目以及四個英語敘述之後，選出與所看到的圖畫最相符的答案，每題只播出一遍。

A. Question 1

1. ＿＿＿＿

B. Question 2

2. ＿＿＿＿

C. Question 3

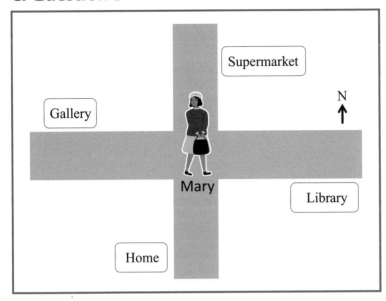

3. _____

D. Questions 4 and 5

4. _____
5. _____

第二部份：問答

共 10 題，每題請聽音檔播出一英語問句或直述句之後，從試題冊上 A、B、C、D 四個回答或回應中，選出一個最適合者作答。每題只播出一遍。

_____ 6. A. We haven't decided on a date yet.

B. We got married in Hawaii.

C. We'll go out to a nice restaurant.

D. We've been married nearly ten years.

_____ 7. A. I don't have medical insurance.

B. Let me talk to him.

C. Someone call an ambulance!

D. It's not on me.

_____ 8. A. Three hours.

B. NT$30,000.

C. An international airline.

D. Four hundred kilometers.

_____ 9. A. He may need surgery.

B. He signed the contract.

C. He gave me some medicine.

D. He's the director of this hospital.

_____ 10. A. Sure, here's her number.

B. Yes, but the line was busy.

C. OK. Coming right up.

D. No, not anymore.

_____ 11. A. Well, we've decided to sue them.

B. Not bad. I'll graduate next summer.

C. Thanks! This loan will really help.

D. Pretty good, thanks. We are starting to turn a profit.

_____ 12. A. Just a few slices, thanks.

B. Please pass the salt and pepper.

C. Pretty good! I like its flavor.

D. A little mustard, but hold the ketchup.

_____ 13. A. No big deal!

B. Oh, it's OK!

C. How rude you are!

D. Well, I'm flattered!

_____ 14. A. Sure! I'll help you apply.

B. Never mind! You'll get another one.

C. Great! You deserve it!

D. Oh dear! I shouldn't have told you.

_____ 15. A. It's obviously fake.

B. Thanks for the compliment.

C. Sorry, but that's not my problem.

D. I'm trying to lose weight.

🎧 TRACK 7-3

第三部份：簡短對話

共 10 題，每題請聽音檔播出一段對話及一個相關的問題後，從試題冊上 A、
B、C、D 四個選項中選出一個最適合者作答。每段對話及問題只播出一遍。

_____ 16. A. The brother's sons.

B. The woman's twin sons.

C. The man's sisters.

D. The woman's nephews.

_____ 17. A. She is feeding her pet.

B. She is asking to see the manager.

C. She is ordering a drink.

D. She is paying for the meal.

_____ 18. A. At a gas station.

　　 B. At a bakery.

　　 C. In an ice cream shop.

　　 D. At a fish market.

_____ 19. A. Take a nap.

　　 B. Learn a language.

　　 C. Walk his dog.

　　 D. Read a novel.

_____ 20. A. She is still in the hospital.

　　 B. She will make a full recovery.

　　 C. She'll never be able to move her legs again.

　　 D. She needs to use a wheelchair from now on.

_____ 21. A. There has been an accident.

　　 B. The man is not a good driver.

　　 C. The woman has missed her plane.

　　 D. They might miss their flight.

_____ 22. A. The woman is trying to lose weight.

　　 B. The woman is trying to gain weight.

　　 C. The meal is too spicy for her.

　　 D. The waiter is too busy to take orders.

_____ 23. A. They both feel time passes fast.

　　 B. They both enjoy being grown-ups.

　　 C. Both of them would like to be children again.

　　 D. The woman likes the man better when he was young.

_____ 24.

Shopping List
1. biscuits
2. milk
3. Coke/juice
4. beef
5. potatoes
6. beans
7. carrots

A. 4.

B. 5.

C. 6.

D. 7.

_____ 25.

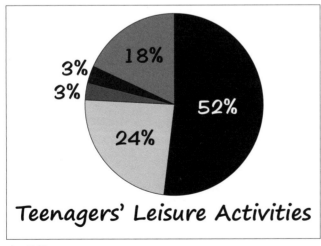

Teenagers' Leisure Activities

A. 3%.

B. 18%.

C. 24%.

D. 52%.

第四部份：簡短談話

共 10 題，每題請聽音檔播出一段談話及一個相關的問題後，從試題冊上 A、B、C、D 四個選項中選出一個最適合者作答。每段談話及問題只播出一遍。

_____ 26. A. Open a new branch in July.

B. Celebrate the 10th anniversary of the store.

C. Combine a bookstore with a coffee shop.

D. Try to design a brand-new menu.

_____ 27. A. To plant new trees in the park.

B. To complain about neighbors' pets.

C. To ask for help to take care of their children.

D. To donate money to build a new playground.

_____ 28. A. Local people.

B. Foggy weather.

C. The tourism industry.

D. Oil leak.

_____ 29. A. A healthier coffee with no caffeine.

B. A new type of exercise program.

C. A natural health product for energy.

D. A cream for smoother skin.

_____ 30. A. A movie director.

B. A hit movie.

C. An annual festival.

D. A resident of this town.

_____ 31. A. We can't understand foreign languages.

B. The radio waves can't travel very far.

C. The traditional radios don't have enough power.

D. Radio stations from other countries require a fee to listen.

_____ 32. A. Work experience.

B. Wage.

C. Personality traits.

D. Medical skills.

_____ 33. A. Get free Internet service after signing a three-year service contract.

B. Catch a flight, and get the meal for free.

C. Buy a new smartphone, and get the next new phone for free.

D. Get two sets of designer phones that will never be out of fashion.

_____ 34.

Brand New Products

A. Clean Water Straw

B. Cake Knife

C. Mini Safe

D. Baby Mopper

_____ 35.

A. $8.

B. $10.

C. $15.

D. $30.

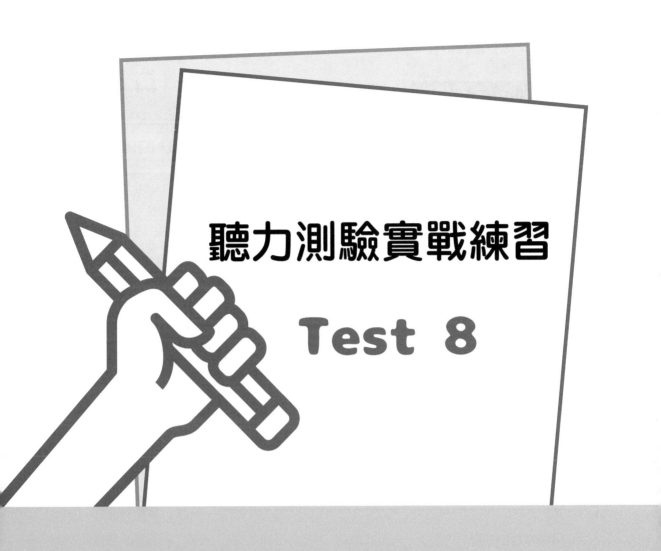

聽力測驗實戰練習

Test 8

本測驗分四部份，全為四選一之選擇題，共 35 題，作答
時間約 30 分鐘。

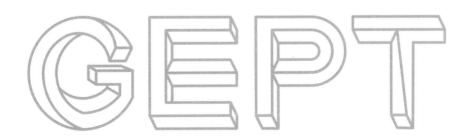

🎧 TRACK 8-1

第一部份：看圖辨義

共 5 題，試題冊上有數幅圖畫，每一圖畫有 1～3 個描述該圖的題目，每題請聽音檔播出題目以及四個英語敘述之後，選出與所看到的圖畫最相符的答案，每題只播出一遍。

A. Question 1

1. _____

B. Question 2

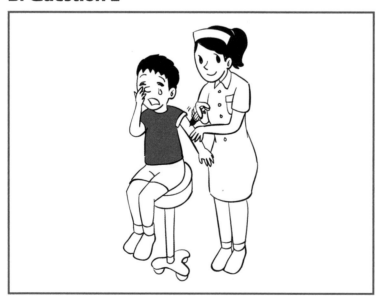

2. _____

C. Question 3

3. ____

D. Questions 4 and 5

4. ____

5. ____

第二部份：問答

共 10 題，每題請聽音檔播出一英語問句或直述句之後，從試題冊上 A、B、C、D 四個回答或回應中，選出一個最適合者作答。每題只播出一遍。

_____ 6. A. Yes, it's one of my favorite jeans.

B. I prefer the other pair, to be honest.

C. Not bad, but the sleeves are a bit too long.

D. You can only take three items into the fitting room.

_____ 7. A. No, I'm downstairs in the lobby.

B. No, I'm just suffering from jet lag.

C. No, I'm an exchange student.

D. No, I had called in advance.

_____ 8. A. It's on the best-seller list.

B. May I have your library card?

C. Please return the books to the library.

D. May I have your room number, please?

_____ 9. A. Neither! They make me sneeze.

B. I take him for a walk once a day after dinner.

C. The vet gave her all the necessary shots.

D. I think training them would be the hardest part.

_____ 10. A. I've been unemployed for over a year.

B. I want to negotiate for a higher salary.

C. I have brought my résumé.

D. I have previous experience of this work.

_____ 11. A. A table for four, please.

B. I'd like a seafood pasta.

C. A single room for October 8th.

D. I'd like to book a seat in business class, please.

_____ 12. A. Yes, I want to be a lawyer.

B. Yes, I've applied for a job in marketing.

C. Yes, I graduated from New York University.

D. Yes, I babysat for my neighbor's children.

_____ 13. A. Yes, he certainly does.

B. Yes, she's very attractive.

C. Yes, but he's not my type.

D. Yes, I'm so proud of you.

_____ 14. A. I'm Mary. Pleased to meet you, Jennifer.

B. That sounds incredible, Jennifer. I can't wait.

C. Jennifer! I almost didn't recognize you!

D. So, Jennifer, are you ready for the big exam today?

_____ 15. A. I think it really suits you.

B. I'm already dressed for work.

C. I usually wear a dark suit to work.

D. The other pair of shoes looks better.

🎧 TRACK 8-3

第三部份：簡短對話

　　共 10 題，每題請聽音檔播出一段對話及一個相關的問題後，從試題冊上 A、B、C、D 四個選項中選出一個最適合者作答。每段對話及問題只播出一遍。

_____ 16. A. Easy but rewarding.

B. Enjoyable but challenging.

C. Difficult and boring.

D. Luxurious and comfortable.

_____ 17. A. There is a car accident.

B. She needs an ice pack.

C. The man was attacked.

D. She is going crazy.

_____ 18. A. Once.

B. Twice.

C. Three times.

D. Four times.

_____ 19. A. In New Zealand.

B. In their own house.

C. They haven't decided yet.

D. They will spend the vacation apart.

_____ 20. A. In the dresser.

B. On the balcony.

C. In the dryer.

D. In the washing machine.

_____ 21. A. Right now, his grades are fine.

B. He can't keep up with his schoolwork.

C. His mother has taken away all his comic books.

D. He mostly reads comic books on Saturdays and Sundays.

_____ 22. A. Shrimp pasta.

B. Mapo tofu.

C. Mushroom pizza.

D. Fried rice.

_____ 23. A. He isn't a photographer.

B. The woman was offended.

C. The police recognized him.

D. It is a regulation.

24.

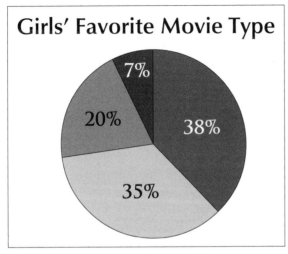

A. 7%.

B. 20%.

C. 35%.

D. 38%.

25.

A. $9.

B. $10.

C. $11.

D. $12.

第四部份：簡短談話

共 10 題，每題請聽音檔播出一段談話及一個相關的問題後，從試題冊上 A、B、C、D 四個選項中選出一個最適合者作答。每段談話及問題只播出一遍。

_____ 26. A. A truck driver.

B. A newscaster.

C. A student.

D. An adopter.

_____ 27. A. It is important to every generation.

B. Only kids have to be aware of that.

C. Actions speak louder than words.

D. Parents should always say "Please" and "Thank you" to their children.

_____ 28. A. To share an interesting video.

B. To promote a video website.

C. To teach you how to make a video.

D. To sell a useful file cabinet.

_____ 29. A. An award-winning chef.

B. An athlete.

C. A science major.

D. A vegetarian.

_____ 30. A. To make children be nicer to each other.

B. To help the hospital make money.

C. To assist children with cancer.

D. To build new children's hospitals.

_____ 31. A. They are watching an award ceremony.

B. They are watching *Hunters*.

C. They are watching *The Talk Show*.

D. They are watching Kevin's new movie.

_____ 32. A. He couldn't afford the rent.

B. He sold drugs.

C. Someone stole his property.

D. He lost his job.

_____ 33. A. Knowing how to run your own grocery store.

B. Learning how to build a beautiful garden.

C. Finding a place to grow flowers.

D. Gaining your confidence in doing things by yourself.

_____ 34.

Who Killed John?

put on by Drama Club

Characters
John: the former and dead CEO
Oscar: son of the dead CEO
Gloria: mother of Oscar
Tony: the new CEO
Mary: lover of Oscar
Bill: best friend of Oscar

A. The new CEO.

B. Oscar's mother.

C. Oscar's lover.

D. Oscar's best friend.

_____ 35.

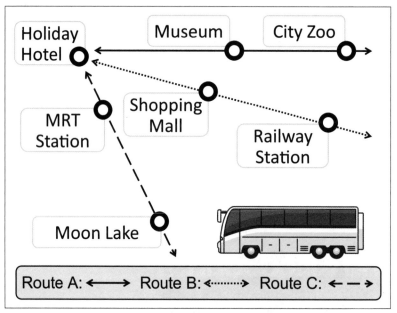

A. Museum.
B. Shopping Mall.
C. MRT Station.
D. Railway Station.

NOTE

Answer Key

Test 1

1. B	2. A	3. B	4. D	5. C	6. C	7. B	8. D	9. B	10. C
11. D	12. B	13. D	14. D	15. C	16. A	17. A	18. D	19. A	20. D
21. B	22. C	23. B	24. C	25. C	26. D	27. C	28. A	29. D	30. B
31. B	32. C	33. A	34. B	35. C					

Test 2

1. C	2. D	3. D	4. A	5. C	6. D	7. D	8. C	9. A	10. D
11. C	12. C	13. D	14. D	15. B	16. B	17. A	18. C	19. D	20. B
21. D	22. D	23. C	24. B	25. D	26. A	27. B	28. B	29. A	30. D
31. B	32. D	33. C	34. C	35. C					

Test 3

1. C	2. C	3. A	4. B	5. A	6. D	7. B	8. D	9. D	10. D
11. C	12. B	13. A	14. D	15. C	16. C	17. B	18. A	19. B	20. D
21. A	22. A	23. D	24. A	25. A	26. A	27. C	28. D	29. D	30. B
31. A	32. D	33. C	34. A	35. D					

Test 4

1. A	2. A	3. B	4. C	5. D	6. A	7. D	8. D	9. B	10. C
11. B	12. A	13. A	14. D	15. C	16. D	17. D	18. D	19. C	20. D
21. B	22. A	23. A	24. B	25. B	26. C	27. A	28. B	29. A	30. D
31. C	32. D	33. D	34. B	35. B					

Test 5

1. B	2. C	3. C	4. C	5. A	6. A	7. D	8. C	9. D	10. B
11. C	12. B	13. B	14. C	15. C	16. C	17. C	18. D	19. B	20. D
21. C	22. A	23. A	24. D	25. B	26. D	27. B	28. C	29. A	30. B
31. C	32. A	33. C	34. D	35. D					

Test 6

1. D	2. C	3. D	4. C	5. D	6. D	7. C	8. B	9. D	10. A
11. B	12. C	13. B	14. B	15. D	16. D	17. D	18. A	19. B	20. C
21. A	22. A	23. C	24. C	25. B	26. C	27. B	28. C	29. C	30. A
31. A	32. A	33. D	34. D	35. D					

Test 7

1. C	2. D	3. C	4. C	5. C	6. C	7. C	8. A	9. A	10. B
11. D	12. D	13. D	14. C	15. B	16. D	17. D	18. B	19. D	20. B
21. D	22. A	23. A	24. B	25. C	26. C	27. D	28. B	29. C	30. A
31. B	32. D	33. C	34. C	35. C					

Test 8

1. C	2. B	3. C	4. C	5. B	6. C	7. C	8. B	9. A	10. D
11. B	12. D	13. C	14. C	15. A	16. B	17. C	18. C	19. B	20. B
21. A	22. C	23. D	24. B	25. C	26. B	27. A	28. B	29. D	30. C
31. C	32. A	33. B	34. B	35. A					

國家圖書館出版品預行編目資料

全民英檢聽力測驗SO EASY (中級篇)／三民英語編
輯小組彙編.——初版一刷.——臺北市: 三民，2022
面；　公分

ISBN 978-957-14-7370-3　（平裝）
1. 英語 2. 問題集

805.1892　　　　　　　　　　　110022285

全民英檢聽力測驗 SO EASY (中級篇)

彙　　　編	三民英語編輯小組
責任編輯	謝佳恩
美術編輯	黃顯喬
內頁繪圖	古佩純　李吳宏

發 行 人	劉振強
出 版 者	三民書局股份有限公司
地　　　址	臺北市復興北路 386 號 (復北門市)
	臺北市重慶南路一段 61 號 (重南門市)
電　　　話	(02)25006600
網　　　址	三民網路書店 https://www.sanmin.com.tw

出版日期	初版一刷 2022 年 4 月
書籍編號	S871770
I S B N	978-957-14-7370-3

三民書局

全民英檢
聽力測驗
SO EASY

中級篇

三民英語編輯小組　彙編

解答本

最新穎！符合全新改版英檢題型
最逼真！模擬試題提升應試能力
最精闢！範例分析傾授高分技巧

三民書局

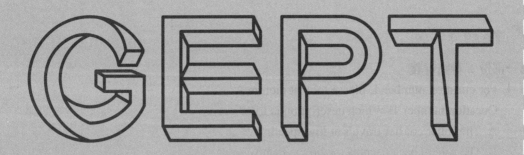

GEPT

聽力測驗

腳本與解答

第一部份：看圖辨義

B 1. For question number 1, please look at picture A.

Question number 1: Which description is true?

A. The roller coaster travels at low speed.

B. The roller coaster scares the boy to death.

C. Only one person goes for a ride on the roller coaster.

D. Everyone hates to ride the roller coaster.

第一題，請看圖片 A。

第一題：哪一個敘述是正確的？

選項：A. 雲霄飛車慢速行進。　　　　　　B. 雲霄飛車把男孩嚇得半死。

　　　C. 只有一人搭乘雲霄飛車。　　　　D. 大家都討厭搭雲霄飛車。

A 2. For question number 2, please look at picture B.

Question number 2: What can be inferred from the picture?

A. The woman is on trial.

B. This is taking place in a prison.

C. The man on the left is being sued.

D. A boss is asking the woman some questions.

第二題，請看圖片 B。

第二題：從圖中可以推測什麼？

選項：A. 女子正在受審。　　　　　　　B. 這場景發生在監獄裡。

　　　C. 左方的男子被提出控告。　　　D. 一位老闆正在問女子一些問題。

B 3. For questions number 3 and 4, please look at picture C.

Question number 3: What will take place on June 1st?

A. A negotiation.　　　　　　　　B. A contest.

C. A psychological test.　　　　　D. A boxing match.

第三題及第四題，請看圖片 C。

第三題：什麼事情將在六月一日舉行？

選項：A. 一場協商。　　B. 一場競賽。　　　C. 一個心理測驗。　　D. 一場拳擊賽。

D 4. Question number 4: Please look at picture C again. How many people will take part in the tug-of-war?

A. 10.　　　　　　B. 20.　　　　　　C. 30.　　　　　　D. 40.

第四題：請再看一次圖片 C。將會有多少人參加拔河？

選項：A. 十人。　　　B. 二十人。　　　C. 三十人。　　　D. 四十人。

C 5. For question number 5, please look at picture D.

Question number 5: What has happened to Lucky?

A. It was adopted.　　B. It was abandoned.　　C. It has gone missing.　　D. It has lost its collar.

第五題，請看圖片 D。

第五題：Lucky 發生什麼事？

選項：A. 牠被領養了。 B. 牠被拋棄了。　　C. 牠走失了。　　　　D. 牠弄丟牠的項圈。

第二部份：問答

C 6. Let's have dinner at that new Italian restaurant.

A. No way. I haven't been to Italy.

B. Why not? Sushi is always the best.

C. Cool! I'll call and make a reservation.

D. Sure! I would love to travel there one day.

問題：我們去那家新的義大利餐廳吃晚餐。

選項：A. 不行。我沒去過義大利。　　　　B. 好啊！壽司最棒了。

　　　　C. 沒問題！我來打電話訂位。　　D. 當然！我希望有一天能到那裡旅行。

B 7. Give me a call when you have time.

A. Thank you.　　　　　　　　　　B. You bet!

C. Do I have to call him?　　　　　D. I think so.

問題：當你有時間時，致電給我。

選項：A. 謝謝你。　　　B. 當然！　　　　C. 我一定要打給他嗎？ D. 我想也是。

D 8. How was the game last night?

A. The one is the latest version.　　　B. My parents like to play games.

C. I played games last weekend.　　　D. It's the best game I have ever seen.

問題：昨晚的比賽如何？

選項：A. 那一個是最新的版本。　　　　B. 我的父母喜歡玩遊戲。

　　　　C. 我上週末玩遊戲。　　　　　　D. 它是我所看過最棒的一場比賽了。

B 9. So, what do you do?

A. I am learning to cook.　　　　　B. I run a toy company.

C. I'm very well, thanks.　　　　　D. I finally found my smartphone.

問題：那麼，你是做什麼的呢？

選項：A. 我正在學習烹飪。　　　　　　B. 我經營一家玩具公司。

　　　　C. 我很好，謝謝。　　　　　　　D. 我終於找到我的智慧型手機了。

C 10. Have you got the time?

A. I'm available now.　　　　　　　B. I don't have the slightest idea.

C. My watch says 1 p.m.　　　　　D. I am late for work.

問題：你知道現在幾點嗎？

選項：A. 我現在有空。　　　　　　　　B. 我一點概念都沒有。

　　　　C. 我的手錶是下午一點。　　　　D. 我上班遲到了。

D 11. That's a beautiful ring you have.

A. It's all Greek to me.　　　　　　B. Sorry, I missed your phone.

C. Yeah, you deserve a medal.   D. Thank you. That's my birthday present.

問題：你的戒指真漂亮。

選項：A. 對我來說是天書。   B. 抱歉，我沒有接到你的來電。

       C. 對呀，你值得表揚。   D. 謝謝你。那是我的生日禮物。

B 12. The printer is out of paper.

    A. I'll call the technician.   B. I'll see if I can get some.

    C. The machine doesn't work.   D. The battery needs to be charged.

問題：印表機沒有紙了。

選項：A. 我致電給技術人員。   B. 我去看看能否找到一些。

       C. 這個機器沒辦法運轉了。   D. 電池需要被充電。

D 13. Why are you transferring to another school?

    A. It is a suitable place to live.   B. I can't wait to go to the new school.

    C. I decide to transfer to a new office.   D. I am not happy with the environment here.

問題：你為什麼要轉到另一所學校？

選項：A. 它是一個適合居住的地方。   B. 我迫不及待要去新的學校。

       C. 我決定調到新的辦公室。   D. 我不滿意這裡的環境。

D 14. I don't believe you.

    A. I'm jealous!   B. We've had enough.

    C. Stop lying to me!   D. I'm not making it up!

問題：我不相信你。

選項：A. 我在嫉妒！   B. 我們受夠了。

       C. 不要再對我說謊！   D. 這不是我憑空捏造的！

C 15. Let's get some strawberry ice cream!

    A. Watch your step.   B. What's the matter?

    C. No way! I'm on a diet.   D. All right. Just one sip.

問題：我們去買些草莓冰淇淋來吃吧！

選項：A. 走路小心。   B. 怎麼啦？

       C. 絕對不行！我正在節食。   D. 好吧。只能喝一小口喔。

第三部份：簡短對話

A 16. M: How do you like my vegetable garden?

    W: It's fantastic. So you don't use any chemicals at all, right?

    M: Nope! It's 100% natural.

    W: Wonderful! I've heard that some chemicals may threaten our health.

    M: Right. It's much better for you to eat vegetables that haven't been sprayed with harmful stuff.

    Q: Which of the following opinions would the man agree with?

       A. Organic food is healthier.

B. Chemicals help plants grow better.

C. Chemicals are necessary in vegetable gardens.

D. Not all vegetables are good for you.

男：你覺得我的菜園如何？

女：太驚人了。那麼，你沒有使用任何化學物質，對嗎？

男：沒有！這 100% 純天然。

女：太棒了！我聽聞有些化學物質可能對我們的健康有害。

男：是的。食用沒有噴灑有害物質的蔬菜對你較有益處。

問題：男子可能會認同下列何種觀點？

選項：A. 有機食物較健康。　　　　　　B. 化學物質幫助植物長得較好。

　　　C. 在菜園裡化學物質是必要的。　　D. 並非所有蔬菜都對你有好處。

A 17. W: I heard that Mary was offered a job with a new company. When will she leave?

M: I'm not certain. She didn't give me a straight answer.

W: Let's invite her to lunch, so we can ask her in private.

M: That's a good idea. She may not want it to be publicly known.

Q: Why doesn't the man know when Mary will leave?

A. Mary didn't provide a clear statement.

B. Mary will work in an office straight down the road.

C. He doesn't know what type of job Mary was offered.

D. He owes Mary a lunch for giving him a lift.

女：聽說一家新公司提供工作機會給 Mary。她什麼時候離職？

男：我不確定。她沒給我直接的答案。

女：我們邀她吃午餐好了，這樣我們就可以私下問她。

男：好主意。她可能不想讓大家知道。

問題：男子為什麼不知道 Mary 何時離職？

選項：A. Mary 未提供明確的說法。

　　　B. Mary 要在街底的一家公司上班。

　　　C. 他不知道 Mary 謀得什麼樣的工作。

　　　D. 他該請 Mary 一頓午餐，因為 Mary 順路載他一程。

D 18. M: What happened to your finger?

W: Well, I was chopping some onions and oops!

M: That must have been painful. Was it a deep cut?

W: No, I didn't need stitches. Just a Band-Aid.

M: Well, make sure it heals well and doesn't get infected.

W: Don't worry! I am a nurse, remember?

Q: What happened to the woman?

A. She worked as a nurse.

B. She chopped off one of her fingers.

C. She burned her hand while cooking.

D. She injured herself accidentally.

男：你的手指怎麼了？

女：哦，我正在切洋蔥，然後就唉唷！

男：那一定很痛。傷口很深嗎？

女：不會，我不需要縫合傷口。只要 OK 繃。

男：嗯，要確認傷口癒合良好，且不要感染了。

女：別擔心！我是護理師，記得嗎？

問題：女子發生什麼事？

選項：A. 她曾任職為護理師。　　　　　　B. 她切下自己一根手指。

　　　C. 她做菜時燒傷了手。　　　　　　D. 她不小心傷了自己。

A 19. W: What would you like to drink?

M: I've never been to this tea shop before. What is your specialty?

W: Our coffee bean milk tea is very tasty.

M: Does it have real coffee in it? I don't want to stay up all night.

W: OK. Then you'd better just order fruit tea.

Q: Where is the man?

    A. At a tea shop.　　　　　　　　　B. At a coffee shop.

    C. In a convenience store.　　　　　　D. In a supermarket.

女：想要喝點什麼？

男：我之前沒到過這家飲料店。你們的招牌飲料是什麼？

女：我們的咖啡豆奶茶非常好喝。

男：裡面真的有咖啡嗎？我不想整晚睡不著。

女：好的。那麼你還是點水果茶比較好。

問題：男子在哪裡？

選項：A. 在飲料店。　　B. 在咖啡店。　　　　C. 在便利商店。　　　　D. 在超市。

D 20. M: I think I have a cold coming on.

W: You should see my doctor. The last time I had a bad cough, she gave me some special herbs. They really seemed to help.

M: You're talking about Chinese medicine. I think I'll have something from the pharmacy.

W: I don't recommend doing that. My Chinese medical physician says that many Western medicines have side effects.

M: Well, of course she says that.

W: Have it your way. I'm only trying to help.

Q: What will the man probably do?

    A. Take nothing.

    B. Take some special herbs.

    C. Go to see the Chinese medical physician.

D. Get some medicine from the pharmacy.

男：我覺得我快感冒了。

女：你應該去看看我的醫生。上次我咳嗽很嚴重，她給我一些特別的藥草。它們似乎很有幫助。

男：你說的是中藥。我想我會去藥房買點藥吃。

女：我不建議你這樣做。我的中醫師說許多西藥都有副作用。

男：哦，她當然這麼說啊。

女：你高興就好。我只是想要幫忙而已。

問題：男子可能會做什麼？

選項：A. 什麼都不服用。　　　　　　　B. 服用一些特別的藥草。

　　　　C. 去看中醫。　　　　　　　　D. 從藥房裡買些藥。

B 21. W: I really don't know what I should study at university. How about you?

M: I'm thinking of going where lots of money is: business law.

W: There's more to life than earning money. You should do what you love.

M: Well, I would love to gain a lot of money.

W: I think you're missing the point.

Q: Why does the man want to study business law?

A. He doesn't know what else to do.

B. He wants to make a fortune.

C. He agrees with the woman's suggestion.

D. He is interested in doing business.

女：我真的不知道我大學要讀什麼？你呢？

男：我想要攻讀錢潮最多的地方，也就是商業法。

女：人生並不是只有賺大錢而已。你應該做你喜愛的事。

男：嗯，我想要得到很多錢。

女：我想你沒有理解重點。

問題：男子為什麼想讀商業法？

選項：A. 他不知道還有什麼可以做的。　　B. 他想賺取財富。

　　　　C. 他同意女子的建議。　　　　　D. 他對做生意有興趣。

C 22. M: Do you know the blender I bought at the electronics store the other day? It isn't working.

W: Take it back. Do you have the receipt?

M: That's the thing. I can't find it. I was wondering if you'd seen it anywhere.

W: If you kept your desk tidy, you might have a chance to find things when you need them.

M: I was actually trying to be more organized, so I threw out a bunch of stuff this morning.
Oh, I think I accidentally threw away the receipt.

Q: Where does the man think the receipt might be?

A. At the electronics store.　　　　　B. On his desk.

C. In the trash can.　　　　　　　　D. In the blender.

男：你知道我前幾天在電器行買的果汁機嗎？它壞掉了。

女：退回去吧。你有收據嗎？

男：這就是我要說的。我找不到它。我在想你有沒有在哪裡看到它。

女：如果你的桌子保持整潔的話，你可能就有機會在需要東西的時候找到它們。

男：我的確試著要更有條理，所以我今天早上丟了一堆東西。喔，我想我不小心丟掉收據了。

問題：男子認為收據可能會在哪裡？

選項：A. 在電器行。　　B. 在他桌上。　　　　C. 在垃圾桶裡。　　　　D. 在果汁機裡。

B 23. W: I've decided to do something about my weight. Starting from today, I'm going on a diet.

M: Wow! What's going on?

W: I just tried to put on an old pair of jeans, and I couldn't fasten the button.

M: Just buy a new pair of jeans. Problem solved!

W: And keep buying larger sizes as I'm putting on on weight? No, thanks!

M: It works for me.

Q: What made the woman want to lose weight?

　　A. She wants to try a new diet.

　　B. Her jeans are now too tight.

　　C. The man teased her about her figure.

　　D. She bought a pair of large-sized jeans.

女：我決定要對我的體重採取行動。從今天開始，我要節食。

男：哇！發生什麼事了？

女：我試著穿上一條舊的牛仔褲，而我無法扣上鈕扣。

男：買一條新的牛仔褲就行了。問題解決啦！

女：然後隨著我的體重越來越重，就一直買越來越大的尺寸的褲子？謝了，我才不要！

男：對我來說很有用。

問題：是什麼原因讓這女子想減肥？

選項：A. 她想要嘗試新的飲食。　　　　B. 她的牛仔褲現在太緊了。

　　　C. 男子嘲笑她的身材。　　　　D. 她買了件大尺寸的牛仔褲。

C 24.

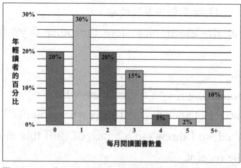

For question number 24, please look at the bar chart.

M: Have you read today's newspaper? On this page, the bar chart shows information about young people's reading habits in our country in the past year.

W: Yes, I've read. According to the chart, about 80% of young people in our country read regularly.

M: Yes. Though most of them read only one book per month, a large number read two or three books.

W: After that, the number of young people who read five books a month became much smaller, falling to merely 2%.

M: However, much to my surprise, 10% of young people read more than five books per month!

Q: When the woman said "read regularly," what did she mean?

    A. Reading 1 book every day.

    B. Reading less than 1 book a month.

    C. Reading more than 1 book a month.

    D. Reading more than 5 books a month.

第二十四題,請看長條圖。

男:你看過今天的報紙了嗎?在這一頁,這個長條圖顯示過去一年我國年輕人閱讀習慣的資訊。

女:有,我看過。根據這張圖表,我國大約 80% 的年輕人經常閱讀。

男:是的。雖然他們大部份人每個月只讀一本書,但也有很多人讀二或三本書。

女:在那之後,每個月讀五本書的年輕人的數字變小很多,掉到只有 2%。

男:然而,令我很驚訝的是,10% 的年輕人每個月讀超過五本書!

問題:當女子說「經常閱讀」時,她是指什麼意思?

選項:A. 每天讀一本書。   B. 每個月讀少於一本書。

      C. 每個月讀超過一本書。   D. 每個月讀超過五本書。

解析 由對話可知 80% 的年輕人經常閱讀;而根據長條圖,不讀書的年輕人佔 20%,可推知女子認為每個月讀超過一本書就算經常閱讀,故答案選 C。

C 25. For question number 25, please look at the school timetable.

課 表	
8:10–9:00	數學
9:10–10:00	歷史
10:10–11:00	地理
11:10–12:00	英文

W: I came to school late and missed the first class this morning.

M: Was it because of the heavy rain?

W: Yes. What's today's math homework?

M: I'll show it to you later. It's 10:05. Hurry up, or we'll be late for class.

Q: Which class are the speakers going to attend?

    A. The math class.   B. The history class.

    C. The geography class.   D. The English class.

第二十五題,請看課表。

女:今天早上我晚到校且錯過了第一堂課。

男:是因為下大雨嗎?

女:是啊。今天的數學作業是什麼?

男：我晚點會給你看。十點五分了。快一點，不然我們上課會遲到。

問題：說話者們將要上哪一堂課？

選項：A. 數學課。　　　B. 歷史課。　　　C. 地理課。　　　D. 英文課。

解析　由對話可知說話者們說話的時間是十點五分；而根據課表，十點十分是地理課，故答案選 C。

....

第四部份：簡短談話

D 26. Do you believe that our own universe could be just one of countless other universes? It is known as the multiverse. It's an incredible theory that has not been proven yet. However, some scientists not only think that the multiverse is possible, but also believe that our universe is affected by other universes. It may be many decades before scientists figure out whether or not the multiverse truly exists, no matter what.

Q: What would the speaker say about the multiverse?

　　A. It is nonsense.　　　　　　　　B. It is a weird theory.

　　C. It has countless stars.　　　　　D. It has not been proven yet.

你相信我們的宇宙可能只是其他數不盡的宇宙的其中之一嗎？這就是知名的多重宇宙論。這是還沒被證實的驚人理論。然而，有些科學家不僅相信多重宇宙論是有可能的，而且還相信我們的宇宙受其他的宇宙影響。不管怎樣，在科學家找出是否有多重宇宙論的真相之前，可能還要花上數十年的時間。

問題：說話者是怎麼看多重宇宙論？

選項：A. 它是胡說八道。　　　　　　B. 它是一個奇怪的理論。

　　　C. 它有數不清的星星。　　　　D. 它還沒被證實。

C 27. How do you feel when your friends always use their smartphones and completely ignore you? Drive you crazy? The problem of "phubbing" seems to affect many people. More and more people prefer to use their smartphones than pay attention to their friends and family. Some people say smartphones can kill off basic social skills such as how to carry on a conversation.

Q: According to the report, what is the disadvantage of using smartphones?

　　A. Paying more attention to advertisements.

　　B. Paying a lot of money for mobile games.

　　C. Losing the ability to hold a conversation.

　　D. Losing temper with close friends.

你的朋友總是使用他們的智慧型手機，並完全地忽視你，你會感覺如何？讓你抓狂？「低頭族」的問題似乎影響許多人。越來越多人喜歡使用手機而不把注意力放在他們的親朋好友上。有些人說智慧型手機可能扼殺像是如何進行對話等的基礎社交技巧。

問題：根據報導，使用智慧型手機的缺點是什麼？

選項：A. 花更多注意力在廣告上。　　　B. 為了手機遊戲花大錢。

　　　C. 失去與人談話的能力。　　　　D. 對好朋友發脾氣。

A 28. A vegetarian is someone who doesn't eat meat. However, some vegetarians do eat animal products such as eggs, milk, and cheese. Some Taiwanese vegans, on the other hand, don't eat meat, animal products, and specific spices. Be careful when ordering food in vegan restaurants overseas because dishes often contain onion and garlic. If there's any doubt about food, ask the staff. They will be more than happy to answer your questions.

Q: What advice is given to the listeners?

    A. To pay attention to the ingredients.

    B. To eat animal products carefully.

    C. To mix together the meat, onion, and garlic.

    D. To enjoy cheese and eggs from Taiwan.

素食者是不吃肉的人。然而，有些素食者的確會食用蛋、牛奶、起司等動物製品。另一方面，一些臺灣的純素食主義者是不吃肉、動物製品和特定的辛香料。在國外的素食餐廳點餐時應格外小心，因為餐點常有洋蔥或大蒜。如果對食物有任何疑慮，就問工作人員。他們會非常樂意回答你的問題。

問題：何項建議提供給聽者？

選項：A. 注意食材。   B. 小心食用動物製品。

           C. 將肉、洋蔥和大蒜混合在一起。   D. 享用來自臺灣的起司和蛋。

D 29. A massive earthquake claimed over 8,000 lives and injured more than 18,000. Many people were left homeless. In addition to the tragic loss of life, numerous great cultural treasures were completely destroyed or severely damaged in the earthquake, including many historically important temples and towers. For the nation, the road to recovery will be a long one, and there will always be the fear that another large earthquake will strike at any time.

Q: What is mainly discussed in this passage?

    A. The influence on the local culture.

    B. The difficult rescues after the earthquake.

    C. The reasons why the death rate was so high.

    D. The death and destruction caused by the earthquake.

一場巨大的地震奪走超過八千人的生命，並有超過一萬八千人受傷。許多人都無家可歸。除了人員傷亡的慘劇之外，無數珍貴的文化遺產在地震中不是全毀就是嚴重毀損，其中還包括許多歷史上重要的寺廟和塔。對於國民來說，重建之路將很漫長，而且也伴隨著另一場大地震會隨時發生的恐懼。

問題：本文主要在討論什麼？

選項：A. 對當地文化的影響。   B. 地震過後困難的救援任務。

           C. 死亡率如此高的原因。   D. 地震所造成的傷亡及毀滅。

B 30. Being a senior high school student is not very easy. In addition to my homework and preparation for the class, I have a tight schedule after school. Every day, I have two hours of English conversation at a language school nearby. At first, I didn't like going there because my grades were terrible. But now I really look forward to it, and learning English is more like a hobby than a subject.

Q: What is the speaker's attitude toward English?

    A. He tries to avoid it.   B. He enjoys learning it.

    C. He finds it easy to learn.   D. He improves his English.

當個高中生是相當不容易的。除了我的功課和課堂準備之外，我放學後還有緊湊的行程。每天，我在附近的語言學校有兩小時的英語會話課。一開始，我不喜歡去那裡上課，因為我的分數很糟糕。但現在我真的很期待去上課，而且學習英文更像是興趣，而非科目。

問題：說話者對於英文的態度是什麼？

選項：A. 他試著避免它。   B. 他喜歡學習它。

         C. 他發現它容易學習。   D. 他改進他的英文。

B 31. Are you a dog person or a cat person? If you have to choose between cats and dogs, which do you prefer? I'm a cat person. The reason I like cats is that they are quite independent and quiet. They don't lick your face with the tongue and bark noisily. Instead, they enjoy a nap on the sofa, or walk around the house with calm dignity. Cats can sometimes seem to be a little bit cold, but there are also many cats that are warm.

Q: Why doesn't the speaker seem to like dogs?

    A. They are dirty.   B. They lick your face.

    C. They are always hungry.   D. They follow you everywhere.

你是愛狗人士還是愛貓人士呢？如果你必須在貓和狗中間選一個，你會選哪一個？我是個愛貓人士。我喜歡貓的原因是牠們相當獨立且安靜。牠們不會用舌頭舔你的臉還有吵鬧地吠叫。相反地，牠們喜歡在沙發上小睡片刻或莊重沉穩地在家中走動。貓有時候會讓人覺得有點冷酷，但還是有很多貓是溫暖的。

問題：說話者為什麼似乎不喜歡狗？

選項：A. 牠們很髒。   B. 牠們會舔你的臉。   C. 牠們總是很餓。   D. 牠們總是跟著你。

C 32. Have you noticed that selfie drones are on trend now? Instead of holding selfie sticks, using selfie drones are getting popular. Selfie drones are small devices, and they could fly around like mini helicopters. They follow tracking devices on users. For example, your selfie drone automatically takes photos of you while you ski down the hill. Selfie drones are certainly not cheap. However, the cost is sure to go down as the market grows.

Q: According to the speaker, what is likely to happen in the future?

    A. Flying helicopters will cost much.   B. More people will use selfie sticks.

    C. Selfie drones will become cheaper.   D. People will be good at photography.

你有注意到空拍機現在正流行嗎？不再是拿著自拍棒，使用空拍機逐漸流行。空拍機是小型裝置，它們能到處飛來飛去，就像迷你直升機。它們會追蹤使用者的偵測裝置。例如，當你自山上滑雪而下時，你的空拍機自動給你拍照。空拍機肯定不便宜。然而，隨著市場成長，價格一定會跟著降低。

問題：根據說話者，未來很可能發生什麼事？

選項：A. 開直升機會花太多錢。   B. 更多人會使用自拍棒。

C. 空拍機將會變便宜。   D. 人們將會善於攝影。

A 33. Sports are an important part of children's education. However, many schools are cutting back on time spent doing sports in order to give students more time in the classroom. One possible consequence of this is that students are becoming increasingly unhealthy. Some teachers often put the blame on smartphones and the Internet. But if you ask students why they don't exercise much, you will usually hear the same answer—too many math classes and Chinese classes! Perhaps schools should consider letting students have more PE lessons during school hours.

Q: What is one reason given by some teachers for students' lack of exercise?

    A. Smartphones.   B. Education.   C. Homework.   D. PE classes.

運動是兒童教育重要的一環。然而，許多學校為了要讓學生有更多時間待在教室裡，正在減少運動的時間。其中一個可能的後果是學生變得越來越不健康。有一些老師常將此歸罪於智慧型手機和網路。但若是你問學生為什麼他們這麼少運動的話，你通常會聽到一樣的回答——太多數學課和國文課了！或許學校應該考慮讓學生在學校上課時多上點體育課。

問題：一些老師對於學生缺乏運動所給的理由是什麼？

選項：A. 智慧型手機。 B. 教育。   C. 家庭作業。   D. 體育課。

B 34. For question number 34, please look at the recipe.

Today, I'll show you how to make cookies. First, preheat the oven to 160°C. Next, stir melted butter and white sugar together. Then, add 1 egg to the mixture. The fourth step is to put the flour into the mixture to make a dough and make different shapes of cookies you want. Last, bake at 160°C for about 15 minutes. Take the cookies out of the oven, and let them cool down. Now, you can enjoy cookies with your family or friends.

Q: What is the last ingredient that should be put into the mixture?

    A. 1 egg.   B. Flour.   C. White sugar.   D. Unsalted butter.

第三十四題，請看食譜。

今天，我將為你們展示如何做餅乾。首先，將烤箱預熱到攝氏 160 度。接著，把融化的奶油和白糖攪拌在一起。然後，加一顆蛋到混合物裡。第四步是將麵粉放入混合物裡做成麵團，並做出你想要的不同形狀的餅乾。最後，用攝氏 160 度烤大約 15 分鐘。將餅乾移出烤箱讓它們冷卻。現在，你可以和你的家人或朋友享用餅乾了。

問題：最後應該被放入混合物的材料是什麼？

選項：A. 一顆蛋。   B. 麵粉。   C. 白糖。   D. 無鹽奶油。

解 析   由談話內容可知最後加入混合物的材料是食譜上的麵粉，故答案選 B。

C 35. For question number 35, please look at the invitation card.

We're pleased to inform you that you are invited to the party honoring Jerry White as the new president of Sanmin University. The party will be held on January 26th, at 6:30 p.m.–9:30 p.m. at MCA Center. The evening will begin with a wine reception from 6:45 p.m., followed by lectures at 7:15 p.m. Please tell us if you are available before January 20th by contacting us at (025)0743-8161 or by emailing us at sanmin@smail.com.tw. We look forward to your arrival.

你被邀請
參加派對
以向三民大學的
新校長
Jerry White
致敬

週六，1月26日
晚上6點30分至9點30分
MCA中心

Q: Which of the following information is NOT provided?

A. The time of the party.　　B. The location of the party.
C. The entrance fee to the party.　　D. The purpose of the party.

第三十五題，請看邀請函。

我們很高興地通知你，你被邀請參加向三民大學新校長 Jerry White 致敬的派對。派對將於一月二十六日，晚上六點三十分至九點三十分在 MCA 中心舉行。晚上從六點四十五分將以酒會開場，隨後七點十五分是演講。請在一月二十日前確認你是否能出席，以電話 (025)0743-8161 或電子郵件 sanmin@smail.com.tw 聯繫我們。我們期待你的到來。

問題：以下何項資訊沒有被提供？

選項：A. 派對的時間。 B. 派對的地點。　　C. 派對的入場費。　　D. 派對的目的。

解析 談話內容有提到派對時間、地點、舉行目的以及會進行酒會和演講，而邀請函裡並無提到入場費，故答案選 C。

第一部份：看圖辨義

C 1. For questions number 1 and 2, please look at picture A.

Question number 1: Where will this letter be sent?

A. To the United States.   B. To New Zealand.

C. To the United Kingdom.   D. To the Republic of India.

第一題及第二題，請看圖片 A。

第一題：這封信將被寄往何處？

選項：A. 到美國。   B. 到紐西蘭。   C. 到英國。   D. 到印度。

D 2. Question number 2: Please look at picture A again. What else do we know about this letter?

A. It's an urgent package.

B. It will be shipped by cargo ship.

C. It probably contains a photograph.

D. The sender hasn't put a stamp on it.

第二題：請再看一次圖片 A。關於這封信，我們還知道哪些資訊？

選項：A. 它是個緊急包裹。   B. 它將由貨船運送。

     C. 它可能裝著照片。   D. 寄件人尚未在上面貼一張郵票。

D 3. For question number 3, please look at picture B.

Question number 3: What can be inferred from the picture?

A. They are playing tennis.

B. They are playing mixed doubles.

C. The player on the left is frustrated.

D. The player on the right has been defeated.

第三題，請看圖片 B。

第三題：從圖中可以推測什麼？

選項：A. 他們在打網球。   B. 他們在打混合雙打。

     C. 左邊的選手很沮喪。   D. 右邊的選手被擊敗了。

A 4. For question number 4, please look at picture C.

Question number 4: What is true about the picture?

A. The woman is putting on her make-up.

B. The woman is not good at eye make-up.

C. The woman is wearing too much perfume.

D. The woman may have a dinner with her boyfriend later.

第四題，請看圖片 C。

第四題：關於這張圖片何者正確？

選項：A. 女子正在上妝。   B. 女子不擅長眼妝。

     C. 女子噴了太多香水。   D. 女子稍後可能會與男友共進晚餐。

C 5. For question number 5, please look at picture D.

　　Question number 5: What is the farmer doing?

　　A. He is cooking grain.　　　　　　　B. He is staying up late.

　　C. He is keeping the poultry.　　　　D. He is waking the rooster up.

　　第五題，請看圖片 D。

　　第五題：農夫在做什麼？

　　選項：A. 他正在烹調穀物。　　　　　B. 他正在熬夜。

　　　　　C. 他正在飼養家禽。　　　　　D. 他正在叫公雞起床。

第二部份：問答

D 6. Could you turn the air conditioner up?

　　A. I will put it on.　　　　　　　　B. OK. I am freezing.

　　C. Do you feel cold?　　　　　　　　D. Sure. No problem.

　　問題：你能把冷氣機開強一點嗎？

　　選項：A. 我會穿上它。　 B. 好。我都凍僵了。　 C. 你感到冷嗎？　　　 D. 當然。沒問題。

D 7. Let's do something this weekend!

　　A. It's a piece of cake.　　　　　　B. Sorry, life is too short.

　　C. What about tomorrow?　　　　　　D. Sure. What do you have in mind?

　　問題：我們這週末一起做些什麼吧！

　　選項：A. 這輕而易舉。　　　　　　　B. 對不起，人生短暫。

　　　　　C. 明天如何？　　　　　　　　D. 當然。你有什麼想法？

C 8. How about having dinner together after work this Friday night?

　　A. What time on Saturday?　　　　　B. How about another cup of coffee?

　　C. I won't be available that day.　　D. Something suddenly came up at home.

　　問題：這週五晚上下班後一起吃晚餐如何？

　　選項：A. 週六什麼時間？　　　　　　B. 再來一杯咖啡如何？

　　　　　C. 我那天不方便。　　　　　　D. 家裡突然有事。

A 9. I'm waiting for you in front of the movie theater.

　　A. Sorry, but I'll be 10 minutes late.　B. It starts at seven o'clock.

　　C. What's the name of the movie?　　D. The theater is around the corner.

　　問題：我正在電影院前等你。

　　選項：A. 抱歉，我會遲到十分鐘。　　B. 它七點開始。

　　　　　C. 電影的名字是什麼？　　　　D. 電影院就在轉角。

D 10. I'd like to invite you over for dinner next week.

　　A. The food there is great.　　　　　B. Please show me the way.

　　C. I had a good time last weekend.　D. Did you talk to your parents first?

　　問題：下週我想邀請你到我家吃晚餐。

　　選項：A. 那裡的食物很棒。　　　　　B. 請告訴我怎麼走。

C. 上週末我玩得很愉快。　　　　　　　　D. 你有先和你父母說了嗎？

C 11. Who's going to win the election?

    A. Get lost!　　　　B. Hang on!　　　C. Beats me!　　　　D. Get down!

    問題：誰會贏得大選呀？

    選項：A. 走開啦！　　B. 稍等一會兒！　　C. 我不知道！　　　D. 記下來！

C 12. I'd like a pound of beef, please.

    A. To go, please.　　　　　　　　　　B. Here's your change.

    C. I'm afraid we've sold out.　　　　　D. Do you take credit cards?

    問題：請給我一磅牛肉。

    選項：A. 外帶，謝謝。　　　　　　　　B. 你的零錢。

    　　　　C. 抱歉，我們賣完了。　　　　D. 你們接受刷卡嗎？

D 13. I'm so sorry about the other day.

    A. My goodness!　　　　　　　　　　B. We had a blast.

    C. You're welcome.　　　　　　　　　D. Apology accepted.

    問題：關於前幾天我真的很抱歉。

    選項：A. 天哪！　　B. 我們玩得很愉快。　　C. 不客氣。　　　D. 我接受你的道歉。

D 14. Where the heck is Brian?

    A. I've lost my place in the book.　　　B. Check your route on this online map.

    C. It's on the top shelf in the storeroom.　　D. He called to say he's stuck in traffic.

    問題：Brian 到底在哪裡？

    選項：A. 我忘了書看到哪裡了。　　　　B. 在電子地圖上確認你的路線。

    　　　　C. 在貯藏室裡架子的最上層。　　D. 他打電話來說他塞在車陣裡。

B 15. My skin feels so itchy.

    A. Put this mask on.　　　　　　　　B. Try this cream.

    C. Go to the dentist now!　　　　　　D. There are germs everywhere!

    問題：我的皮膚好癢。

    選項：A. 戴上這個面具。　　　　　　　B. 試試看這個乳霜。

    　　　　C. 現在看牙醫！　　　　　　　D. 到處都是細菌！

第三部份：簡短對話

B 16. M: Turn down your music, please!

    W: What? I've got my headphones on. Sorry, what was that?

    M: I said turn down your music. I can hear your music from here. That can't be good for
       your ears, you know.

    Q: What does the man tell the woman?

      A. She was born deaf.　　　　　　　B. The volume is too loud.

      C. She has terrible taste in music.　　D. He can't tell what she's saying.

    男：請把你的音樂關小一點！

女：什麼？我戴著我的耳機。抱歉，你剛說什麼？

男：我說把你的音樂關小一點。我從這裡就可以聽到你的音樂。你知道這樣對你的耳朵不好。

問題：男子跟女子說什麼？

選項：A. 她天生耳聾。　　　　　　　　B. 音量太大了。

　　　C. 她對音樂的品味很糟。　　　　D. 他分辨不清她在說什麼。

A 17. W: Can you believe that driver? It's very dangerous to overtake on a bend, especially on the freeway.

M: You're right. But maybe we should slow down a bit as people say, "Better safe than sorry."

W: It's not a good idea. The speed limit here is 50 mph.

Q: What might the woman want to do?

　　A. Keep driving at the same speed.　　B. Catch up with the other driver.

　　C. Ask the man to drive instead.　　　D. Take medicine to calm down.

女：你相信有這樣的駕駛嗎？在彎道超車太危險了，特別是在高速公路上。

男：你說得沒錯。但或許我們應該慢一點，就像人家說「防範於未然。」

女：這不是個好主意。這邊限速每小時 50 英里。

問題：女子可能想做什麼？

選項：A. 繼續保持原來的速度。　　　　B. 追上另一名駕駛。

　　　C. 要求換男子開車。　　　　　　D. 吃點藥冷靜一下。

C 18. M: Look at those poor lions. They look so weak and bored.

W: It's a kind of torture to keep these amazing animals locked up in such a small space.

M: Exactly! They should be living free in the wild, not in a zoo.

Q: What does the man imply about the zoo?

　　A. It is illegal.　　　　　　　　　　B. It is dangerous.

　　C. It is quite cruel.　　　　　　　　D. It is environmentally friendly.

男：快看那些可憐的獅子。牠們看起來很虛弱又煩悶。

女：把那些了不起的動物關在這麼小的空間裡算是一種折磨。

男：沒錯！牠們應該自由自在地住在野外，而不是在動物園裡。

問題：關於動物園，男子暗示什麼？

選項：A. 它是違法的。　　　　　　　　B. 它是危險的。

　　　C. 它是相當殘忍的。　　　　　　D. 它是對環境友善的。

D 19. W: I want to do something more exciting this summer vacation.

M: What do you have in mind?

W: I don't know. Something like hiking in Spain or camping in the rainforest in Brazil.

M: Doesn't sound like much fun to me.

W: You know what? Maybe we should consider going on separate holidays this year.

Q: What can we say about the man?

　　A. He has been to Tibet.

B. He doesn't have his own travel plans.

C. He'd like to go with the woman.

D. He is not interested in the woman's idea.

女：我今年暑假想要做點更刺激的事。

男：你有什麼想法呢？

女：我不知道。像是去西班牙健行或是在巴西雨林裡露營。

男：怎麼我聽起來沒有很有趣。

女：你知道嗎？或許今年我們應該考慮分開旅行。

問題：關於男子我們可以怎麼說？

選項：A. 他去過西藏了。　　　　　　　　B. 他沒有自己的旅行計畫。

　　　　C. 他想跟女子一起去。　　　　　D. 他對女子的想法不感興趣。

B 20. M: Ouch, the skin on my back is so sore. I can't lie on my back.

W: Wow! It's really red. Why did you fall asleep on the beach?

M: I was too sleepy. Can you help me put some gel on my back?

W: All right then.

Q: What's wrong with the man?

　　A. He had a stroke.　　　　　　　　B. He's got sunburn.

　　C. He's got a skin disease.　　　　　D. He pulled a muscle in his back.

男：噢，我背上的皮膚好痛。我無法躺下。

女：哇！它真的好紅。你為什麼要在沙灘上睡著？

男：我太睏了。你可以幫我在背上擦些凝膠嗎？

女：好啊。

問題：男子怎麼了？

選項：A. 他中風了。　　　　　　　　　B. 他皮膚曬傷。

　　　　C. 他得了皮膚病。　　　　　　　D. 他拉傷了背部的肌肉。

D 21. W: My mother is coming to visit this weekend.

M: Oh, OK. Any special reason?

W: Actually, she wants to visit my father's grave. It's been a year since he passed away.

M: Got it. We can get some flowers in town and then go together.

W: Sure!

Q: What do we learn about the woman's mother?

　　A. She is unwell.　　　　　　　　　B. She is in grave danger.

　　C. She got divorced.　　　　　　　　D. She will come this weekend.

女：我的母親這週末要過來一趟。

男：噢，好啊。有什麼特別的原因嗎？

女：事實上是，她想去看我父親的墓。他已經過世一年了。

男：了解。我們去城裡買些花，然後一起過去。

女：當然！

問題：關於女子的母親，我們知道什麼？

選項：A. 她身體不舒服。　　　　　　　　B. 她身陷危險。

　　　C. 她離婚了。　　　　　　　　　　D. 她這週末會來。

D 22. M: Hello, Ms. Chen. I am calling about this month's rent. You are supposed to pay before the 5th of each month and it's already the 10th now.

W: I'm really sorry about that. The thing is that I was just laid off last week. I'm short of cash right now. Can you give me a couple more weeks?

M: I'll give you until the 20th. Otherwise, I'm going to ask you to move out.

Q: Who is the man?

　　A. The woman's ex-husband.　　　　B. The woman's supervisor.

　　C. The woman's bank manager.　　　D. The woman's landlord.

男：哈囉，陳女士。我打電話來是要說關於這個月房租的事。你應該要在每月的五號前付款，現在都已經十號了。

女：我真的很抱歉。事情是這樣的，我上週剛被裁員。我現在沒有這麼多現金。你可以多給我幾週的時間嗎？

男：我會寬限你到二十號。不然的話，我就只好請你搬走。

問題：男子是誰？

選項：A. 女子的前夫。　B. 女子的主管。　　　C. 女子的銀行經理。　D. 女子的房東。

C 23. W: Our neighbor is playing his drums again!

M: It's no use getting mad. Shouting through the wall isn't going to help either.

W: Then, what do you suggest?

M: I'm going to bake some delicious cookies and go there for a friendly little chat. I think I can make him see our point of view.

W: It's worth a try, I suppose.

Q: How will the man stop the neighbor making so much noise?

　　A. He will tell him to move.　　　　B. He will take away his drums.

　　C. He will communicate with him.　　D. He will teach him how to bake.

女：我們的鄰居又再打他的鼓！

男：生氣是沒用的。對牆吼叫也於事無補。

女：那麼，你有什麼建議呢？

男：我要烤些美味的餅乾過去，然後親切地跟他談談。我想我可以讓他了解我們的感受。

女：我想那值得一試。

問題：男子會如何阻止那位製造很多噪音的鄰居呢？

選項：A. 他會叫他搬走。　　　　　　　　B. 他會拿走他的鼓。

　　　C. 他會和他溝通。　　　　　　　　D. 他會教他如何烘焙。

B 24. For question number 24, please look at the bar chart.

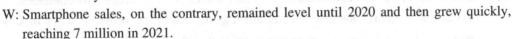

M: Look at this report! The bar chart illustrates information about the number of notebook computers and smartphones sold in our country between 2018 and 2021.

W: According to the chart, there were upward trends in both products.

M: Notebook sales increased steadily by 2 million each year.

W: Smartphone sales, on the contrary, remained level until 2020 and then grew quickly, reaching 7 million in 2021.

M: They were still less than the sales of notebooks, but they were only 1 million behind.

W: Generally speaking, the sales of both products increased.

Q: How many smartphones were sold in the country between 2018 and 2019?

    A. 2 million.   B. 4 million.   C. 6 million.   D. 7 million.

第二十四題,請看長條圖。

男:看看這份報告!這張長條圖說明我國 2018 到 2021 年間筆記型電腦和智慧型手機的銷售數量。

女:根據這張圖表,兩項產品都有上升的趨勢。

男:筆記型電腦的銷售每年穩定增加兩百萬臺。

女:相反地,智慧型手機的銷售直到 2020 年都持平,然後快速成長,在 2021 年達到七百萬臺。

男:它們還是少於筆記型電腦的銷售量,但是只少一百萬臺。

女:普遍來說,兩項產品的銷售都增加了。

問題:2018 年到 2019 年間智慧型手機在該國賣出多少臺?

選項:A. 兩百萬臺。   B. 四百萬臺。   C. 六百萬臺。   D. 七百萬臺。

解析 對話中提到智慧型手機的銷售直到 2020 年都沒變,由此可知右邊的長條代表智慧型手機。智慧型手機在 2018 年和 2019 年的銷售量皆為兩百萬臺,相加即為四百萬臺,故答案選 B。

D 25. For question number 25, please look at the room card.

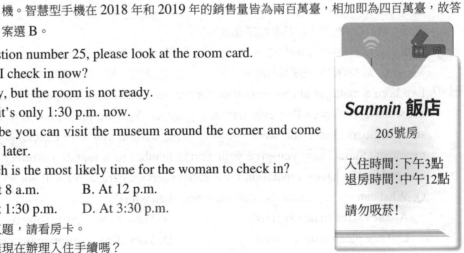

W: Can I check in now?

M: Sorry, but the room is not ready.

W: Oh, it's only 1:30 p.m. now.

M: Maybe you can visit the museum around the corner and come back later.

Q: Which is the most likely time for the woman to check in?

    A. At 8 a.m.   B. At 12 p.m.

    C. At 1:30 p.m.   D. At 3:30 p.m.

第二十五題,請看房卡。

女:我能現在辦理入住手續嗎?

男：抱歉，但房間還沒準備好。

女：噢，現在才下午一點三十分。

男：也許你可以參觀轉角的博物館，晚點再回來。

問題：何者是女子最有可能辦理入住手續的時間？

選項：A. 上午八點。　　B. 中午十二點。　　C. 下午一點三十分。　　D. 下午三點三十分。

解析 由房卡可知下午三點開始可以辦理入住手續；而根據對話，可知下午一點三十分時，房間尚未準備好，故答案選 D。

第四部份：簡短談話

A 26. Global warming has been in the news a lot these days. As average temperatures around the world reach record highs, scientists are urgently exploring different ways of producing power without releasing more carbon dioxide into the atmosphere. As a result, solar panel technology has advanced at a remarkable pace over the past decade. One of the disadvantages of solar panels is that they are expensive. However, thanks to the recent discovery of a new material, solar panel production might soon become much cheaper. It is hoped that greater use of solar panel technology will reduce our need for fossil fuels, which produce enormous amounts of carbon dioxide.

Q: What does the speaker say about fossil fuels?

 A. We rely on them for power.

 B. They are replacing solar energy.

 C. A new type of fuel has been invented.

 D. New technology removes carbon dioxide from them.

最近全球暖化占據了許多新聞版面。隨著全球平均溫度創新高，科學家們急迫地拓展不同的方法創造無須釋放更多二氧化碳到大氣裡的能源。因此，太陽能板科技在過去十年來有著驚人的先進發展。太陽能板其中一個缺點是它們很貴。然而，多虧了最近發現的新材料，太陽能板的生產可能很快就會變得更便宜。希望大量使用太陽能板科技能降低我們對那些產生大量二氧化碳的石油燃料的需求。

問題：關於石油燃料，說話者做何表示？

選項：A. 我們依賴它們取得能源。　　B. 它們正在取代太陽能。

  C. 新型的燃料已經發明出來了。　　D. 新科技將二氧化碳從中除去。

B 27. I've been a manager at this restaurant for ten years, and what happened tonight was one of the worst experiences I've ever had in my career. You are all supposed to be professional staff members. Judy, you were chewing gum. Darren, you kept checking your phone for messages. Sam, I saw you give your phone number to a female customer. These are not acceptable. We have a reputation for excellent service here, and I will not let you ruin that.

Q: What can we say about the staff members' behaviors?

 A. They were to be expected.　　B. They were unprofessional.

 C. They pleased the customers.　　D. They did not surprise the manager.

我已經在這家餐廳當了十年的經理了，今晚發生的事是我職業生涯中最糟的其中一個經驗。你們都應該是專業的工作人員。Judy，你在嚼口香糖。Darren，你一直查看手機簡訊。Sam，我看到你把你的電話號碼給了一位女性客人。這些是無法被接受的。我們以良好的服務著稱，我不會讓你們毀了它。

問題：我們可以怎麼看工作人員的行為？

選項：A. 他們在預期之中。　　　　　　B. 他們很不專業。

　　　C. 他們讓客人滿意。　　　　　　D. 他們沒有使經理訝異。

B 28. My favorite pastime is baking cookies. Whenever I have free time, I search the Internet for interesting recipes. Then, I stay in the kitchen and simply start mixing the ingredients together to make different cookies. What I love about baking cookies is that it's pretty hard to mess up. As long as you follow the recipe and make sure that you don't bake them for too long, cookies will come out really well every time. I've rarely had any total failure.

Q: Why does the speaker enjoy baking cookies?

　　A. They cost little to make.　　　　B. It is not difficult to make them.

　　C. It is an activity you can do alone.　D. He can try his own cookie recipes.

我最喜愛的消遣是烤餅乾。每當我有空閒時間，我會在網路上搜尋有趣的食譜。然後，我就會待在廚房並開始混合所有食材做出不同的餅乾。我愛烤餅乾的原因是因為它很難搞砸。只要你遵循食譜，並且確認你沒有烤太久，餅乾每次都會很不錯。我很少有徹底失敗的時候。

問題：為什麼說話者喜歡烤餅乾？

選項：A. 製作它們花費很少。　　　　　B. 製作它們並不困難。

　　　C. 它是個你可以獨自完成的活動。　D. 他可以試做他自己的餅乾食譜。

A 29. Have you ever considered keeping your own hens? You might think that keeping hens is difficult and expensive. In fact, in many ways, it is a lot easier and cheaper to keep chickens than it is to have pets like cats and dogs. Of course, hens can also give you something that dogs and cats can't — delicious eggs! Another advantage of keeping chickens is that they can eat bugs and weeds in your backyard. What's more, they will provide you with free and natural fertilizers! So, if you have a backyard, why not try keeping a few chickens?

Q: What does the speaker explain about raising hens?

　　A. It's not as hard as you think.

　　B. It brings bugs and weeds.

　　C. Hens can give you artificial fertilizers.

　　D. Hens get along well with your other pets.

你有考慮過飼養自己的母雞嗎？你或許會認為養母雞又難又貴。事實上，從許多方面來看，養雞比養像是貓或狗這類寵物來得簡單和便宜。當然，母雞可以提供你狗和貓無法給你的——美味的雞蛋！養雞的另一個優點是牠們會吃你們家後院的蟲子和雜草。而且，牠們還會提供你免費又天然的肥料！所以，如果你有個後院的話，何不試著養幾隻雞呢？

問題：關於飼養母雞，說話者有何解釋？

選項：A. 它並不如你所想的困難。　　　　B. 它帶來蟲子和雜草。

　　　　C. 母雞可以給你人工肥料。　　　D. 母雞與你的其他寵物相處愉快。

D 30. When I was in elementary school, there was a short and skinny boy in my class called Jeremy. No one liked him. Whenever we had to do work in groups, Jeremy would sit by himself until the teacher forced one of the groups to take him. One day while going down the stairs, he tripped and fell. He wasn't hurt, but some people laughed at him there. Then, one of his classmates helped him pick up his things. At that moment I suddenly felt ashamed of how we had all been treating him. What had he ever done to us, I wondered? How I wish I had been the one to offer him help.

Q: How does the speaker feel about Jeremy?

　　A. He forgives him for what he did.　　B. He thinks he deserved what he got.

　　C. He feels confused about his emotions.　　D. He deeply regrets how he treated him.

在我國小的時候，班上有一個叫做 Jeremy 的瘦小男孩。沒有人喜歡他。每當我們要分組活動時，Jeremy 會獨自坐在一旁，直到老師要求某一組讓他成為組員。有一天下樓梯的時候，他絆倒並摔跤了。他沒有受傷，但有些人在那裡嘲笑他。然後，其中一位同學幫他撿起他的東西。那一刻，我突然為我們一直以來對待他的方式感到羞愧。我思索著，他到底對我們做了什麼？我多麼希望我是那個提供他協助的人。

問題：說話者對 Jeremy 有何感想？

選項：A. 他原諒他所做的事。　　　　　B. 他覺得他罪有應得。

　　　　C. 他對他的感受感到困惑。　　　D. 他為自己對待他的方式感到抱歉。

B 31. For many years, doctors warned about the dangers of eating too much sugar. It was thought that too much sugar in the diet would increase the risk of developing heart disease and cancer. Thus, we were told to limit sugar intake, especially from drinks and sweets. Otherwise, we will most likely get many diseases when we are still so young!

Q: What is the speaker's conclusion?

　　A. Don't trust the advice of so-called experts.

　　B. Don't have too much sugar in your diet.

　　C. Foods containing salt and pepper are still risky.

　　D. Sugar is a major cause of stroke and heart disease.

多年以來，醫生都在警告攝取過多糖分的危險。飲食中過量的糖被認為會提高得心臟疾病和癌症的危險。因此，我們被告誡要限制對尤其是從飲料和甜食而來的糖分攝取。不然，我們很有可能在我們仍很年輕的時候，就得到很多疾病！

問題：說話者的結論為何？

選項：A. 不要相信所謂的專家的建議。　　B. 你的飲食中別吃太多糖。

　　　　C. 含鹽和胡椒粉的食物還是很危險。　　D. 糖是導致中風及心臟病的主因。

D 32. Good afternoon, passengers. This is your captain speaking. This is Flight CY537 from Chicago to San Francisco. The weather looks good and we are expecting to land in San

Francisco approximately 15 minutes ahead of schedule. The cabin crew will be coming around to offer you a light snack and beverage. I'll talk to you again before we reach our destination. Once again, welcome aboard and have a pleasant trip!

Q: Who most likely is the listener?

    A. Residents of Chicago.   B. Captain and his crew.

    C. Residents of San Francisco.   D. Passengers heading to San Francisco.

各位乘客午安。我是機長。這是從芝加哥飛往舊金山的 CY537 班機。今天天氣很好，我們預計會比預定的時間提早十五分鐘抵達舊金山。機組人員稍後會提供點心和飲料。抵達目的地前我也會再次廣播。再次歡迎搭乘，敬祝旅途愉快！

問題：誰最有可能是聽眾？

選項：A. 芝加哥的居民。   B. 機長及機組人員。

       C. 舊金山的居民。   D. 前往舊金山的旅客。

C 33. In many parts of the world, the average annual rainfall is very low. The Atacama Desert in Chile, South America, is particularly dry. For the residents, getting enough water is a big challenge. Despite the lack of rain, there is water contained in clouds that blow in from the coast. This often creates a thick fog over the mountains. Unfortunately, the drops of water in the fog are so tiny that they don't fall out of the air.

Q: Where does the water come from?

    A. Sea fog.   B. Wind power.   C. Coastal clouds.   D. Mountain streams.

世界上許多地方年平均降雨量是非常低的。在南美洲智利的阿他加馬沙漠特別的乾燥。對居民來說，要取得足夠的水是個大挑戰。除了缺雨之外，含水氣的雲由海岸吹入。這常常造成山區霧氣濃厚。不幸的是，霧裡的水滴太少了，無法從空中落下。

問題：水分從何而來？

選項：A. 海霧。   B. 風力。   C. 沿岸的雲。   D. 山區小溪。

C 34. For question number 34, please look at the score sheet.

I was one of the judges for this year's Singing Contest. I tried to follow the rating instructions carefully. However, compared with those of the other three judges, the score that I gave to Abbie Lin was relatively high. In my opinion, if a competitor does a great job, he or she gets a grade A regardless of how good other competitors' performance is.

Q: Who is probably the speaker?

    A. Simon Smith.   B. David Mitchell.

    C. Thomas Dave.   D. Bob Tyler.

參賽者： Abbie Lin	*Singing Contest*
評審	**分數**
Simon Smith	82
David Mitchell	80
Thomas Dave	96
Bob Tyler	79

第三十四題，請看計分單。

我是今年歌唱比賽的評審之一。我試著小心遵守評分指示。然而，相較於其他三位評審給的分數，我給 Abbie Lin 的分數較高。依我所見，如果一名參賽者表現優異，他或她就得高分，不管其他參賽者的表現有多好。

問題：說話者可能是誰？

選項：A. Simon Smith。　　　　　　　　B. David Mitchell。
　　　C. Thomas Dave。　　　　　　　　D. Bod Tyler。

解析　由談話內容可知說話者給的分數比其他三位評審高；而根據計分單，給最高分的是 Thomas Dave，故答案選 C。

C 35. For question number 35, please look at the leaflet.

Hi, I'm Hanna Lee. I'd like to go for a holiday next month, but I haven't decided where to go yet. I want a 4-day and 3-night tour. I am looking forward to a cooler vacation. Besides, I'm not a nature lover. I would rather stay indoors than spend hours walking in the woods and fighting against bugs. All I want to do is to take a good rest.

行程 A	行程 B
*三天行程 *觀賞絢麗的櫻花	*四天行程 *享受熱帶氣候及水上運動

行程 C	行程 D
*四天行程 *W 水療度假酒店 *享受放鬆的時光	*三天行程 *絕佳健行步道 *森林浴並放鬆

Q: If you were a travel agent, which tour would you recommend Hanna to book?

　　A. Tour A.　　　　B. Tour B.　　　　C. Tour C.　　　　D. Tour D.

第三十五題，請看傳單。

嗨，我是 Hanna Lee。下個月我想度假，但我還沒決定要去哪裡。我想要四天三夜的行程。我期盼一個清涼的假期。此外，我不是自然愛好者。我寧願待在室內，也不願花幾個小時在樹林中行走並與蟲子對抗。我想要做的就是好好休息一下。

問題：如果你是旅行社職員，你會推薦哪一個行程給 Hanna？

選項：A. 行程 A。　　B. 行程 B。　　　C. 行程 C。　　　D. 行程 D。

解析　由談話內容可知女子想要四天三夜的行程；根據傳單內容，行程 A 和 D 只有三天，所以不符；此外，女子期盼清涼又放鬆的假期，所以傳單上享受熱帶氣候的行程 B 不符，故答案選 C。

第一部份：看圖辨義

C 1. For question number 1, please look at picture A.

Question number 1: Which description matches the picture?

A. The captain is using his phone.　　B. The weather conditions are severe.

C. There is a lighthouse on the cliff.　　D. A submarine is approaching the coast.

第一題，請看圖片 A。

第一題：哪一個敘述符合這張圖片？

選項：A. 船長正在使用電話。　　B. 天氣很嚴峻。

　　　　C. 有一座燈塔在懸崖上。　　D. 有一艘潛水艇正在靠近海岸。

C 2. For question number 2, please look at picture B.

Question number 2: What might the man be saying?

A. It was all in your mind.

B. May I help you, ma'am?

C. Your condition is serious.

D. I'm afraid you'll have to cancel the appointment.

第二題，請看圖片 B。

第二題：男子可能正在說什麼？

選項：A. 只是心理作用罷了。　　B. 女士，我能幫你的忙嗎？

　　　　C. 你的情況很嚴重。　　D. 恐怕你要取消預約。

A 3. For question number 3, please look at picture C.

Question number 3: Where are these people?

A. In a mine.　　　B. In a laboratory.　　　C. At an aquarium.　　　D. At a stadium.

第三題，請看圖片 C。

第三題：這些人在哪裡？

選項：A. 在礦坑。　　B. 在實驗室。　　　C. 在水族館。　　　　D. 在體育館。

B 4. For questions number 4 and 5, please look at picture D.

Question number 4: To buy a bottle of orange juice that costs NT$100, how much would you have to pay if you use this coupon?

A. NT$100.　　　　B. NT$60.　　　　C. NT$40.　　　　D. NT$80.

第四題及第五題，請看圖片 D。

第四題：若使用這張折價券買要價新臺幣 100 元的柳橙汁需付多少錢？

選項：A. 新臺幣 100 元。　　B. 新臺幣 60 元。

　　　　C. 新臺幣 40 元。　　D. 新臺幣 80 元。

A 5. Question number 5: Please look at picture D again. Who might be interested in this coupon?

A. People who want to shop for groceries.　　B. People who miss their baggage.

C. People who try to hire new employees.　　D. People who have the flu.

第五題：請再看一次圖片 D。誰會對這張折價券感興趣？

選項：A. 想要買食品雜貨的人。　　　　　　B. 行李不見的人。

　　　C. 試著找到新員工的人。　　　　　　D. 患有流感的人。

第二部份：問答

D 6. How was your meal?

A. No dessert. Just black tea.　　　　　B. Can I have the check, please?

C. All right. Let's go Dutch this time.　　D. Actually, the steak was a bit tough.

問題：你的餐點如何？

選項：A. 不要甜點。紅茶就好。　　　　　B. 請幫我結帳，好嗎？

　　　C. 好吧。這次我們各付各的。　　　D. 事實上，牛排有點老。

B 7. Would you like to have coffee with me sometime?

A. I'd like two spoons of sugar.　　　　B. Sorry. I'm seeing someone.

C. Yes, I've collected ten coupons.　　　D. No. I usually have milk for breakfast.

問題：要不要找時間跟我一起去喝杯咖啡？

選項：A. 我想要加兩匙糖。　　　　　　　B. 抱歉。我有交往的對象了。

　　　C. 是的，我已經收集十張優惠券。　D. 不。我早餐通常是喝牛奶。

D 8. Is something wrong?

A. Sure! Let's grab a bite to eat.　　　　B. No! Don't even think about it.

C. Not really. It's not my cup of tea.　　D. Yes. Someone just stole my bicycle!

問題：發生什麼事了嗎？

選項：A. 當然！我們趕快吃點東西吧。　　B. 不行！想都別想。

　　　C. 不太喜歡。那不合我的胃口。　　D. 是的。有人偷了我的腳踏車！

D 9. Hello. I'd like to make an appointment to see Dr. Lin.

A. Please enter your password.　　　　　B. I have been busy these days.

C. You can't cut in line like that.　　　　D. How about the 12th at 10 a.m.?

問題：你好。我想要預約看林醫師的門診。

選項：A. 請輸入你的密碼。　　　　　　　B. 我最近很忙。

　　　C. 你不能這樣子插隊。　　　　　　D. 十二號早上十點可以嗎？

D 10. It's been a really long day.

A. No way. I don't have time.　　　　　B. Cut it out. I'm in a bad mood.

C. Never mind! I'll try again tomorrow.　D. It sure has been. I'm completely exhausted.

問題：今天真是漫長的一天。

選項：A. 不行。我沒有時間。　　　　　　B. 別鬧了。我沒心情。

　　　C. 別在意！我明天會再試一次。　　D. 的確是。我筋疲力盡。

C 11. How come you failed the test again?

A. I took it yesterday.　　　　　　　　B. I wrote a great essay.

C. My mind just went blank.　　　　　　D. I think the answer was either C or D.

問題：你怎麼又沒通過考試？

選項：A. 我昨天考的試。　　　　　　　B. 我寫了一篇很棒的短文。

　　　C. 我的腦中一片空白。　　　　　D. 我想答案不是 C 就是 D。

B 12. Where to, sir?

　　A. I'm from Texas.　　　　　　　　B. The train station.

　　C. Here's my bus pass.　　　　　　　D. A return ticket to Boston.

問題：先生，你要去哪裡？

選項：A. 我來自德州。　　　　　　　　B. 到火車站。

　　　C. 這是我的公車通行證。　　　　D. 一張回程車票到波士頓。

A 13. How would you like your steak, ma'am?

　　A. Medium, please.　　　　　　　　B. A glass of red wine.

　　C. Just a little bit. Thank you.　　　　D. Tea with one sugar, please.

問題：女士，你的牛排要幾分熟？

選項：A. 五分熟，麻煩你。　　　　　　B. 一杯紅酒。

　　　C. 一點點就好。謝謝你。　　　　D. 請給我一杯茶，加一匙糖。

D 14. I can't thank you enough for your help.

　　A. I appreciate it.　　　　　　　　B. My darling!

　　C. Thank you for coming.　　　　　　D. It's my pleasure!

問題：對於你的協助，我真是感激不盡。

選項：A. 我很感激。　　B. 我親愛的！　　C. 謝謝你來。　　　　D. 我的榮幸！

C 15. Hello. I'd like a single room for tomorrow night.

　　A. Sign here, please. Have a good journey.

　　B. I'm afraid not. The restaurant closes at 10 p.m.

　　C. I'm sorry. We don't have any rooms available.

　　D. Let me see. There's a seat available in business class.

問題：你好。我想訂明晚一間單人房。

選項：A. 請在此處簽名。祝你旅途愉快。　　B. 恐怕不行。餐廳晚上十點關門。

　　　C. 抱歉。我們沒有任何空房了。　　　D. 我看看。還有一個在商務艙的位子。

第三部份：簡短對話

C 16. M: I've just booked a table for two at the finest French restaurant in town.

　　W: Are you talking about that restaurant we went to last year on Valentine's Day?

　　M: That's the one!

　　W: Oh, no. I had a bad argument with the manager of that restaurant.

　　M: So you would feel embarrassed about seeing her again?

　　W: Exactly! Who knows what she'll do to my food?

　　Q: Why did the woman mention the restaurant manager?

A. The restaurant manager helped her get a table.

B. The restaurant manager refused to let them eat there.

C. The restaurant manager didn't get along with her.

D. The restaurant manager invited them for dinner on Valentine's Day.

男：我剛在本鎮最好的法式餐廳訂兩個人的位置了。

女：你說的是我們去年情人節去的那家嗎？

男：就是那家沒錯！

女：噢，不。我跟那家餐廳的經理有過嚴重的爭吵。

男：所以再次見到她，你會感到尷尬？

女：沒錯！誰知道她會對我的食物做什麼？

問題：女子為什麼提及餐廳經理？

選項：A. 餐廳經理幫她訂到位子。　　　　B. 餐廳經理拒絕讓他們在此用餐。
　　　　C. 餐廳經理無法與她和平共處。　　　D. 餐廳經理在情人節時邀請他們共進晚餐。

B 17. W: Hi, it's Mandy. Sorry, boss. I've got a heavy cold. Can I take a day off, please?

M: All right, but we really need you in the office. If you feel well enough this afternoon, please try to come in.

W: No problem!

M: Don't forget to see a doctor now.

Q: Why did the woman call the man?

A. To seek help.　　　　　　　　B. To ask for sick leave.

C. To ask for a promotion.　　　　D. To let him know she's busy.

女：嗨，我是 Mandy。抱歉，老闆。我得了重感冒。請讓我休一天假，好嗎？

男：好吧，但我們真的很需要你在公司裡。如果你下午覺得好多了的話，請試著進公司上班。

女：沒問題！

男：別忘了現在去看個醫生。

問題：女子為什麼要打電話給男子？

選項：A. 尋求協助。　　B. 要求請病假。　　　C. 要求升遷。　　　　D. 讓他知道她很忙。

A 18. M: Who was that on the phone?

W: What? Oh! Wrong number.

M: How come it's always you who picks up the phone when we have a wrong number? And why have we been getting so many wrong numbers lately?

W: Did you mean that I was lying?

Q: What is the man implying about the woman?

A. She's being dishonest.　　　　B. She always gets confused.

C. She is using the phone too much.　　D. She can't use the phone properly.

男：是誰打來的電話？

女：什麼？哦！打錯的。

男：為什麼每當有人打錯電話來時，你總是接到的那個人？還有，為什麼最近有這麼多通打錯的電話？

女：你是指我在說謊嗎？

問題：關於女子，男子做何暗示？

選項：A. 她總是不誠實。　　　　　　B. 她總是搞糊塗。

　　　C. 她太常使用電話。　　　　　D. 她無法正確地使用電話。

B 19. W: Hello, Steve! What seems to be the problem?

M: I've got a terrible stomachache.

W: How long have you had it?

M: Since yesterday morning.

W: I see. Let me listen to your chest. Take a deep breath. Good. Any fever?

M: I'm not sure. Maybe. And I've got these weird red spots all over my neck and on my back.

Q: What is the relationship between the man and the woman?

A. They are mother and son.　　　B. They are doctor and patient.

C. They are teacher and student.　D. They are clerk and customer.

女：哈囉，Steve！哪裡出了問題嗎？

男：我的胃痛得很厲害。

女：這個症狀持續多久了呢？

男：從昨天早上開始。

女：我知道了。讓我聽聽你的胸腔。深呼吸。很好。有發燒嗎？

男：我不確定。可能有。而且我的脖子和背部都是這種怪異的紅斑點。

問題：男子跟女子的關係是什麼？

選項：A. 他們是母親和兒子。　　　　B. 他們是醫生和病患。

　　　C. 他們是老師和學生。　　　　D. 他們是店員和顧客。

D 20. M: Oh, no! My laptop keeps crashing.

W: Well, it is kind of old now. Why not buy a new one?

M: No, I'll have someone take a look at it. I bet it just needs to replace some parts.

W: If you think so.

Q: What will the man probably do later?

A. Recycle some parts.　　　　　B. Fix his laptop on his own.

C. Purchase a brand-new laptop.　D. Have his laptop repaired.

男：噢，不！我的筆記型電腦一直當機。

女：嗯，它現在看起來有點舊了。何不買一臺新的電腦呢？

男：不，我會找人檢查一下。我猜它只是需要更換一些零件。

女：如果你這樣覺得的話。

問題：男子稍後可能會做什麼？

選項：A. 回收一些零件。　　　　　　B. 自己修電腦。

　　　C. 買一臺全新的筆電。　　　　D. 請人修理他的電腦。

A 21. W: Why is our door open? What's going on?

M: Look! The lock is broken.

W: I guess we've been robbed. I heard that there's a gang of burglars in the neighborhood.

M: Let's go and see what they've taken.

W: Wait! Don't go in. They might still be in there.

M: Good point. I didn't think of that. I'm calling the police.

Q: What has happened to the man and woman?

A. Their house was broken into.

B. The door of their house is missing.

C. They have been locked out of their house.

D. They were threatened by a gang of burglars.

女：為什麼我們的門是開著的？發生什麼事？

男：看！門鎖壞了。

女：我想我們被偷了。我聽說這附近有一群竊賊。

男：我們去看看他們偷走了什麼。

女：等等！不要進去。他們可能還在裡面。

男：有道理。我沒想到那一點。我要報警。

問題：男子與女子發生什麼事？

選項：A. 他們的房子遭人闖入。　　　　　B. 他們房子的門不見了。

　　　C. 他們被鎖在屋子外面。　　　　　D. 他們被一群竊賊威脅。

A 22. M: I've made a decision. From now on, I will never drink any alcohol. No beer, no wine, and no whiskey.

W: Wow! It's a big deal. But you don't seem to have a problem with alcohol.

M: No, I don't. I just think it will be better for my health in the long run.

W: You could just have a drink on special occasions such as weddings and birthday parties. You don't have to give it up altogether.

M: That won't work for me.

W: All right.

Q: What did the man announce?

A. He has quit drinking.　　　　　B. He has had health issues.

C. He has taken up jogging.　　　　D. He has an alcohol problem.

男：我做了一個決定。從現在開始，我不會再喝任何酒。不喝啤酒、葡萄酒、和威士忌。

女：哇！這是很重要的事。但是你似乎沒有酗酒的問題。

男：不，我沒有。我只是覺得長遠來說這樣對我的健康較好。

女：你可以在特殊的場合像是婚禮或慶生派對上喝一杯。你不用完全放棄。

男：那樣對我來說行不通。

女：好吧。

問題：男子宣布什麼？

選項：A. 他戒酒。　　　B. 他有健康問題。　　　C. 他開始慢跑。　　　D. 他酗酒。

D 23. W: I'm thinking of moving overseas.

M: OK. Any special reason?

W: I can give you two good reasons. First, I can't stand my job, and secondly, my boyfriend dumped me.

M: So do you have any particular country in mind?

W: Yes! I'm going to Brazil. I've been having Spanish lessons these past six weeks.

M: Spanish? But they don't speak Spanish there!

W: What? What do they speak then?

Q: What do we know about the woman?

　A. She is going to South Africa.

　B. She speaks Spanish very well.

　C. She will travel to Brazil with her boyfriend.

　D. She doesn't know what the official language of Brazil is.

女：我打算搬到國外去。

男：好的。有什麼特別的原因嗎？

女：我可以給你兩個很好的理由。首先，我無法忍受我的工作；其次，我男朋友甩了我。

男：那麼你心裡有什麼特定的國家嗎？

女：有！我要去巴西。過去這六週我都在上西班牙語課。

男：西班牙語？但他們不說西班牙語啊！

女：什麼？不然他們到底說什麼語言呢？

問題：關於女子我們知道什麼？

選項：A. 她要去南非。　　　　　　　B. 她西班牙語說得很流利。

　　　C. 她將跟男朋友到巴西旅遊。　　　D. 她不知道巴西的官方語言是什麼。

A 24. For question number 24, please look at the bar chart.

M: Hey, what are you doing now?

W: I'm looking at the educational website. It gives information about the number of male and female students studying medicine at our university between 2017 and 2020.

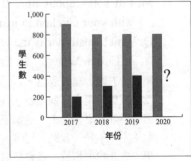

M: In 2018, the number of male students slightly fell.

W: And then it remained level through the following years.

M: Relatively speaking, the number of female students was quite low in 2017.

W: But when the number of male students decreased, the number of female students grew.

M: And afterward female students increased by 100 each year.

W: This resulted in a rise in the total number of medical students from 1,100 in 2017 to 1,300 in 2020.

M: Although men still made up the majority of medical students, the proportion of female students grew steadily.

Q: How many female students studied medicine at the university in 2020?

    A. 500.   B. 800.   C. 1,100.   D. 1,200.

第二十四題，請看長條圖。

男：嘿，你在做什麼呢？

女：我正在看教育網站。它提供在 2017 年到 2020 年之間我們大學學醫的男女學生數量的資訊。

男：在 2018 年，男性學生數量稍微下降了。

女：然後接下來幾年數字都持平。

男：相對來說，女性學生數量在 2017 年相當低。

女：但是當男性學生數量降低時，女性學生數量成長了。

男：之後女性學生每年增加一百人。

女：這使得醫學系學生的總數量從 2017 年的一千一百人上升到 2020 年的一千三百人。

男：雖然男性學生仍占醫學系學生中的大多數，但女性學生的比例穩定成長。

問題：在 2020 年學醫的女學生有多少人？

選項：A. 五百人。   B. 八百人。   C. 一千一百人。   D. 一千兩百人。

解析 由對話可知當 2018 年男性學生數量降低時，女性學生數量成長了，且之後女性學生數量每年穩定增加一百人；根據長條圖內容可推知符合女性學生數量為右邊的長條。2017 年女性學生數量為兩百人，因此可推知 2020 年會到達五百人，故答案選 A。

A 25. For question number 25, please look at the form.

W: I think there's a problem right now. I didn't order steak.

M: Excuse me, ma'am. Isn't this New York strip steak yours?

W: No, it isn't. I ordered roasted chicken.

M: I'm sorry about this. I'll take this away and be back with your chicken in just a moment.

顧客	抱怨
Lillian Wang	送錯餐
Emily Lin	湯有怪味
Helen Liu	煮過頭的牛排
Cathy Chang	桌子有髒汙

Q: Which customer is the waiter talking to?

    A. Lillian Wang.   B. Emily Lin.   C. Helen Liu.   D. Cathy Chang.

第二十五題，請看表格。

女：我覺得現在有個問題。我沒有點牛排。

男：不好意思，女士。這個紐約客牛排不是你的？

女：不，不是。我點了烤雞。

男：對此我很抱歉。我會把這個拿走並馬上端上你的烤雞。

問題：服務生在跟哪一位顧客講話？

選項：A. Lillian Wang。   B. Emily Lin。

       C. Helen Liu。   D. Cathy Chang。

解析 由對話可知顧客是在抱怨上錯菜；而根據表格內容，抱怨上錯菜的顧客是 Lillian Wang，故答案選 A。

A 26. Good morning! I'm Andrew, and right now it's coming up to 8 o'clock. For southbound traffic on the freeway is heavy due to an accident involving a tour bus and several cars. Fortunately, no one has been seriously hurt. That's the traffic report on the radio. Thank you for listening.

Q: What can drivers going south on the freeway expect?

    A. They will be stuck in a traffic jam.   B. Andrew will be on the scene.

    C. The police will ask them to pull over.   D. The traffic will be light.

早安！我是 Andrew，現在時間是八點整。因為一起遊覽車與多輛小客車的事故，高速公路往南下的車流是壅塞的。幸運的是沒有人嚴重受傷。以上是車況廣播。謝謝你的收聽。

問題：高速公路南下的駕駛可以預期有什麼狀況？

選項：A. 他們會塞在車陣中。   B. Andrew 會在現場。

    C. 警方會要求他們車停在路邊。   D. 交通流量小。

C 27. Good morning, everyone. I'm going to inform you that our company is no longer offering free English lessons to our employees after work. We found the employees have shown no measurable improvement in their English language ability. If you think that English language skills are important for your job, we recommend that you take English classes in other languages schools.

Q: What is the purpose of this announcement?

    A. To fire an employee.

    B. To offer medical benefits.

    C. To cancel English lessons.

    D. To give tips on learning English.

早安，各位。我要通知大家，公司不再於下班後提供員工免費的英語課程。我們發現員工們的英語能力無明顯進步。如果你認為英語技能對你的工作很重要，我們建議你到其他語言學校上英語課程。

問題：這則廣播的目的是什麼？

選項：A. 解僱一名員工。   B. 提供醫療保險。

    C. 取消英語課程。   D. 提供學習英文的祕訣。

D 28. Ladies and gentlemen, welcome to today's lecture. Recent research shows that lung cancer can be caused by second-hand smoke. If you are exposed to second-hand smoke frequently, you may get lung cancer even if you don't smoke. Fortunately, in order to protect people from this risk, the government has passed laws to forbid people from smoking in public places like hotels and restaurants. However, there are still risks to children because some smokers will smoke in their houses and cars with children nearby.

Q: Which of the following may pose a threat to children's health?

    A. The government.   B. The hotel guests.

    C. The lawmaker.   D. Their parents.

各位先生、小姐，歡迎蒞臨今天的講座。最近的研究顯示肺癌可為二手菸所致。如果你經常接觸二手菸，即使你不吸菸，你還是很有可能會得肺癌。幸好，為了保護民眾免於這項風險，政府已經通過法案，禁止民眾在像是旅館及餐廳等公共場所吸菸。然而，對孩童來說還是有風險，因為有些吸菸者會在家中或車上吸菸，而孩童就在旁邊。

問題：下列何者可能對孩童健康造成威脅？

選項：A. 政府。　　　　B. 飯店房客。　　　　C. 立法委員。　　　　D. 他們的父母。

D 29. This is a special news report. A group of city workers went to the city hall to occupy the lobby, refusing to leave until the mayor responds to their demands. According to their leader, the city government has refused to give anyone a raise for the past five years, and some workers say they have been treated poorly. The leader says they will stay in the location for days or even weeks if they need to.

Q: Which of the following is the main reason the group is occupying the city hall?

　A. Their working conditions were very poor.

　B. The city government has heard their complaints.

　C. The group was forced by their leader to protest.

　D. They have not received a raise for a long time.

這是一篇特別報導。一群市區工人前往市政府占領大廳，並表示在市長回應他們的訴求前絕不散去。根據他們領導人的說法，過去五年來，市政府拒絕給任何一位工人加薪，而且也有一些工人表示他們一直遭受惡劣對待。該領導人表示，如果有需要，他們會在該地待上數天，甚至數週之久。

問題：下列何者為該團體占據市政府的主要理由？

選項：A. 他們的工作環境很差。

　　　B. 市政府已聽到他們的抱怨。

　　　C. 該團體是因為被他們的領袖強迫才會去抗議。

　　　D. 他們的薪資已經很久沒有調高了。

B 30. Although we have won our freedom, we are still facing some serious problems. There is a water shortage and a lack of food from drought. On the positive side, some are creating new businesses and jobs. However, lack of daily necessities has made quite a negative impact on the nation. Who can the people turn to? The government has offered support, but is it enough?

Q: What do the people in this country need?

　A. Jobs and money.　　　　　　　B. Water and food.

　C. Roads and railroads.　　　　　D. Soldiers and weapons.

雖然我們已經獲得我們的自由，但是我們仍正面臨一些嚴重問題。乾旱引起的供水不足與糧食短缺。從正面來看，有些人正在開創新的事業及工作。然而，缺乏民生物資已經對國民造成很大的負面影響。人們能向誰求助呢？政府已提供支援，但是足夠嗎？

問題：這國家的人民需要什麼？

選項：A. 工作及金錢。　B. 水及食物。　　　　C. 道路及鐵路。　　　　D. 士兵及武器。

A 31. Your country needs you! If you are a healthy and young person between the ages of 18 and

24, your army needs you. Join us and make sure our citizens are safe. If you join, you can enjoy many benefits, including skills training, a monthly salary, and scholarships for college. Apart from that, you'll have the thanks and appreciation of those you protect.

Q: What kind of job is being advertised?

    A. Soldier.   B. Coach.   C. Firefighter.   D. Physician.

你的國家需要你！如果你是十八至二十四歲之間的健康年輕人，你的軍隊需要你。加入我們並確保人民安全。你若加入，就能享受多項福利，包括技能訓練、月薪及大學獎學金。此外，你還能贏得受你保護的人對你的感謝與激賞。

問題：何種工作正在徵聘？

選項：A. 軍人。   B. 教練。   C. 消防隊員。   D. 外科醫師。

D 32. Students, please listen to this important announcement from the principal. For safety reasons, students will not be allowed to play dodgeball near the buildings at the school at any time. Students may only play this sport on the soccer field. A window of the school cafeteria was broken this morning while students were playing dodgeball nearby. If anyone knows who is responsible for this damage, please come to the principal's office right away.

Q: Which is true about this announcement?

    A. No one broke the window.

    B. A window was broken in the principal's office.

    C. Students need permission to play basketball at the school.

    D. Students are forbidden to play dodgeball near the school buildings.

同學們，請注意聽校長的重要宣布。為了安全起見，同學們無論何時都不能在學校建築物附近打躲避球。只能在足球場從事這項運動。今天早上，學生餐廳有一面窗戶被打破了，當時有同學在附近打躲避球。如果有人知道誰該負責損壞賠償，請立刻到校長室。

問題：關於這則廣播，何者為真？

選項：A. 沒有人打破窗戶。   B. 校長辦公室裡的一扇窗戶被打破。

    C. 學生須得到允許才能在學校打籃球。   D. 禁止學生在學校建築物附近玩躲避球。

C 33. Do you want to improve your English listening and speaking skills? Do you want to experience western culture and make friends from other countries? We offer many exciting study tours in the United States, Canada, and Australia. This year, join other students on a monthly trip to study English in famous universities in Boston!

Q: What is the commercial offering to the listeners?

    A. An English listening workshop.   B. A working holiday visa.

    C. A one-month study program in Boston. D. A chance to be a language instructor.

你想要增進英文聽與說的能力嗎？你要體驗西方文化和結交來自其他國家的朋友嗎？我們提供許多在美國、加拿大及澳洲令人興奮的遊學。今年，就和其他學生一起參加我們到波士頓著名大學的一個月英語遊學團隊！

問題：廣告要提供聽眾的是什麼？

選項：A. 英語聽力研習會。   B. 打工度假的簽證。

C. 一個月的波士頓學習計畫。 D. 成為語言教師的機會。

A 34. For question number 34, please look at the map.

There's one near here. It's within walking distance, maybe about 350 meters. It's this way. Take this road. Go straight ahead until you reach the traffic lights. Then, turn left and go along the street. You'll pass a convenience store and keep going straight, and you'll see it on your left.

Q: Which place is the speaker giving directions to?

  A. A bank.   B. A bakery.   C. A park.   D. A post office.

第三十四題，請看地圖。

這裡附近有一家。它在走路就能到的距離，也許大約三百五十公尺的距離。是往這邊走。走這條路。往前直走，直到你走到紅綠燈的地方。然後，左轉並沿著街直走。你會經過一家便利商店，繼續直走，你會看到它就在你的左邊。

問題：說話者指引方向到何處？

選項：A. 一間銀行。 B. 一間麵包店。   C. 一座公園。   D. 一間郵局。

解 析 由談話內容並根據地圖可知，問路人從下方位置直走到紅綠燈，再左轉直走，會先經過一家便利商店，再直走，左手邊是一間銀行，故答案選 A。

D 35. For question number 35, please look at the bus route map.

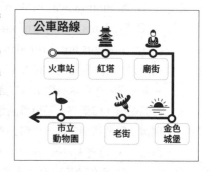

Our sightseeing bus runs every 30 minutes between 9 a.m. and 6 p.m., starting at the bus stop outside the Railway Station. It stops at several tourist spots. The region is known for its historic buildings, beautiful sunset, and delicious street snacks. With the one-day pass, you can get on and off at any of these stops to enjoy different tourist attractions.

Q: A tourist wants to try some local food. At which stop should he get off the bus?

  A. Red Tower. B. Temple Street. C. Golden Castle. D. Old Street.

第三十五題，請看公車路線圖。

我們的觀光公車從上午九點到下午六點每三十分鐘運行一班，從火車站外的公車站出發。它停靠幾個觀光景點。此地區以它的歷史建物、美麗夕陽及美味的街邊小吃聞名。有了這張一日票，你可以在這些站中任何一站上下車，欣賞不同的觀光景點。

問題：一位觀光客想嘗嘗一些當地的食物。他應該在哪一站下車？

選項：A. 紅塔。   B. 廟街。   C. 金色城堡。   D. 老街。

解 析 由談話可知要吃街邊小吃要在老街站下車，故答案選 D。

第一部份：看圖辨義

A 1. For question number 1, please look at picture A.

Question number 1: Which description matches the picture?

A. The spectators are cheering.　　　B. They are jogging in the park.

C. The race record has been broken.　　D. One of the competitors has tripped.

第一題，請看圖片 A。

第一題：哪一個敘述與圖片相符？

選項：A. 觀眾們在歡呼。　　　　　　B. 他們在公園慢跑。

　　　C. 比賽紀錄已經被打破了。　　D. 其中一名參賽者跌倒了。

A 2. For question number 2, please look at picture B.

Question number 2: What is the man doing?

A. He is pouring cement.　　　　　B. He is washing the floor.

C. He is creating a new product.　　D. He is lifting some building materials.

第二題，請看圖片 B。

第二題：男子正在做什麼？

選項：A. 他正在倒水泥。　　　　　B. 他正在洗地板。

　　　C. 他正在創造一個新產品。　D. 他正在舉一些建材。

B 3. For question number 3, please look at picture C.

Question number 3: What can be inferred from the picture?

A. The woman is quite happy.　　　B. The woman is a fortune-teller.

C. The man has been cured of an illness.　D. The man is confused about what he hears.

第三題，請看圖片 C。

第三題：從圖中可以推測什麼？

選項：A. 女子相當開心。　　　　　B. 女子是位算命師。

　　　C. 男子的疾病被治癒了。　　D. 男子對他所聽到的感到困惑。

C 4. For questions number 4 and 5, please look at picture D.

Question number 4: What does the shop owner need?

A. A police officer.　　B. A plumber.　　C. New employees.　　D. Some volunteers.

第四題及第五題，請看圖片 D。

第四題：老闆需要什麼？

選項：A. 一名警察。　　B. 一名水電工。　　C. 一些新員工。　　D. 一些志工。

D 5. Question number 5: Please look at picture D again. What can be bought at BEST MART?

A. Fresh tuna.　　　B. Tomato soup.　　C. An oil can.　　D. Cookies.

第五題：請再看一次圖片 D。能在好棒商店買到什麼？

選項：A. 新鮮鮪魚。　　B. 番茄湯。　　C. 油壺。　　D. 餅乾。

第二部份：問答

A 6. What was your best subject in high school?

A. Physics.   B. Essay.   C. Engineer.   D. Passion.

問題：你在高中最拿手的科目是什麼？

選項：A. 物理。   B. 短文。   C. 工程師。   D. 熱情。

D 7. I'm so nervous about the exam tomorrow!

A. Stay here!   B. Get off!   C. Wake up!   D. Calm down!

問題：明天的考試我好緊張哦！

選項：A. 待在這裡！   B. 走開！   C. 起床！   D. 冷靜！

D 8. Doctor, I have a terrible sore throat.

A. Put this sunscreen on.   B. You will feel better.

C. What kind of excuse is that?   D. Do you have any other symptoms?

問題：醫生，我的喉嚨超痛。

選項：A. 擦上這個防曬乳。   B. 你會感覺好一點。

         C. 這是哪門子的藉口？   D. 你還有其他症狀嗎？

B 9. What do you think of my new jeans?

A. It looks good on me.   B. They really suit you.

C. They were on sale.   D. It's a lovely dress.

問題：你覺得我的新牛仔褲如何？

選項：A. 我穿起來很好看。   B. 它們很適合你。

         C. 它們在特價。   D. 它是件可愛的裙子。

C 10. Waiter, there's a fly in my soup.

A. Our special today is roast duck.   B. Are you ready to order?

C. Oh dear. I'll get you another one.   D. I'll bring you the wine menu.

問題：服務生，我的湯裡有隻蒼蠅。

選項：A. 我們的今日特餐是烤鴨。   B. 你準備好要點餐了嗎？

         C. 天啊。我會換另一碗給你。   D. 我會拿酒單給你。

B 11. Could you hand me that hairbrush?

A. Nicely done.   B. Here you go.   C. That's it.   D. Take it easy.

問題：你能遞給我那把梳子嗎？

選項：A. 做得漂亮。   B. 拿去吧。   C. 就這樣。   D. 放輕鬆。

A 12. When is the next bus to the school?

A. There's one every half hour.   B. We'll arrive there in an hour.

C. You need to be on platform 3.   D. I booked a seat in business class.

問題：下一班到學校的公車是什麼時候？

選項：A. 每半小時一班。   B. 我們一小時內會抵達那裡。

         C. 你要到 3 號月臺。   D. 我訂了一個商務艙的位子。

A 13. I heard that Diane is getting divorced.

    A. Don't believe that rumor.   B. He proposed to me on the beach.

    C. I am sure it was a touching moment.   D. The wedding will be held in the summer.

    問題：我聽說 Diane 即將要離婚了。

    選項：A. 不要相信那個流言。   B. 他在沙灘上向我求婚。

            C. 我確信那是個動人時刻。   D. 婚禮將在夏天舉行。

D 14. These cookies don't taste right.

    A. Thank you for your compliment!

    B. No, thanks. I'm cutting back on snacks.

    C. Yes! I used my grandmother's recipe.

    D. Oh! Check the expiration date on the package.

    問題：這些餅乾吃起來不太對勁。

    選項：A. 謝謝你的讚美！   B. 不，謝了。我現在少吃零食了。

            C. 是！我用我祖母的食譜。   D. 哦！檢查包裝袋上的有效期限。

C 15. What super power would you like to have?

    A. I'm not a movie fan.   B. I can do some magic tricks.

    C. I wish I could be invisible.   D. The new movie is awesome.

    問題：你想要有什麼樣的超能力呢？

    選項：A. 我不是電影迷。   B. 我會一些魔術。

            C. 我希望我能隱形。   D. 新的電影超棒的。

第三部份：簡短對話

D 16. M: Lovely juicy apples! Only $10 for four apples!

    W: Are they organic?

    M: Yes, ma'am, they are! I grow them myself on my farm nearby.

    W: Lovely. I'll take 4 apples, please.

    Q: What does the woman want to avoid?

    A. Imported fruit.   B. Being cheated.

    C. Paying too much.   D. Eating chemicals.

    男：美味多汁的蘋果！四顆蘋果只要 10 美元！

    女：它們是有機的嗎？

    男：是的，女士，它們是的！我在我自己的農場種的，就在附近。

    女：太好了。我要四顆蘋果。

    問題：女子想要避免什麼？

    選項：A. 進口的水果。 B. 上當受騙。   C. 付太多錢。   D. 吃到化學物質。

D 17. W: Oh, no! What have you done to the curry? How much chili powder did you put in?

    M: One cup. It's all right, isn't it?

    W: No, it says here one teaspoon! Can't you read?

M: I just thought that was a mistake. I mean, one teaspoon isn't much, is it?

W: It's enough for a mild curry. I don't know what you were thinking.

M: Hey, don't try to act like you've never messed up in the kitchen.

Q: What mistake did the man make?

    A. He used a teaspoon.

    B. He made a mild curry.

    C. He bought the wrong kind of spice.

    D. He didn't follow the recipe exactly.

女：噢，不！你把咖哩怎麼了？你放了多少辣椒粉進去？

男：一杯。應該還可以，不是嗎？

女：不對，這裡說要放一茶匙！你不會看嗎？

男：我以為那是個錯誤。我是說一茶匙沒有太多，是嗎？

女：對於微辣的咖哩來說，就已經足夠了。我真的不知道你在想什麼。

男：嘿，不要說得好像你從未在廚房裡搞砸任何事。

問題：男子犯了什麼錯？

選項：A. 他使用了一枝茶匙。   B. 他做了微辣的咖哩。

      C. 他買到錯誤的香料。   D. 他沒有明確地遵照著食譜。

D 18. M: My goodness! Your suitcase weighs a ton! What have you got in there?

W: Clothes, shoes, and all the usual stuff I take on vacation.

M: Do you realize that we'll have to pay extra if it's over 23 kilograms?

W: Well, let's put it on the scale and find it out.

Q: What does the man inform the woman?

    A. She's put on a lot of weight lately.

    B. He will make all the travel arrangements.

    C. She won't be able to put her bag on the plane.

    D. There's a weight limit for luggage.

男：我的天啊！你的行李箱超重的！你裡面裝了什麼啊？

女：衣服、鞋子和所有通常我會帶去旅行的東西。

男：你知道如果它超過二十三公斤的話，我們要額外付費嗎？

女：嗯，我們把它秤一下就知道了。

問題：男子告知女子什麼？

選項：A. 她最近增重很多。   B. 他會做好所有旅遊規畫。

      C. 她無法將包包放在飛機上。   D. 行李有重量限制。

C 19. W: I think it's Dana's birthday on Saturday. We should get her something.

M: I don't think so. She's going to a fancy restaurant with some friends and then afterward they're going to a nightclub.

W: Oh, I guess that means we were not invited.

M: Correct! So a birthday gift might put us in an awkward position.

W: It's a good thing to find out, otherwise I might have made a fool of myself.

Q: What would have happened if the woman had given Dana a birthday gift?

    A. The gift would have been rejected.

    B. Dana would have been jealous.

    C. The woman would have felt embarrassed.

    D. Dana would have invited her to join her party.

女：我想 Dana 的生日是在週六。我們應該買點東西給她。

男：我不這麼認為。她要跟朋友去一家高級餐廳，之後他們會去夜店。

女：哦，我猜那表示我們沒有被邀請。

男：沒錯！所以一個生日禮物對我們來說可能會很尷尬。

女：能知道這事真好，否則我可能會讓我自己變成傻瓜。

問題：如果女子給了 Dana 一個生日禮物會發生什麼事？

選項：A. 禮物會被退回。   B. Dana 會嫉妒。

    C. 女子會感到尷尬。   D. Dana 會邀請她參加她的派對。

D 20. M: I'm thinking of moving out of the city.

W: How come? Because of the poor air quality?

M: Right. It's really affecting my health.

W: Oh, that's too bad.

Q: What is affecting the man's health?

    A. Stress.   B. His job.   C. City life.   D. Air pollution.

男：我在想要搬到城外。

女：為什麼？因為空氣品質很差嗎？

男：是啊。它真的影響到我的健康了。

女：喔，真是太糟了。

問題：什麼影響到男子的健康？

選項：A. 壓力。   B. 他的工作。   C. 城市生活。   D. 空氣汙染。

B 21. W: I hope the chicken wings are not too spicy for you.

M: No, they're perfect. The spicier the better.

W: All right! I'll remember that for next time I make Mexican food.

M: I'm looking forward to it!

Q: What is one of the ingredients the woman probably used?

    A. Wine.   B. Chilies.   C. Red pepper.   D. Chicken breast.

女：希望雞翅對你來說不會太辣。

男：不，它們很棒。越辣越好。

女：好！下次我做墨西哥料理的時候會記住這點。

男：我很期待！

問題：女子可能用了哪一個食材？

選項：A. 紅酒。   B. 辣椒。   C. 紅椒。   D. 雞胸肉。

A 22. M: Do you think I should get a part-time job?

W: But you already have a full-time job.

M: I know, but if I worked in a bar or something after work, I could make some extra money.

W: What for? Both of us are on quite decent salaries. We can afford the bills and still have some left for savings every month.

M: True, but what if we wanted to buy a house?

Q: What do we learn about the woman?

A. She also has a job.　　　　　　B. She has trouble saving money.

C. She wants the man to work less.　D. She can't pay her bills on time.

男：你覺得我該找份打工嗎？

女：但你已經有一份正職工作了。

男：我知道，但如果我下班時在一家酒吧或是其他地方工作，我可以賺更多的錢。

女：為了什麼？我們兩個都有不錯的收入。每個月我們也能支付帳單和存一點錢。

男：是沒錯，但是如果我們想要買房子的話呢？

問題：關於女子我們得知什麼？

選項：A. 她也有一份工作。　　　　B. 她存錢有困難。

C. 她要男子工作少一點。　D. 她無法準時付帳單。

A 23. W: Hello. How may I help you?

M: Hi, I want to buy a birthday gift for my wife. What do you recommend?

W: How about this necklace? It's the best-seller. And, we can wrap it up for you.

M: Sounds great.

Q: Where are the speakers?

A. In a jewelry store.　　　　　B. In a liquor store.

C. In a cosmetic store.　　　　D. In a furniture store.

女：你好。有什麼我可以幫忙的嗎？

男：嗨，我想要買生日禮物給我太太。你有什麼推薦的嗎？

女：這條項鍊如何？這是暢銷款。而且，我們可以替你包裝。

男：聽起來不錯。

問題：說話者們在哪裡？

選項：A. 在首飾店。　　B. 在酒行。　　　　C. 在化妝品店。　　　D. 在家具行。

B 24. For question number 24, please look at the line graph.

M: Cindy, I passed the English exam this time!

W: Congratulations! All your hard work finally paid off.

M: But I know there is still much room for improvement. Bob got the highest score, and you

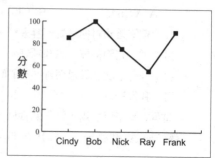

scored 85 out of 100. You both did much better than me.

W: What do you think you could improve?

M: I think I could take better notes and study harder.

W: I believe you can do better next time.

Q: Who is talking to Cindy?

    A. Bob.   B. Nick.   C. Ray.   D. Frank.

第二十四題，請看折線圖。

男：Cindy，我這次通過英文考試了！

女：恭喜！你所有的努力終於有收穫了。

男：但我知道還有很大的改善空間。Bob 考了最高分，你 100 分中也拿了 85 分。你們都考得比我好多了。

女：你覺得你可以改進什麼呢？

男：我想我可以筆記做好一點並更加用功。

女：我相信你下次可以做得更好。

問題：誰在和 Cindy 說話？

選項：A. Bob。   B. Nick。   C. Ray。   D. Frank。

解析　由對話可知男孩通過考試，但不是最高分且分數比 Cindy 的 85 分低；而根據折線圖，符合此狀況為 75 分的 Nick，故答案選 B。

B 25. For question number 25, please look at the floor guide.

W: I want to buy a lipstick on this floor first.

M: Then, I'm going to Men's Wear myself. I need a new tie for work.

W: OK, but don't forget we have to get a new dress for your mom.

M: In that case, why don't we meet at the information desk on the second floor one hour later?

W: All right. And before we leave the mall, let's get some ice cream at the supermarket.

Q: Where are the speakers now?

    A. B1.   B. 1F.   C. 2F.   D. 3F.

樓層導引	
3F	男裝
2F	女裝
1F	化妝品
B1	超市

第二十五題，請看樓層導引。

女：我想先在這層樓買一支口紅。

男：那我自己會去男裝部。我上班需要一條新領帶。

女：好的，但別忘記我們得幫你母親買一件新洋裝。

男：那樣的話，我們何不一個小時後在二樓服務臺碰面？

女：好啊。然後在離開購物中心前，我們去超市買些冰淇淋。

問題：說話者們現在在哪裡？

選項：A. 地下一樓。   B. 一樓。   C. 二樓。   D. 三樓。

解析　由對話可知說話者們所在的樓層可以買到口紅；而根據樓層導引，化妝品在一樓，故答案選 B。

第四部份：簡短談話

C 26. A typhoon will be approaching our coastline during this weekend. Residents are advised to limit their outdoor activities and stay indoors. Because of the chance of heavy rains and high winds, people are encouraged to stay off the roads. If you live on the coast, the authorities encourage you to evacuate to higher ground before this weekend.

Q: What is the announcement about?

    A. A busy holiday weekend.   B. The Central Weather Bureau.

    C. An approaching typhoon.   D. The official's outdoor activities.

颱風將於這週末接近我們的沿海地帶。建議居民避免戶外活動，待在室內。因為可能帶來強風豪雨，希望民眾不要到路上。你若住在海邊，有關當局希望你能於這週末前撤至地勢較高處。

問題：這則宣布是關於什麼？

選項：A. 忙碌的週末假期。   B. 中央氣象局。

       C. 接近中的颱風。   D. 官員的戶外活動。

A 27. Are you looking for a unique gift for your friends or family? Do they love chocolate? We offer chocolate gifts that are customized with the names of the people you are giving the gift to. You can fill out the order form on our website, and choose one of our many designs. Type in a person's name and your message, and it will be printed on high quality Swiss chocolate.

Q: According to the advertisement, what makes this product special?

    A. The chocolate gift can be more personalized.

    B. A chocolate gift is certain to make everyone happy.

    C. The customized notebooks will have your name on it.

    D. Switzerland produces the best chocolate in the world.

你在找送給親朋好友的獨特禮物嗎？他們喜愛巧克力嗎？我們提供客製化的巧克力禮物，可將收禮人的名字放在上面。你可以在我們的網站上填寫訂單，然後從眾多設計中挑選一款。打上姓名及你的訊息，這些就會印在高品質的瑞士巧克力上面。

問題：根據這則廣告，是什麼讓這個產品變得獨特？

選項：A. 這個巧克力禮物能夠更加特製。   B. 巧克力禮物一定會讓每個人都快樂。

       C. 客製化的筆記本上面會有你的名字。   D. 瑞士生產世界上最棒的巧克力。

B 28. Thank you for attending this course on business marketing. There are many ways to let people know what your company offers. You can show them a website or provide them a brochure. But often, people don't have time to read what you give them. That's why a business card is an essential tool for men and women in the business world. It is easy to carry and hold a person's most important information. A business card allows people to know you and your products with a quick glance. It can give potential customers your company's name, your job position, and how to contact you. No matter where you go, always carry enough business cards. You never know when you will meet the most important person for your business.

Q: What is this talk about?

    A. How to reach your sales targets.   B. The importance of business cards.

    C. The difference between two products.   D. Effective methods to serve customers.

感謝大家參加企業行銷課程。有許多方法可以讓大家知道你公司銷售的產品。你可以請他們看網站或提供手冊。但人們時常沒空看你給的東西。這就是為什麼名片對商場上的男士或女士來說是重要的工具。它方便攜帶，記載個人最重要的資訊。一張名片能讓人快速看一眼便了解你與你的產品。它可以提供潛在客戶你的公司名稱、你的工作職位及連絡方式。不論你去哪裡，一定要攜帶足夠的名片。你永遠不知道自己何時會遇到事業上的貴人。

問題：這個談話的主旨是什麼？

選項：A. 如何達到你的銷售目標。   B. 名片的重要性。

    C. 兩項產品間的差異。   D. 服務客戶的有效方法。

A 29. Good afternoon, everyone. The animal exhibits will be open today until 6 p.m. Be sure to visit our gift shops and restaurants in the zoo. They will remain open until 7 p.m. Because of the recent cold weather, the reptiles have been removed from their exhibits temporarily to keep them safe. The Reptile House will be open as soon as the weather becomes warmer. Please enjoy the rest of the animal exhibits.

Q: Where is the speaker?

    A. In a zoo.   B. In a library.   C. In a pet shop.   D. In a laboratory.

大家午安。今天的動物展示開放到晚上六點。務必要到我們動物園內的禮品店及餐廳看一看。這些地方將持續開放到晚上七點。由於最近天氣寒冷，為維護爬行動物的安全，我們暫時將牠們移出展示區。天氣較為暖和時，爬行動物區將立即開放。敬請盡情參觀其餘動物展示。

問題：說話者在哪裡？

選項：A. 在動物園。   B. 在圖書館。   C. 在寵物店。   D. 在實驗室。

D 30. In the City of London in the United Kingdom, an elementary school student found what appeared to be a bomb in the playground yesterday morning. The police have evacuated the school and the surrounding buildings. They are searching for any other possible bombs and have sent out the bomb disposal team.

Q: According to the report, who found this bomb?

    A. A local police chief.   B. A bomb disposal team.

    C. A British commander.   D. A pupil.

昨天早上，英國倫敦市一名小學生在操場發現一個類似炸彈的東西。警方已撤離學校及周圍建築物裡的人員。他們正在搜尋任何其他可能的炸彈，同時派出拆彈部隊。

問題：根據這篇新聞報導，誰發現這顆炸彈？

選項：A. 一名當地的警長。   B. 拆彈部隊。

    C. 一名英國指揮官。   D. 一名小學生。

C 31. Next week, Alice will show us how to make classic brownies. Brownies are like a combination of chocolate cake and cookies. They are crispier than cakes, but are softer and moister than cookies. Brownies don't cost too much to make, and the ingredients are easy to find in a supermarket. Another advantage of brownies is that they can be cut into small pieces and are easy to carry. You can bring them to work to eat as a snack to get more energy.

Q: Which of the following statements is true?

    A. Ingredients for brownies are hard to find.

    B. You can learn how to make brownies today.

    C. It is easy to carry brownies wherever you go.

    D. Brownies are more expensive than cakes and cookies.

下週，Alice 將為我們示範如何製作經典的布朗尼。布朗尼像是巧克力蛋糕和餅乾的綜合體。口感比蛋糕脆，卻又比餅乾鬆軟滑潤。製作布朗尼無需太多花費，材料在超級市場就能輕易買到。布朗尼的另一好處是能夠切成小塊，便於攜帶。你可以帶去上班當作點心補充體力。

問題：下列敘述何者正確？

選項：A. 不易買到製作布朗尼的材料。   B. 你今天可以學到如何製作布朗尼。

    C. 不論你去哪裡都能輕易帶著布朗尼。   D. 布朗尼比蛋糕及餅乾還貴。

D 32. People often compliment me on my smooth skin. Good skin is important for my career as a model. Do you want to know how to take care of your skin and make every bath a pleasant experience? Wash with Everbeauty Soap! Combined with natural herbs and essential oils from Germany, this is the only soap available from Europe that will naturally make your skin clean and healthy. This soap is produced with high quality you would expect from German manufacturers.

Q: What benefit does this product provide?

    A. Provide nutrition for your body.

    B. A discount on traveling to Germany.

    C. Wash your clothes without harmful chemicals.

    D. Naturally make your skin clean and healthy.

人們時常稱讚我滑潤的肌膚。好的皮膚對我的模特兒職業來說非常重要。你想知道要如何照顧你的皮膚，讓每次洗澡都成為愉悅的經驗嗎？用 Everbeauty 肥皂沐浴吧！加入來自德國的天然藥草及精油，這是唯一來自歐洲，能夠天然地使肌膚乾淨健康的肥皂。這款肥皂的高品質製程會符合你對德國廠商的期待。

問題：這個產品提供何項益處？

選項：A. 提供身體營養素。   B. 到德國旅遊的折扣。

    C. 不以有害的化學物質洗衣服。   D. 以天然方式使肌膚乾淨健康。

D 33. Japan has increased its tourism over the past few years with successful international marketing; therefore, we sent a research group to Japan to study its marketing methods. I am pleased to welcome a guest speaker, Annie, to our travel conference. She was one of the members of the research group, and she just completed an amazing journey. She has a lot of information to share with us. I believe what she learned from Japan can help our tourism industry. Please welcome Annie.

Q: What is the purpose for Annie's visit to Japan?

    A. To help increase tourism in Japan.

    B. To attend a conference in the foreign country.

    C. To share her experiences of traveling in Japan.

    D. To study Japan's successful methods of tourism marketing.

由於過去幾年成功的國際行銷，日本觀光業已有成長；因此，我們派出一個研究小組到日本去學習它的行銷方式。我很高興能歡迎特邀講者 Annie 來到我們的旅遊會議。她是研究小組的一員，才剛完成一趟奇幻旅程。她有許多資訊要跟我們分享。我相信她從日本學到的能幫助我們的觀光業。請歡迎 Annie。

問題：Annie 造訪日本的目的是什麼？

選項：A. 幫助日本提升觀光業。   B. 參加國外的會議。

       C. 分享她在日本旅遊的經驗。   D. 學習日本成功的觀光行銷方式。

B 34.

For question number 34, please look at the voucher.

A gift that everyone loves, our voucher is ideal for celebrations or just to say thank you. With it, you may delight your loved ones with meals. And you may also cheer them with a cup of hot cappuccino. It can be also used for coffee beans and other products in our store. It's available in any value you'd like above $50.

Q: Which store is most likely to offer the voucher?

    A. Pizza Papa.   B. Sunny Café.   C. Big Burgers.   D. Jason's Mart.

第三十四題，請看禮券。

大家都喜愛的禮物，我們的禮券用來慶祝或只是表達感謝都是很理想的。有了它，你可以用餐點讓你心愛的人感到開心。而且你也可以用一杯熱卡布奇諾使他們振作起來。它也可以用在我們店裡買咖啡豆和其他商品。五十美元以上，你想要的任何金額都有。

問題：哪一家店最有可能提供這張禮券？

選項：A. 老爹披薩。   B. 陽光咖啡店。   C. 大漢堡。   D. 傑森超市。

解析   由談話可知禮券可買餐點、咖啡、咖啡豆和零售品，可推知應該是咖啡店推出的，故答案選 B。

B 35. For question number 35, please look at the leaflet.

Dear customers, our department store is having a Thanksgiving sale now. You will get a 30% discount if you buy a scarf today. Sweaters are also on sale. You can buy one and get the second one 20% off. Our shirts are 50% off if you buy three. The winter coat is 10% off. And you'll receive an additional 10% discount if you pay in cash.

Q: Nelson is going to buy three shirts in cash. How much should he pay?

A. $40.　　　　　B. $54.

C. $60.　　　　　D. $150.

第三十五題，請看傳單。

親愛的顧客你好，現在我們百貨公司正在進行感恩節大特賣。如果你今天買一條圍巾，會打七折。毛衣也在特價。你可以買一件，而後第二件打八折。如果你買三件我們的襯衫可以打五折。冬季大衣打九折。如果你用現金結帳，可以再打九折。

問題：Nelson 要用現金買三件襯衫。他應該付多少錢？

選項：A. 40 美元。　　　B. 54 美元。　　　　C. 60 美元。　　　　D. 150 美元。

解析　由談話可知買三件襯衫打五折，用現金結帳可以再打九折；而根據傳單內容，襯衫一件 40 美元，所以 $40 \times 3 \times 50\% \times 90\% = 54$，故答案選 B。

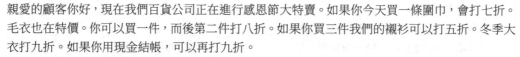

第一部份：看圖辨義

B 1. For question number 1, please look at picture A.

Question number 1: What are the people on the stage doing?

A. They are applauding.

B. They are bowing.

C. They are grinning.

D. They are playing their instruments.

第一題，請看圖片 A。

第一題：舞臺上的人正在做什麼？

選項：A. 他們正在拍手。

B. 他們正在鞠躬。

C. 他們正在咧嘴笑。

D. 他們正在演奏他們的樂器。

C 2. For question number 2, please look at picture B.

Question number 2: What information is provided in the receipt?

A. The shopper provided the exact change.

B. A toothbrush costs NT$300.

C. The shopper bought a dozen eggs.

D. One of the items is toothpaste.

第二題，請看圖片 B。

第二題：收據提供什麼訊息？

選項：A. 購物者給剛好的錢。

B. 一枝牙刷花費新臺幣 300 元。

C. 購物者買了一打蛋。

D. 其中一個品項是牙膏。

C 3. For question number 3, please look at picture C.

Question number 3: What can be inferred from the picture?

A. The nurse has back pain.

B. The patient is about to give birth.

C. The patient broke her leg.

D. The doctor had taken a walk.

第三題，請看圖片 C。

第三題：從圖中可以推測什麼？

選項：A. 護理師有背痛。

B. 病患快要生產了。

C. 病患摔斷她的腿。

D. 醫生已經去散過步。

C 4. For questions number 4 and 5, please look at picture D.

Question number 4: Why do they come to the park?

A. To play games.

B. To lift weights.

C. To do some exercise.

D. To meet with friends.

第四題及第五題，請看圖片 D。

第四題：他們為什麼要來公園？

選項：A. 來玩遊戲。　　B. 來舉重。　　　　C. 來做些運動。　　　D. 來見朋友。

A 5. Question number 5: Please look at picture D again. Why is no one playing ball on the grass?

A. It is forbidden.

B. There are no balls.

C. People prefer to exercise.

D. It is probably not popular here.

第五題：請再看一次圖片 D。為什麼沒有人在草地上玩球？

選項：A. 它遭到禁止的。　　　　　　　　B. 那裡沒有球。

　　　C. 人們寧可做運動。　　　　　　D. 它可能在這裡不受到歡迎。

第二部份：問答

A 6. Do you think this shirt would be OK to wear for business trips?

A. I don't think so. It's a little too casual.

B. Well, it's certainly fashionable.

C. I've never worn a suit before.

D. 50% off all neckties. Not a bad deal!

問題：你覺得這件襯衫出差穿適合嗎？

選項：A. 我不這麼覺得。它有一點太休閒了。　　B. 嗯，它當然非常流行。

　　　C. 我從沒穿過西裝。　　　　　　　　　D. 領帶全部五折。還蠻划算的！

D 7. How do I apply for gym membership?

A. The ship is approaching the port.

B. We close on Saturdays.

C. Please print an extra copy for me.

D. Just fill out this form and sign at the bottom.

問題：我要如何申請健身房會員？

選項：A. 船正在靠近港口。　　　　　　　B. 我們每週六休息。

　　　C. 請多影印一份給我。　　　　　　D. 只要填寫表格，並在下面簽名。

C 8. I can't believe how much sugar Jenny puts in her drink.

A. I usually prepare my own lunch.　　B. I much prefer iced coffee to iced tea.

C. No wonder she has to visit the dentist.　D. No doubt she'll expect me to pay the bill.

問題：我真不敢相信 Jenny 放了那麼多糖在她的飲料裡。

選項：A. 我通常會準備我自己的午餐。　　B. 我喜歡冰咖啡更勝於冰茶。

　　　C. 難怪她需要看牙醫。　　　　　　D. 難怪她還奢望我付帳單。

D 9. I feel so stressed out.

A. What have I ever done to you?　　　B. How on earth should I know?

C. Where have you been recently?　　　D. Why not take a long hot bath?

問題：我覺得壓力好大。

選項：A. 我到底對你做了什麼？　　　　　B. 我怎麼會知道？

　　　C. 你最近去哪呢？　　　　　　　　D. 何不洗個熱水澡呢？

B 10. Did you complete the project on time?

A. Yes, we caught the train just in time.　B. No, we missed the deadline by one day.

C. Well, the final decision is not up to me.　D. If we hurry, I think we can catch up.

問題：你們有準時完成這個計畫嗎？

選項：A. 是的，我們及時搭上了火車。　　B. 沒有，我們超過了期限一天。

C. 嗯，最終的決定權不在我身上。　　D. 如果我們加快的話，我想我們能趕上。

C 11. Which work of art won the art contest?

    A. The piano concert.　　　　　　　B. The modern art museum.

    C. A sculpture of an ant.　　　　　　D. Digital photography.

問題：哪一件藝術品贏得藝術大賽？

選項：A. 鋼琴演奏會。　B. 現代藝術美術館。　　C. 螞蟻的雕塑。　　　　D. 數位攝影。

B 12. How much should I tip the waiter?

    A. Pay at the end of the meal.　　　　B. 15% of the total bill.

    C. My advice is to book early.　　　　D. The service was wonderful, thanks.

問題：我該給服務生多少小費？

選項：A. 用餐結束時付帳。　　　　　　B. 帳單的 15%。

    C. 我的建議是早一點訂位。　　　　D. 服務很棒，謝啦。

B 13. I didn't know you were into jazz.

    A. Why didn't you let me know sooner?　　B. Oh, sure! I'm a huge jazz fan.

    C. Don't forget to return my CD!　　　D. I watch videos on YouTube.

問題：我不知道你喜歡爵士樂。

選項：A. 為什麼你不早點讓我知道？　　B. 哦，當然！我是個超級爵士樂迷。

    C. 別忘了把 CD 還給我！　　　　　D. 我在 YouTube 上看影片。

C 14. Are there any ferries to the island after 9 p.m.?

    A. I must have dropped my map.　　　B. I joined a tour group.

    C. Let's ask at the information desk.　　D. There may be a bank along this street.

問題：晚上九點過後有任何渡輪到這座島嗎？

選項：A. 我一定是把我的地圖弄丟了。　　B. 我參加了旅行團。

    C. 我們到服務櫃臺問。　　　　　　D. 這條街上可能有家銀行。

C 15. Thank you so much! How can I thank you?

    A. The interest rate is set at 5%.

    B. Thanks a million. I owe you big time.

    C. There's no need. It was the very least I could do.

    D. I make it a rule never to borrow money from friends.

問題：非常謝謝你！我要如何謝謝你呢？

選項：A. 利率設在 5%。

    B. 太感謝了。我欠你一個大人情。

    C. 不用啦。至少這是我能做的。

    D. 我自己訂了一個規則就是永遠不要跟朋友借錢。

....

第三部份：簡短對話

C 16. M: Excuse me. What is the fastest way to send a package to Canada?

    W: Sending it by airmail is the fastest way.

M: How much is the postage for this package?

W: It is NT$500.

Q: Where might this conversation take place?

    A. On a bus.   B. At a train station.   C. In a post office.   D. In a travel agency.

男：不好意思。寄包裹到加拿大的最快方式是什麼？

女：航空郵件最快。

男：這件包裹郵資要多少錢？

女：新臺幣 500 元。

問題：這段對話可能發生在哪裡？

選項：A. 在公車上。   B. 在火車站。   C. 在郵局。   D. 在旅行社。

C 17. W: Did you hear that Bob and Susan are getting married?

M: Yeah. It is really a surprise.

W: I didn't even know they were dating.

M: No one knows that Susan would end up marrying her boss.

Q: What do we know about Bob and Susan?

    A. Susan is Bob's manager.

    B. Bob and Susan are going to get divorced.

    C. Bob and Susan work together.

    D. Susan had never seen Bob before.

女：你聽說 Bob 和 Susan 要結婚了嗎？

男：有啊。這真是令人驚訝。

女：我連他們在約會都不知道。

男：沒有人想到 Susan 最後是嫁給自己的老闆。

問題：關於 Bob 和 Susan 我們知道什麼？

選項：A. Susan 是 Bob 的經理。   B. Bob 和 Susan 打算離婚。

        C. Bob 和 Susan 一起工作。   D. Susan 未曾見過 Bob。

D 18. M: Welcome home. Oh dear! What happened to your arm?

W: Ouch! Easy! It really hurts. Nick teased me and pushed me off the swing at school.

M: Did you tell your teacher about this?

W: No. I think he just wanted to play a joke on me. He said he was sorry and took me to the health center right away.

M: If he does anything like this again, let the teacher know and call me, all right?

W: All right.

M: OK, let me check your wound again.

Q: Where did the girl get hurt?

    A. At home.   B. In the health center.

    C. In the classroom.   D. In the school playground.

男：歡迎回家。天哪！你的手臂怎麼了？

女：哎喲！輕一點！真的很痛。Nick 捉弄我，在學校把我從鞦韆上推下去。

男：你有告訴你的老師嗎？

女：沒有，我想他只是想跟我玩笑。他說他很抱歉，並立刻帶我到健康中心。

男：如果他再犯類似的事情，就要讓老師知道並打電話給我，知道嗎？

女：知道了。

男：好，再讓我看看你的傷口。

問題：女孩在哪裡受傷的？

選項：A. 在家裡。　　　B. 在健康中心。　　　C. 在教室。　　　D. 在學校操場。

B 19. W: Alex! Hey, Alex! Watch out!

M: That was close! The truck almost hit me.

W: No! It was you that almost hit the truck! You shouldn't just stare at your smartphone while you are walking across the street! What were you doing?

M: Well, you know, using Facebook and Instagram . . . .

W: And it's dangerous to do so!

M: I know. I won't do it again.

W: Keep that in your mind. Next time you won't be so lucky.

M: Thank you. I owe you one.

Q: What happened to Alex?

A. His smartphone was ringing.

B. He almost had a car accident.

C. He kept in touch with his friends all the time.

D. The truck driver was staring at his smartphone.

女：Alex！嘿，Alex！小心！

男：差一點！那輛卡車差點撞到我。

女：不對！是你差點撞到卡車！你過馬路時不該一直盯著智慧型手機看！你在做什麼啊？

男：嗯，你知道的，就是用 Facebook 和 Instagram……

女：還有這樣做很危險！

男：知道了。我不會再犯了。

女：記住你說過的話。下次你就不會這麼幸運了。

男：謝謝你。我欠你一次。

問題：Alex 發生什麼事？

選項：A. 他的智慧型手機正在響。　　　B. 他差點發生車禍。

　　　C. 他向來都會與朋友保持連絡。　　　D. 卡車司機正盯著他的智慧型手機看。

D 20. M: Hi. I'd like to order a cup of iced coffee and a bowl of ice cream with berries on top.

W: I'm sorry, but we're out of berries. How about chocolate syrup?

M: That sounds great! Can you bring me two spoons? I want to share it with my friend.

W: Sure, no problem.

Q: Why does the man want two spoons?

A. The ice cream is too big to eat.

B. The woman promises to give him two spoons.

C. He likes to eat ice cream with two spoons.

D. His friend will eat the ice cream together with him.

男：嗨。我要點一杯冰咖啡和一碗莓果冰淇淋。

女：抱歉，我們莓果用完了。要不要換巧克力醬？

男：聽起來不錯！可以給我兩枝湯匙嗎？我要和我朋友一起吃。

女：當然，沒問題。

問題：男子為什麼要兩枝湯匙？

選項：A. 冰淇淋太大了，無法食用。　　　B. 女子答應給他兩枝湯匙。

　　　C. 他喜歡用兩枝湯匙吃冰淇淋。　　D. 他的朋友會跟他一起吃冰淇淋。

C 21. W: Oh, I need to find another part-time job. I have to earn more money.

M: I thought your parents would give you an allowance.

W: They do, but that's not enough!

M: Why?

W: I am saving up for my trip to Australia.

M: Oh, in that case, you really need to save a lot of money.

W: Yeah. I am looking for a job in the newspaper.

M: Why don't you check the job search website? I think you will find more options there.

W: That's a good idea. Thanks!

Q: Why is the girl looking for another part-time job?

A. She wants to kill time.

B. Her parents never give her an allowance.

C. She wants to save up for her trip to Australia.

D. Ask her parents to increase her allowance.

女：哦，我需要再找一份兼職工作。我必須賺更多的錢。

男：我以為你父母有給你零用錢。

女：有啊，但那不夠！

男：怎麼會呢？

女：我正在存錢去澳洲旅遊。

男：哦，那樣的話，你的確是需要存上一大筆錢。

女：是啊。我正在報紙上尋找工作。

男：你怎麼不去求職網站看看呢？我想在那裡你會有更多的選擇。

女：真是個好主意。謝謝！

問題：為什麼女孩在找另一份兼職工作？

選項：A. 她想要打發時間。　　　　　　B. 她的父母從沒有給過她零用錢。

　　　C. 她想要為了澳洲旅遊存錢。　　D. 要求她父母多給零用錢。

A 22. M: I heard you are an excellent piano teacher.

W: Thank you.

M: I am interested in hiring you for piano lessons.

W: Have you played the piano before?

M: Not at all.

W: Then I can't teach you. I only teach an advanced piano course.

M: I'm afraid you misunderstood. I want to hire you to teach my daughter, and she is a very good student.

Q: What is the most likely reason the woman said she can't teach the man?

    A. He is only a beginner.   B. He doesn't ask her politely.

    C. He is a professional pianist.   D. She is not a good piano teacher.

男：聽說你是一位很棒的鋼琴老師。

女：謝謝。

男：我有意聘請你來上鋼琴課。

女：你之前有彈過鋼琴嗎？

男：從來沒有。

女：這樣我不能教你。我只教授高階鋼琴課程。

男：我想你誤會了。我要請你教我女兒，她是個很好的學生。

問題：女子說她無法教男子鋼琴最有可能的原因是什麼？

選項：A. 他只是個初學者。   B. 他並未有禮地詢問她。

      C. 他是專業鋼琴家。   D. 她不是一位好的鋼琴老師。

A 23. W: Can I have a table for two?

M: Do you have a reservation?

W: No, I don't.

M: I am sorry, but all our customers have to make reservations in advance.

W: Oh, please. Today is my birthday. Can you make an exception for me?

M: I apologize once again. I am afraid I can't do that.

Q: What should the woman do beforehand?

    A. Book a table for two.   B. Break the rule for her friend.

    C. Tell the man today is her birthday.   D. Ask the man to apologize to her.

女：可以給我一張兩人座的餐桌嗎？

男：請問你有訂位嗎？

女：不，我沒有。

男：抱歉，但所有的客人都必須事先訂位。

女：哦，拜託。今天是我的生日。能為我破例嗎？

男：再次向你致歉。恐怕我無法這麼做。

問題：女子應該預先做什麼？

選項：A. 預訂兩人座的餐桌。   B. 為她朋友違反規則。

      C. 告訴男子今天是她的生日。   D. 要求男子向她道歉。

D 24. For question number 24, please look at the train ticket.

M: Oh, no! The departure time is changed to 11:50.

W: The train is delayed for half an hour.

M: We will be late for the meeting in Taichung. What should we do?

W: Let's call the manager to put off the meeting to a later time.

Q: When will the speakers arrive in Taichung?

　A. At 11:20.　　B. At 11:50.　　　C. At 13:05.　　　D. At 13:35.

第二十四題，請看火車票。

男：噢，不！發車時間改成 11:50 了。

女：火車延誤半小時。

男：我們在臺中的會議會遲到。我們該怎麼辦？

女：讓我們打電話給經理把會議延到晚一點的時間。

問題：說話者們何時會抵達臺中？

選項：A. 11:20。　　B. 11:50。　　　C. 13:05。　　　D. 13:35。

解析　由對話可知火車延誤半小時；而根據火車票，原本預定抵達臺中的時間是 13:05，延後半小時的話，會是 13:35，故答案選 D。

B 25. For question number 25, please look at the line graph.

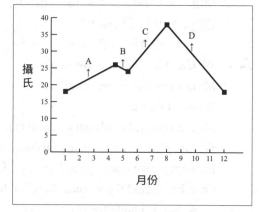

W: Let's see when the best time to visit this island is.

M: It starts from its lowest level in January with about 18°C.

W: And there is a steady increase until April.

M: You know, in early April, thunderstorms begin to occur in the afternoon there, so the weather becomes cooler. It also brings high rainfall throughout the island.

W: After that, it becomes hotter, and temperatures go up and rise to 38°C in August.

M: Summer is too hot for a visit!

W: Then, temperatures go down constantly and reach another lowest level in December.

Q: During which period of time (A, B, C or D), do the temperatures drop due to heavy rain?

第二十五題，請看折線圖。

女：我們來看看何時是造訪這座島嶼的最佳時間。

男：它在一月是最低溫，大約攝氏 18 度。

女：然後直到四月溫度都穩定升高。

男：你知道的，四月初那裡午後會發生雷雨，所以天氣變得比較涼。這也為整座島嶼帶來高的降雨量。

女：在那之後，天氣變得比較熱，氣溫上升並在八月上升到攝氏 38 度。

男：夏天造訪太熱了！

女：然後，氣溫持續下降並在十二月達到另一個低點。

問題：在哪一個時期（A、B、C 或 D）氣溫會因為大雨而下降？

解析 由對話可知四月初該島午後會有雷雨，所以變得比較涼爽；而根據折線圖，四月開始有一段溫度下降期，故答案選 B。

....

第四部份：簡短談話

D 26. An international trading company is seeking an ambitious assistant for the vice president to help him deal with daily activities. The starting salary is NT$200 per hour, but more can be offered, depending on the applicant's experience. The working hours are from 8 a.m. to 5 p.m., 5 days per week. Advanced English skills are required. Good computer skills are a bonus. Please send your résumé to employment@tradecompany.com. We will contact you if you are qualified.

Q: According to the job posting, which of the following is true?

    A. The company is seeking a vice president.

    B. Applicants can't send their résumés by email.

    C. The starting pay is at least NT$400 per hour.

    D. The applicant should be good at English.

一家國際貿易公司正在為副總裁尋找有抱負的助理，以幫助他處理日常事務。起薪是每小時新臺幣 200 元，但薪資可依求職者資歷調升。工作時間是上午八點至下午五點，每週上班五天。需要進階的英語能力。具備良好電腦能力尤佳。請將履歷寄到 employment@tradecompany.com，我們將會與合乎資格者聯繫。

問題：根據這篇職缺公告，下列何者為真？

選項：A. 這家公司在徵副總裁。   B. 求職者無法透過電子郵件寄他們的履歷。

       C. 起薪至少一小時新臺幣 400 元。   D. 求職者需精通英語。

B 27. Are you ready for an enjoyable vacation in a beautiful tropical paradise? V&O Beach Resort offers peaceful relaxation in a beautiful setting. You can enjoy our first-class spa to let your stress and worries melt away. Besides, there are many recreational activities offered at our location, including water sports, horseback riding, and fishing. On the other hand, our restaurant is famous for providing the freshest seafood. The views at sunset are outstanding. Reserve your room in November, and you will get a 50% discount on our regular room rates.

Q: According to the advertisement, what does the resort offer?

    A. Outstanding views of the city.   B. Several outdoor activities.

    C. Tall mountains and great skiing.   D. An Italian restaurant famous for its pasta.

你準備好要到一個美麗的熱帶天堂快度假嗎？V&O 海灘度假勝地的美麗環境能帶給你寧靜的悠閒。你可以享受我們的頂級 spa 服務，消除你的壓力和煩惱。此外，還提供許多休閒活動，包含水上活動、騎馬及釣魚。另一方面，我們的餐廳以供應最新鮮的海產聞名。夕陽景色絕佳。十一月份預訂房間，你將享有一般房價的五折優惠。

問題：根據廣告，該度假勝地提供什麼？

選項：A. 出色的城市景觀。　　　　　　　B. 數種戶外活動。

　　　C. 高山及絕佳滑雪運動。　　　　　D. 以義大利麵聞名的義大利餐廳。

C 28. Ladies and gentlemen, please pay attention to the nearest monitor to you. The video will demonstrate the proper safety tips and directions in case of an emergency. These directions can also be found on the card inserted in the back of the seat in front of you. Please do not ignore this presentation because it might just save your life. Please always stay seated with your seat belt fastened until the captain turns off the fasten seat belt sign. Remember that this is a non-smoking flight. Please do not smoke on this plane. If any emergency happens, please proceed in a calm and orderly manner. Thank you!

Q: Where is this announcement being made?

　　A. On a bus.　　　　　　　　　　B. In an emergency room.

　　C. On an airplane.　　　　　　　　D. At a train station.

各位女士、先生，請注意離你最近的螢幕。影片將解說緊急狀況時正確的安全須知及步驟。這些安全指南也能在你前方椅背上的卡片上找到。請勿輕忽這段說明，因為這可能會救你一命。機長關閉安全帶指示燈之前，請待在你的座位並繫上安全帶。記住，這是禁菸班機。請不要在機上吸菸。如果發生任何緊急狀況，請冷靜並遵守秩序。感謝你！

問題：這則廣播在哪裡播放？

選項：A. 在公車上。　　B. 在急診室。　　　C. 在飛機上。　　　D. 在火車站。

A 29. Hello, Debby, this is Karen. I'm calling because I can't go to school today. My father is on a business trip to New York, and my mother has a very important meeting today, so I have to take care of my little sister. Would you mind helping me with two things? First, could you tell Mr. Lin that I have to take a day off? I don't know why I can't find his phone number. In addition, I have sent my history report to your email address. Could you print it and turn in the report to Mrs. Chen for me? It is my final report, so please make sure that Mrs. Chen gets it. Thank you for your help. I will see you tomorrow.

Q: What does Karen ask Debby to do?

　　A. Turn in her history report.　　　　B. Send her an email.

　　C. Stop by her house.　　　　　　　D. Tell her Mr. Lin's phone number.

哈囉，Debby，我是 Karen。我打電話給你是因為我今天不能去上學。我父親到紐約出差，而我母親今天有一場非常重要的會議，所以我必須照顧我妹妹。你介意幫我兩件事嗎？首先，可以告訴林老師我必須請一天假嗎？不知道為什麼，我找不到他的電話號碼。另外，我已將我的歷史報告寄到你的電子信箱。麻煩你列印出來，然後幫我交給陳老師，好嗎？那是我的期末報告，所以一定要確保陳老師有收到。感謝你的幫忙。明天見。

問題：Karen 要 Debby 做什麼？

選項：A. 繳交她的歷史報告。　　　　　　B. 寄一封電子郵件給她。

　　　C. 到她家坐坐。　　　　　　　　D. 告訴她林老師的電話號碼。

B 30. The college ball will be held in the auditorium at 7 p.m. this Friday night. Tickets can be purchased during lunchtime at the table outside of the school cafeteria. We expect our students to follow a proper dress code and show good behavior during our event. Dresses are recommended for the girls and white shirts for the boys. Please wear leather shoes instead of sneakers, and do not wear jeans. Shirts with offensive language on them are not allowed. When deciding what to wear, just think about how you can show as much class and style as possible. Thank you for your time.

Q: What is this announcement mainly about?

    A. The theme of the college ball.   B. How to dress properly for a ball.

    C. Directions to find the college ball.   D. The class schedule for the new semester.

大學舞會將於這週五晚上七點於禮堂舉行。午餐時間可在學生餐廳外面的攤位買到入場券。我們期待活動期間同學們能夠遵守適當的服裝規範並表現良好的行為。服裝方面，建議女生穿著洋裝，男生穿著白色襯衫。請穿皮鞋而非運動鞋，並請不要穿牛仔褲。印有冒犯性字樣的襯衫也不得穿著。決定穿著時，想想你要如何將自己的格調及風格表現得淋漓盡致。感謝各位的聆聽。

問題：這則廣播的主旨是什麼？

選項：A. 大學舞會的主題。   B. 如何在舞會中穿著得宜。

    C. 找到大學舞會場地的指引。   D. 新學期的課程表。

C 31. Citizens are upset that the cost of electricity has increased by 10% over the previous year. The electric power company explained that the cost of the fuels for its power stations had increased. Furthermore, recent droughts have meant that there is less water in lakes for the power plants. The company is looking for additional methods of producing power to reduce its costs. Moreover, it has invested a great deal of money to research the possibility of using solar and wind energy.

Q: Which of the following statements is true?

    A. There has been plenty of rain in the past year.

    B. People are happy with the new prices for electricity.

    C. The cost of electricity has increased last year.

    D. The company uses only wind power to produce electricity.

民眾對於去年電費上漲 10% 感到生氣。電力公司解釋是發電廠燃料成本上漲。另外，最近的乾旱也代表供應電廠的湖水減少。公司正在尋找其他的發電方式以降低成本。再者，它已經投入大筆經費研究使用太陽能及風力能源的可行性。

問題：下列敘述何者正確？

選項：A. 過去一年雨量充沛。   B. 人們對新電價感到滿意。

    C. 去年電費的花費增加了。   D. 該公司只運用風力發電。

A 32. Good afternoon, everyone. I would like to let you know that there are currently jobs available at the dairy farms outside of the city. I know you may not like the disadvantages of the job. It is hard work and requires long hours. You would need to live far away from the city. However, I will share what I think are the benefits of working in the countryside.

The countryside offers fresh air and a healthier lifestyle. You may find out that you enjoy working with animals. It will be a new experience that you may remember forever. I hope you give it serious a consideration because they need about eight new employees right now. Thank you.

Q: According to the speaker, what is a benefit of working at a dairy farm?

A. Fresh air.   B. High pay.

C. Free milk.   D. Living close to the city.

各位午安。我想讓你們知道，最近在市郊的乳牛場有職缺。我了解你們可能不喜歡這類工作的一些缺點。它既辛苦，工時又長。你們還得住在遠離市區的地方。然而，我想跟你們分享一些鄉間工作的優點。鄉下的空氣新鮮，生活形式也比較健康。你們或許會發現自己其實喜歡工作時有動物為伴。這將是讓你們永生難忘的全新體驗。我希望你們能認真考慮，因為他們現在需要大約八名新工作人員。謝謝。

問題：根據說話者的說法，在乳牛場工作的好處是什麼？

選項：A. 新鮮空氣。　　B. 高薪。　　　　C. 免費的牛奶。　　　D. 住處離市區很近。

C 33. Heidi was an exchange student from Germany. She came to Taiwan to learn Chinese. Even though she had many friends who liked her, she seemed homesick. To help her feel more at home, I learned some German to speak with her. I even treated her to German sausages during lunch one day. She seemed to be touched by my efforts. After that moment, we became the closest friends. Before she went back to Germany, she invited me to visit her hometown during this summer vacation, so she could introduce me to her friends and family. I can't wait to see Heidi again and taste some real German sausages.

Q: Why did Heidi become close friends with the woman?

A. The woman taught her Chinese.

B. The woman was willing to visit Germany.

C. The woman made her feel at home in Taiwan.

D. The woman visited Heidi at the hospital when she was sick.

Heidi 是德國交換學生。她來臺灣學中文。她雖有許多喜歡她的朋友，但她似乎很想家。為了讓她更有家的感覺，我學了些德語與她交談。有一天，我還在午餐時買德國香腸請她吃。她似乎被我的用心感動。從那一刻起，我們成了摯友。在她回德國前，她邀請我今年暑假到她的故鄉一遊，她要介紹我給她的親朋好友認識。我等不及再次見到 Heidi，並品嘗一下道地的德國香腸。

問題：Heidi 為什麼會和該女子成為摯友？

選項：A. 女子教她中文。　　　　　　　B. 女子願意造訪德國。

　　　C. 女子使她在臺灣有家的感覺。　　D. 女子在 Heidi 生病時去醫院看她。

D 34.

乘客姓名	航班	日期
Steve Jones	CY909	31 December 2022

波士頓 ✈ 紐約

座位	登機門	登機時間
38C	D3	18:30

乘客姓名
Steve Jones

航班　　座位
CY909　38C

日期
31 December 2022

登機門
D3

For question number 34, please look at the boarding pass.

Mom, I've boarded the plane. I nearly missed the flight because I didn't notice that the boarding gate had been changed to E5. That was close! I'll arrive in New York half an hour later since the scheduled departure time is delayed due to air traffic control. I just want to tell you that it was great to be back home and spend the Christmas holiday with you and Dad. Don't worry about me. I'll take good care of myself and study hard. Love you!

Q: Which of the following about the speaker is true?

　　A. He boarded Flight CY909 to New York at Gate D3.

　　B. His home is in New York, but he studies in Boston.

　　C. His flight will land in New York on schedule.

　　D. He left the message to his mother after 6:30 p.m.

第三十四題，請看登機證。

媽，我已經登機了。我差點錯過班機，因為我沒有注意到登機門已改到 E5。好險！我會晚半小時抵達紐約，因為航空交通管制的緣故，預定的起飛時間延誤了。我只是想告訴你，回家和你跟爸爸過耶誕假期真棒。不要擔心我。我會好好照顧自己並且認真讀書。愛你喔！

問題：關於說話者，下列何者為真？

選項：A. 他從登機門 D3 登上了飛往紐約的 CY909 航班。

　　　B. 他家在紐約，但他在波士頓讀書。

　　　C. 他的航班會準時降落在紐約。

　　　D. 他在下午六點半後留言給他媽媽。

解析 由談話可知登機門從登機證上的 D3 改到 E5，故不選 A；由談話可知他是回家過節後要回紐約讀書，故不選 B；由談話可知航班會晚半小時抵達紐約，故不選 C；根據登機證，登機時間是 18:30，而他是登機後才留言，故答案選 D。

D 35. For question number 35, please look at the menu.

Good evening! Welcome to Ruby's Kitchen. I'm happy to introduce our latest menu. As you can see from the list, today's specials are Pizza Margherita, Greek Roast Chicken, Pan-Fried Duck Breast, and T-Bone Steak. Our Pizza Margherita and Pan-Fried Duck Breast are very popular! But personally, I love the Greek Roast Chicken, which includes fresh salad and roast potatoes — a winning combination. Now, who loves beef? Well, if you do, don't miss out on our special offer!

Q: Which dish is served at a discount in the restaurant?

    A. Pizza Margherita.

    B. Greek Roast Chicken.

    C. Pan-Fried Duck Breast.

    D. T-Bone Steak.

第三十五題，請看菜單。

晚安！歡迎光臨露比廚房。很高興介紹我們最新的菜單。就如同你在單子上可看到的，今天的特餐是瑪格麗特披薩、希臘烤雞、香煎鴨胸和丁骨牛排。我們的瑪格麗特披薩和香煎鴨胸非常受歡迎！但我個人喜歡希臘烤雞，它包含新鮮沙拉和烤馬鈴薯——最佳組合。現在，誰喜歡牛肉？嗯，如果你喜歡，別錯過我們的特別優惠！

問題：餐廳哪一道菜特價供應？

選項：A. 瑪格麗特披薩。   B. 希臘烤雞。

       C. 香煎鴨胸。   D. 丁骨牛排。

解析   由談話可知牛肉有優惠；根據菜單，有牛肉的特餐是丁骨牛排，故答案選 D。

第一部份：看圖辨義

D 1. For question number 1, please look at picture A.

Question number 1: Which description matches the picture?

A. One of the men is completely bald.

B. The hair on the floor has not been swept yet.

C. The man is sending a message to someone.

D. The customer who is waiting has a beard.

第一題，請看圖片 A。

第一題：哪一個敘述與圖片相符？

選項：A. 其中一位男子是禿頭。　　　　B. 地上的頭髮還沒掃乾淨。

　　　　C. 男子正在傳簡訊給某人。　　　D. 等候的這位客人有鬍子。

C 2. For question number 2, please look at picture B.

Question number 2: What might the woman be saying?

A. You lost lots of blood.　　　　　B. Please provide us your tissue sample.

C. We need to test your kidney function.　　D. Here is your prescription.

第二題，請看圖片 B。

第二題：女子可能正在說什麼？

選項：A. 你大量失血。　　　　　　　B. 請提供你的組織樣本給我們。

　　　　C. 我們需要測試你腎臟的功能。　D. 這是你的處方箋。

D 3. For question number 3, please look at picture C.

Question number 3: What kind of movie is this?

A. Horror movie.　　　　　　　　B. Costume drama.

C. Romantic comedy.　　　　　　　D. Science fiction comedy.

第三題，請看圖片 C。

第三題：這是哪一類型的電影？

選項：A. 恐怖片。　　　B. 古裝劇。　　　　　C. 浪漫喜劇。　　　　D. 科幻喜劇。

C 4. For questions number 4 and 5, please look at picture D.

Question number 4: Why was the sign put there?

A. To encourage people to swim in the river.

B. To block people from entering the park.

C. To prevent people from drowning.

D. To warn people about a penalty.

第四題及第五題，請看圖片 D。

第四題：那個標誌為什麼要放在那裡？

選項：A. 鼓勵人們在河裡游泳。　　　　B. 阻止人們到公園裡。

　　　　C. 防止人們溺水。　　　　　　D. 警告人們有罰責。

D 5. Question number 5: Please look at picture D again. What is true about the people in the river?

    A. They are unable to breathe.   B. They are taking the sign seriously.

    C. They are having a safety lesson.   D. They are breaking the rule.

    第五題：請再看一次圖片 D。關於在河裡的人，何者為真？

    選項：A. 他們無法呼吸。   B. 他們嚴肅地看待這個標誌。

          C. 他們正在上安全課程。   D. 他們違反規定。

第二部份：問答

D 6. Excuse me. Where are the restrooms?

    A. I'll bring one up to your room right away.

    B. There's one on the bottom shelf over there.

    C. We don't have any available rooms at the moment.

    D. Go down to the end of the hall and you'll see them on the left.

    問題：不好意思。洗手間在哪？

    選項：A. 我會立刻送一份到你的房間。

          B. 有一個在那邊架子的最底層。

          C. 我們目前沒有任何空房。

          D. 走到走廊盡頭，你就會看到洗手間在左手邊。

C 7. Learning this stuff is a waste of time.

    A. The schedule has been changed.   B. Check your answers online.

    C. That's not the right attitude.   D. Spend your allowance more wisely.

    問題：學這玩意根本是浪費時間。

    選項：A. 行程已經被改變了。   B. 上網對答案。

          C. 這不是正確的態度。   D. 更聰明地花你的零用錢。

B 8. What is your present occupation?

    A. March 1st.   B. I'm a mechanic.

    C. I have two sons.   D. I live in an apartment.

    問題：你現在的職業是什麼？

    選項：A. 三月一日。   B. 我是個技工。

          C. 我有兩個兒子。   D. 我住在公寓裡。

D 9. You're looking really fit these days.

    A. Great! I'm looking forward to it.   B. Certainly! I'd be honored.

    C. Never mind. It's no big deal.   D. Thanks. I've been working out.

    問題：你最近看起來真的很健康。

    選項：A. 太棒了！我很期待。   B. 當然！我感到很榮幸。

          C. 別在意。沒什麼大不了的。   D. 謝謝。我有在健身。

A 10. I thought there was supposed to be a meeting this morning.

A. It was canceled.　　　　　　　　　B. I'm the head of sales.

C. The line is busy.　　　　　　　　　D. You'll get a promotion!

問題：我以為今天早上有一場會議。

選項：A. 它被取消了。 B. 我是業務部的主管。 C. 線路忙線。　　　D. 你會得到升遷！

B 11. What kind of restaurants do you like?

A. I'd like a chicken salad.　　　　　B. I think buffets are my favorite.

C. I had a lunch box and a piece of fruit.　D. I'll have the chocolate pudding, please.

問題：你喜歡什麼樣的餐廳？

選項：A. 我想要一份雞肉沙拉。　　　　B. 我想自助餐廳是我的最愛。

　　　C. 我有午餐便當和一份水果。　　D. 請給我一份巧克力布丁。

C 12. What are your long-term goals?

A. To tidy up my bedroom and wash my socks.

B. To make dinner and get an early night.

C. To get a PhD and buy an apartment.

D. To have a beer and surf the Internet.

問題：你長期的目標是什麼？

選項：A. 清理我的房間和洗我的襪子。　　B. 做晚餐和早點睡。

　　　C. 得到博士學位和買間公寓。　　D. 喝杯啤酒和上網。

B 13. Doctor, I have a terrible stomachache.

A. This skin cream should help.

B. Take one of these pills every four hours.

C. I need to clean the wound first.

D. I've scheduled a meeting for next month.

問題：醫生，我有嚴重的胃痛。

選項：A. 這個皮膚乳膏應該會有幫助。　　B. 這些藥丸每四小時服用一顆。

　　　C. 我需要先清理傷口。　　　　　D. 下個月我已經安排了會議。

B 14. Hello. There aren't any towels in our room.

A. I'm afraid we don't take checks anymore.

B. I'm sorry. I'll send some up right away.

C. Good morning! How may I help you?

D. All right. So that's a single room for April 14th.

問題：喂，我們的房間裡沒有任何毛巾。

選項：A. 恐怕我們不再收支票了。　　　　B. 抱歉。我會立刻送一些上去。

　　　C. 早安！有什麼需要協助的嗎？　　D. 好的。四月十四日一間單人房。

D 15. I think I'm going to sneeze. Achoo!

A. For goodness' sake!　　　　　　　B. Amen!

C. Good heavens!　　　　　　　　　D. Bless you!

問題：我想我要打噴嚏了。阿嚏！

選項：A. 看在老天的分上！　　　　　　　B. 阿門！

　　　　C. 我的天啊！　　　　　　　　　D. 願神保佑你！

第三部份：簡短對話

D 16. M: Excuse me. Would you please tell me where Room 612 is?

W: Sure. Go around the corner to the elevators and go up to the 6th floor.

M: Thank you.

W: Are you a member of the family?

M: No, I am a friend of the patient.

W: OK. Remember that you have to leave before the doctor comes at 9 p.m.

Q: Where are the speakers?

　　A. In a hotel.　　　B. In Room 612.　　　C. In an elevator.　　　D. In a hospital.

男：不好意思。可以請你告訴我612房在哪裡嗎？

女：沒問題。走過轉角的電梯處後，搭到六樓就是了。

男：謝謝你。

女：你是家屬嗎？

男：不是，我是病患的朋友。

女：好的。記得晚上九點醫師來之前務必離開。

問題：說話者們在哪裡？

選項：A. 在飯店。　　　B. 在612房。　　　C. 在電梯。　　　　D. 在醫院。

D 17. W: I think we can get to our hotel in about two hours.

M: I don't think so. We have to take the traffic into consideration.

W: Are you telling me that there might be a chance that we get stuck in a traffic jam?

M: It's rush hour now.

Q: When does the conversation least likely to take place?

　　A. 7 to 9 a.m.　　　　　　　　　B. 5 to 8 p.m.

　　C. 11 a.m. to 1 p.m.　　　　　　D. 11 p.m. to 2 a.m..

女：我想我們可以在兩個小時內到達旅館。

男：我不這麼認為。我們得把交通狀況列入考慮。

女：你是在告訴我，我們可能陷在車陣中？

男：現在可是尖峰時刻。

問題：這段對話最不可能在何時發生？

選項：A. 早上七點到九點。　　　　　B. 下午五點到八點。

　　　　C. 早上十一點到下午一點。　　D. 晚上十一點到早上二點。

A 18. M: Stand closer together. That's right. 3 . . . 2 . . . 1 . . . Say cheese, everyone!

W: Great! Now we two take a selfie with the waterfall in the background.

M: Do you want to use the selfie stick?

W: No, just a regular selfie will be fine.

Q: What has the man done?

    A. He has taken a group photo.

    B. He has rejected the woman's request.

    C. He has lied to others about the woman.

    D. He has forgotten to bring his selfie stick.

男：站近一點。對。三… 二… 一… 大家，笑一個（說起司）！

女：太棒了！現在我們兩個用瀑布入鏡當背景自拍。

男：你想用自拍棒嗎？

女：不了，一般的自拍就可以。

問題：男子做了什麼？

選項：A. 他照了一張團體照。   B. 他拒絕了女子的要求。

       C. 他和別人說了關於女子的謊話。   D. 他忘記帶自拍棒。

B 19. W: What's the matter with you? You look terrible.

M: I feel sick, and I feel a sharp pain in my stomach.

W: Have you eaten anything different recently?

M: I can't remember, but I did have something really hot last night.

W: That explains everything.

Q: What caused the man to have the stomachache?

    A. Some spoiled food.   B. Some spicy food.

    C. Some greasy food.   D. Some plain food.

女：你怎麼了？你看起來糟透了。

男：我不舒服，而且我胃感到一陣劇痛。

女：你最近有吃什麼不一樣的東西嗎？

男：我不記得，但我昨晚確實有吃很辣的食物。

女：這就說得通了。

問題：造成男子胃痛的原因為何？

選項：A. 腐壞的食物。 B. 辛辣的食物。   C. 油膩的食物。   D. 未經調味的食物。

C 20. M: Good morning! I'd like to send this package to New Zealand.

W: All right. Please place it on the scale.

M: Will it arrive before Christmas?

W: If you send it by express mail, it should arrive on Christmas Eve.

M: How much does that cost?

W: It's double the price of regular airmail, so for this package that comes to NT$1,800.

M: I see.

Q: What does the woman do to the package?

    A. She stamps it.   B. She inspects it.

    C. She checks its weight.   D. She measures its volume.

男：早安！我想將這個包裹寄到紐西蘭。

女：好的。請把它放在秤上。

男：它會在耶誕節前送達嗎？

女：如果你用快遞寄送，它應該會在平安夜送達。

男：那要多少錢？

女：要一般空運郵件的兩倍價格，所以就這個包裹來說要新臺幣 1,800 元。

男：我知道了。

問題：女子對包裹做了什麼處理？

選項：A. 她為包裹貼上郵票。　　　　　B. 她對包裹進行檢查。

　　　C. 她確認包裹的重量。　　　　　D. 她測量包裹的體積。

A 21. W: Tell me why you quit your job.

M: My father is sick, and I have to take over his business.

W: I'm sorry to hear that. Is he feeling better now?

M: He is still in the hospital and will probably stay there for a while.

Q: What is the man's father doing now?

　　A. He is receiving treatment.　　　　B. He is having a routine check-up.

　　C. He is working at home.　　　　　D. He is devoting himself to his business.

女：告訴我你為何辭掉工作。

男：我父親生病，而我必須接下他的事業。

女：很遺憾聽到這個消息。他現在好些了嗎？

男：他還在醫院，而且可能要在醫院待一段時間。

問題：男子的父親現在在做什麼？

選項：A. 他在接受治療。　　　　　　　B. 他正在接受定期的體檢。

　　　C. 他在家裡工作。　　　　　　　D. 他致力於他的事業。

A 22. M: What time does your plane take off?

W: In an hour, 12:30.

M: Does that mean you won't have time for the last-minute shopping?

W: I can always make time for that!

Q: What is the woman going to do next?

　　A. Go shopping.　　　　　　　　　B. Rush to airport lounge.

　　C. Make a phone call.　　　　　　　D. Take off her make-up.

男：你的飛機何時起飛？

女：再一個小時，十二點三十分。

男：那是否代表你不會有時間做購物的最後衝刺？

女：我總是能為買東西挪出時間來！

問題：女子接下來要做什麼？

選項：A. 購物。　　　B. 趕去候機室。　　　C. 打電話。　　　D. 卸妝。

C 23. W: Can you change the channel? This movie is terrible.

M: What are you talking about? This is my favorite comedy.

W: But haven't you seen this already? You could get this movie online and watch it whenever you like.

M: All right then. What do you want to watch?

W: I don't know. Let's see what else is on.

Q: What did the woman say about the movie?

    A. It's her favorite comedy.

    B. She wants to watch it later.

    C. The man had watched it before.

    D. The man will buy a DVD of the film online.

女：你可以切換頻道嗎？這電影糟透了。

男：你在說什麼啊？這是我最喜歡的喜劇。

女：但你不是都已經看過了嗎？你在線上可以看到這部電影，並且隨時要看都可以。

男：好吧。你想看什麼？

女：我不知道。我們來看看還有在播什麼。

問題：關於電影，女子做何表示？

選項：A. 是她最喜歡的喜劇。   B. 她晚一點想看。

      C. 男子之前已經看過了。   D. 男子將會線上購買電影的 DVD。

C 24. For question number 24, please look at the pie chart.

M: Hi, Jenny! How much did you spend on your trip to Tokyo?

W: I spent about NT$40,000 in total. Nearly half of it was spent on transportation, including airline tickets, train and subway tickets.

M: How about accommodations?

W: It's the next biggest expense during my trip though I stayed at B&B's and hostels. Food and drinks cost about NT$4,800, while sightseeing contributed 15% of the total expense.

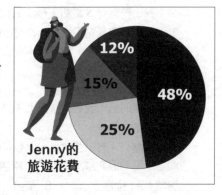

Q: How much money did the woman spend on accommodations?

    A. NT$4,800.   B. NT$6,000.   C. NT$10,000.   D. NT$19,000.

第二十四題，請看圓餅圖。

男：嗨，Jenny！你去東京旅行花了多少錢？

女：我花了大約新臺幣 40,000 元。將近一半的錢都花在交通上，包括機票、火車和地鐵票。

男：那住宿呢？

女：那是我旅行期間第二大花費，雖然我住的是民宿和青年旅館。飲食花費大約是新臺幣 4,800 元，而觀光占了總花費的 15%。

問題：女子在住宿上花了多少錢？

選項：A. 新臺幣 4,800 元。　　　　　　　　B. 新臺幣 6,000 元。

　　　C. 新臺幣 10,000 元。　　　　　　　　D. 新臺幣 19,000 元。

解析　由對話可知總花費為新臺幣 40,000 元、住宿是女子旅行期間第二大花費；根據圓餅圖，第二大花費占總花費 25%，因此算出住宿花費新臺幣 10,000 元，故答案選 C。

B 25. For question number 25, please look at the note.

W: I prefer S Hotel because it's much cheaper.

M: But it's far away from the tourist spots and has no swimming pool.

W: We can rent a car, and I don't think we'll have time for swimming.

M: Do we have the budget to rent a car?

W: Hmm . . . we don't.

M: In that case, we should book L Hotel. It's near the MRT station. We can save time and money if we stay there.

W: But it's expensive.

M: Don't worry. With this membership card, I can get a discount.

Q: Which factor prevents the woman from choosing L Hotel to stay?

　A. Location.　　　B. Price.　　　　　C. Facilities.　　　　D. Reviews.

L 飯店	S 飯店
地點：★★★	地點：★
價錢：★	價錢：★★★
設施：★★	設施：★
評價：★	評價：★★

第二十五題，請看便條。

女：我比較偏好 S 飯店，因為它便宜很多。

男：但是它離景點很遠而且沒有游泳池。

女：我們可以租車，而且我不認為我們會有時間游泳。

男：我們有租車的預算嗎？

女：嗯…我們沒有。

男：那樣的話，我們應該訂 L 飯店。它靠近捷運站。如果住在那裡，我們可以節省時間和金錢。

女：但是它很貴。

男：別擔心。有這張會員卡，我可以拿到折扣。

問題：哪個因素讓女子不選 L 飯店住宿？

選項：A. 位置。　　　B. 價錢。　　　　C. 設施。　　　　D. 評價。

解析　由對話中女子的第四句話可知她覺得住 L 飯店很貴，即為便條上的四個因素中的價錢，故答案選 B。

第四部份：簡短談話

C 26. Attention, students. There is a serious problem of littering outside of the classrooms. Many students like to eat their lunch outdoors on our campus. However, that privilege may be canceled, if you do not do a better job of cleaning up after yourselves during lunchtime. Please throw your lunch box into trash cans after you are done. They can be found next to the basketball courts and each classroom building. If we don't see any improvement during the next two weeks, you will no longer be able to eat outside your classrooms.

Q: According to the announcement, what will happen if the problem is not solved?

    A. Students will have to miss the PE class.

    B. Teachers will have to eat in the cafeteria.

    C. Students will be required to have lunch indoors.

    D. People who litter will pay a fine.

學生們，請注意。教室外面亂丟垃圾的問題很嚴重。許多學生喜歡在校園吃午餐。然而，如果你們沒有在午餐時間將垃圾清理好的話，這項特權就會被取消。請你在用餐後，將餐盒丟入垃圾桶內。垃圾桶在籃球場及每棟教學大樓的旁邊都能找到。未來兩週內若不見任何改善，學生們將不能再到教室外面吃午餐。

問題：根據這則廣播，問題如果沒有解決的話會發生什麼事？

選項：A. 學生必須停上體育課。   B. 老師必須到自助餐廳用餐。

        C. 學生必須在室內吃午餐。   D. 亂丟垃圾的人將繳罰款。

B 27. Sandy and Julia were best friends. Once they got to high school, they became more competitive. They tried to outdo each other on their tests and school competitions. One day, out of frustration, Sandy accused Julia of cheating on a test. Since then, they no longer had a close friendship. One day, Sandy heard that Julia and her family had moved to another city. Not until this moment did she realize that she lost her best friend. After that, Sandy decided not to compete against her friends again.

Q: What did Sandy realize was a bad thing to do to her friends?

    A. Moving away from them.   B. Competing against them.

    C. Accusing them of laziness.   D. Spreading rumors about them.

Sandy 和 Julia 曾是最好的朋友。進入高中之後，彼此變得非常競爭。她們努力在考試及學校競賽上勝過對方。有一天，出於挫折，Sandy 指控 Julia 考試作弊。從那時候開始，她們的友誼不再緊密。有一天，Sandy 聽說 Julia 跟家人搬到另一個城市。直到這一刻她才了解到自己失去了最好的朋友。從此之後，Sandy 決定不再跟朋友競爭。

問題：Sandy 領悟到對朋友做什麼是不好的？

選項：A. 搬離開他們。   B. 與他們競爭。

        C. 指責他們懶散。   D. 散布關於他們的謠言。

C 28. Ladies and gentlemen, thank you for being here to pay your respects to our fallen hero, Captain Chen. We will all miss Captain Chen, who died while protecting citizens against the armed bank robbers. He was a good husband, a devoted father, and a role model for our community. Mr. Chen protected us as a police officer and often volunteered his time as a coach to teach sports to our children. He has inspired us to serve not only the people we care about, but also to do our part to help our neighbors.

Q: Why was the event held for Captain Chen?

    A. He was coaching a basketball team.

    B. He was honored with a medal for being a hero.

C. He died while trying to fight bank robbers.

D. He was considered the most devoted father.

各位女士、先生，謝謝你們來向我們隕落的英雄——陳警官致敬。我們都會懷念陳警官，他為保護市民抵抗武裝銀行搶匪時殉職。他是個好丈夫，盡心的父親，也是我們社區的典範。身為一名警官，陳先生保護我們，也常自願擔任我們孩子的體育教練。他啟發我們不僅為我們在乎的人做出貢獻，也為周遭的人盡一份心力。

問題：為什麼要為陳警官舉辦這場活動？

選項：A. 他在訓練一支籃球隊。　　　　　B. 他是一名英雄，因此獲頒勛章。

　　　　C. 他竭力對抗銀行搶匪時殉職。　　D. 人們認為他是最盡心的父親。

C 29. I enjoyed the Mid-Autumn Festival this year. All my family spent the entire day and night at grandmother's house. I have always enjoyed the traditional foods that my grandmother and my mother made for the Mid-Autumn Festival, but this time our family decided to let grandmother have a rest. Therefore, instead of the traditional feast, we had a barbecue in front of her house this time. We had all kinds of yummy food, including beef, pork, chicken, shrimp and clams. After we were full, we lit fireworks. It was truly a memorable holiday!

Q: Why did the family decide to have a barbecue?

　　A. To save money.　　　　　　　　B. To follow the trend.

　　C. To give the grandmother a rest.　　D. To have more time to chat with each other.

我很喜歡今年的中秋節。我們全家人在祖母家待了一天一夜。我一直都很喜歡我祖母跟我母親為中秋節準備的傳統食物，但這次我們決定讓祖母休息一下。因此不吃傳統大餐，這次我們在祖母家門口烤肉。我們有牛肉、豬肉、雞肉、蝦子及蛤蜊等各式各樣美味的食物。吃飽後，我們放了煙火。這真是個難忘的節慶！

問題：這個家庭為什麼決定要舉辦烤肉？

選項：A. 省錢。　　　　　　　　　　　B. 跟隨潮流。

　　　　C. 讓祖母休息。　　　　　　　D. 可以有更多時間與彼此聊天。

A 30. A fire in the downtown area killed 12 people last night. Dozens of people were sent to the local hospital to be treated for breathing in smoke. Firefighters had to clear residents from the affected buildings at around 1:30 a.m. They were allowed to return to their homes after the fire was put out. This fire was caused by an electric heater being placed too close to a bed. While using electric heaters, keep them at a safe distance away from blankets, clothing, or anything that can easily catch on fire.

Q: According to the news report, which is true?

A. Some people were treated in the hospital.

B. People were moved out in the afternoon.

C. The fire has claimed over 20 lives.

D. The fire was started by someone who was smoking in bed.

昨夜發生於市中心的一場火災，奪走了十二條人命。多名吸入濃煙的民眾被送往當地醫院救治。大約凌晨一點半時，消防人員必須疏散受波及建物中的居民。火勢完全撲滅後，他們已獲准返家。這場火災是因一臺緊靠著床邊的電暖器所引起。在使用電暖器時，務必要與毯子、衣物或是任何易燃物品保持安全距離。

問題：根據這則新聞報導，何者正確？

選項：A. 一些人在醫院接受治療。　　　B. 人們在下午時被撤走。

　　　C. 火災奪走超過二十條人命。　　D. 火災肇因是有人在床上吸菸。

A 31. Are you looking for a relaxing place to spend quality time with your family this summer? We'd like to recommend Hello Campground to you. Why would you spend your hard-earned money on expensive hotels or resorts? For a lot less money, you can rent a camp site for your tent or one of our cabins. Rates start at $30 per day during the summer months, and $20 per day during the other months of the year. Your vacation will be more meaningful when you realize how much you can do for very little cost. Come and enjoy our mountain views and activities at nearby Crystal Lake. Many popular places are within walking distance of Hello Campground.

Q: What is being advertised?

　　A. A campground.　B. A hotel.　　　　C. A resort.　　　　D. A training camp.

你正在尋找今年夏天與家人共度寶貴時光的休閒地點嗎？我們想推薦你 Hello 露營區。為什麼要將你辛苦賺來的錢花在昂貴的飯店或度假勝地呢？少花很多錢，你就可以在我們這裡租到搭帳篷的營地或其中一間小木屋。夏季月份每天最低只要三十美元租金，而其他月份每天最低只需二十美元。當你發現用這麼少的花費卻能做這麼多事時，你的假期就會更有意義。到附近的水晶湖畔來享受我們的山景及活動。許多熱門的景點就在離 Hello 露營區幾步路的地方。

問題：這是主打什麼樣的廣告？

選項：A. 露營區。　　　B. 飯店。　　　　C. 度假勝地。　　　D. 訓練營。

A 32. I would recommend buying this brand of device for your need. It is easy to operate. You can set the air speed to low, medium, or high settings. Furthermore, the heat can be switched to low, medium, or high settings. It's very powerful, so you should be careful when operating this device. I'd like to give you a warning. Do not stand in water when using it or you may get an electric shock. If you use it on your hair for too long, you may damage your hair.

Q: Which of the following products is most likely being described?

　　A. A hairdryer.　　B. An electric fan.　　C. A air fryer.　　　D. An electric toaster.

為符合你的需求，我推薦你這個品牌的器具。它很容易操作。你可以將風速設定調整為弱速、中速或強速。此外，熱度的設定也可轉換至低溫、中溫或高溫。它的功能很強，所以你在操作這個器具時務必要小心。我想特別提醒你。使用這項器具時請勿站在水中，否則可能會觸電。如果你使用它吹頭髮太久的話，頭髮可能會受損。

問題：最有可能描述的產品是下列何者？

選項：A. 吹風機。　　　B. 電風扇。　　　C. 氣炸鍋。　　　D. 烤吐司機。

D 33. A well-known statue of the nation's first President disappeared from Memorial Park overnight. The police are confused about this mystery and can't find a motive for the theft. The bronze statue is 12 feet tall and weighs five tons. Please look at the statue pictured in this report. If you have any clues, please contact the police. A $2,000 reward for any information about the theft will be offered.

Q: What is missing from Memorial Park?

    A. A purse that contained $2,000.   B. A bronze bell that weighs five tons.

    C. The oldest tree in the province.   D. A large bronze statue of the first President.

一尊國家第一任總統的知名雕像一夜之間從紀念公園消失。警方對這起奇案感到不解，也找不到行竊動機。銅像十二英尺高，重達五噸。請看報導中刊出的雕像圖片。如果你有任何線索，請與警方聯繫。提供 2,000 美元的獎金徵求有關行竊的任何線索。

問題：紀念公園遺失了什麼？

選項：A. 裝著 2,000 美元的皮包。   B. 重達五噸的銅鐘。

    C. 該省分最老的樹。   D. 第一任總統的大型銅像。

D 34. For question number 34, please look at the web page.

Our city will be blessed with the performance of the West Wind Trio this weekend. The West Wind Trio consists of three members, including Jenny Wesley on piano, Jack Hooper on violin, and Del Brown on flute. The program will consist of several pieces from various periods. I believe all music lovers will agree that City Concert Hall will be the best place to be this weekend.

≡		市立音樂廳				Q
首頁 | 票券與活動 | 日曆						
Sun	Mon	Tue	Wed	Thr	Fri	Sat
6/2 19:30 Daniel Boodman 鋼琴獨奏會	6/3	6/4 19:30 西風三重奏	6/5	6/6	6/7 19:30 Daniel Boodman 鋼琴獨奏會	6/8 19:30 西風三重奏

Q: Which event is the speaker talking about?

    A. 6/2, Daniel Boodman Piano Recital.   B. 6/4, West Wind Trio.

    C. 6/7, Daniel Boodman Piano Recital.   D. 6/8, West Wind Trio.

第三十四題，請看網站頁面。

本市這週末將有幸欣賞西風三重奏的演出。西風三重奏是由三位成員組成，包括彈鋼琴的 Jenny Wesley、拉小提琴的 Jack Hooper 以及吹長笛的 Del Brown。節目將包含不同時期的作品。我相信所有音樂愛好者都認同市立音樂廳是這週末最佳去處。

問題：說話者正談論的是哪一場活動？

選項：A. 六月二日，Daniel Boodman 鋼琴獨奏會。

    B. 六月四日，西風三重奏。

    C. 六月七日，Daniel Boodman 鋼琴獨奏會。

    D. 六月八日，西風三重奏。

解析   由談話可知活動為週末的西風三重奏，故選 D。

D 35. For question number 35, please look at the poster.

An all-star cast films this slightly overlong but otherwise delightful movie. To many people, *Marry Me* is quite a conventional romantic movie as others, and it offers too little for the actor and actress to do. However, it's directed with a shiver of tension by Steve Hopson. It's a pleasure to be in the hands of such a great storyteller who cares about every aspect of his work.

Scarlet Jefferson　Tony Davis
Allan Willser製片
Steve Hopson擔任導演

Q: According to the speaker, who is the best part of the movie?

　A. The male lead.　B. The female lead.　C. The producer.　D. The director.

第三十五題，請看海報。

一組一流明星卡司演出這部有點冗長，但除此之外令人愉快的電影。對許多人而言，《嫁給我吧》和其他同類型的電影一樣，是部相當傳統的愛情片，而且給男演員和女演員發揮的空間太少。然而，Steve Hopson 卻以緊湊節奏來導這部戲。很高興是由這樣一位照顧自己作品每個面向的傑出說書人來掌控。

問題：根據說話者，誰是這部電影最棒的部份？

選項：A. 男主角。　　B. 女主角。　　C. 製片人。　　D. 導演。

解析　由談話可知男女演員發揮的空間少，而 Steve Hopson 導戲導得好；根據海報內容，Steve Hopson 是本片的導演，故答案選 D。

第一部份：看圖辨義

C 1. For question number 1, please look at picture A.

Question number 1: What can we know about the man?

A. He is losing weight.   B. He is losing his balance.

C. He is lifting weights.   D. He is bending his back.

第一題，請看圖片 A。

第一題：關於男子我們知道什麼？

選項：A. 他正在減重。 B. 他失去平衡。　　C. 他正在舉重。　　D. 他正在彎曲他的背。

D 2. For question number 2, please look at picture B.

Question number 2: What can we learn from this picture?

A. Someone is mopping the floor.   B. The man is drawing the curtains.

C. Wine has spilled onto the sofa.   D. The place is in a mess.

第二題，請看圖片 B。

第二題：我們可以從圖片中知道什麼？

選項：A. 某人正在拖地。　　　　　　　B. 男子正在把窗簾拉上。

　　　C. 酒被灑在沙發上。　　　　　　D. 這個地方一團混亂。

C 3. For question number 3, please look at picture C.

Question number 3: If Mary wants to go home, which direction should she head for?

A. She should head for the east.   B. She should head for the west.

C. She should head for the south.   D. She should head for the north.

第三題，請看圖片 C。

第三題：如果 Mary 要回家的話，她該往哪個方向走？

選項：A. 她應該往東行。　　　　　　　B. 她應該往西行。

　　　C. 她應該往南行。　　　　　　　D. 她應該往北行。

C 4. For questions number 4 and 5, please look at picture D.

Question number 4: Who's the man with a flag in his hand?

A. He's a doctor.   B. He's an artist.   C. He's a tour guide.   D. He's an architect.

第四題及第五題，請看圖片 D。

第四題：那個手上拿著旗子的男子是誰？

選項：A. 他是一位醫生。　　　　　　　B. 他是一位藝術家。

　　　C. 他是一位導遊。　　　　　　　D. 他是一位建築師。

C 5. Question number 5: Please look at picture D again. Why are they here?

A. They like to go gambling.   B. They enjoy the cool climate.

C. They are on a sightseeing tour.   D. They have come to see European culture.

第五題：請再看一次圖片 D。他們為什麼在這裡？

選項：A. 他們想去賭博。　　　　　　　B. 他們喜歡涼爽的氣候。

C. 他們參加景點導覽。　　　　　　D. 他們來看歐洲文化。

第二部份：問答

C 6. How will you celebrate your wedding anniversary?

A. We haven't decided on a date yet.　　B. We got married in Hawaii.

C. We'll go out to a nice restaurant.　　D. We've been married nearly ten years.

問題：你會如何慶祝你的結婚週年紀念日？

選項：A. 我們還沒決定日期。　　　　B. 我們在夏威夷結婚。

　　　C. 我們會去一家不錯的餐廳。　　D. 我們已經結婚快十年了。

C 7. Oh, no! Jeff is having a heart attack.

A. I don't have medical insurance.　　B. Let me talk to him.

C. Someone call an ambulance!　　　　D. It's not on me.

問題：噢，不！Jeff 心臟病發了。

選項：A. 我沒有醫療保險。　　　　　B. 讓我跟他談談。

　　　C. 快叫救護車！　　　　　　　D. 那和我沒關係。

A 8. How long is the flight?

A. Three hours.　　　　　　　　　　B. NT$30,000.

C. An international airline.　　　　　　D. Four hundred kilometers.

問題：飛行航程多久？

選項：A. 三小時。　　　　　　　　　B. 新臺幣 30,000 元。

　　　C. 一間國際航空公司。　　　　　D. 四百公里。

A 9. So what did the doctor say about your son?

A. He may need surgery.　　　　　　B. He signed the contract.

C. He gave me some medicine.　　　　D. He's the director of this hospital.

問題：所以醫生說你兒子怎麼了？

選項：A. 他可能需要手術。　　　　　B. 他簽了合約。

　　　C. 他給我一些藥。　　　　　　D. 他是這家醫院的董事。

B 10. Did you call Anne?

A. Sure, here's her number.　　　　　B. Yes, but the line was busy.

C. OK. Coming right up.　　　　　　D. No, not anymore.

問題：你打電話給 Anne 了嗎？

選項：A. 當然，這是她的號碼。　　　B. 打了，但是電話忙線中。

　　　C. 好的。馬上就來。　　　　　D. 不，再也不會了。

D 11. How's the new business going?

A. Well, we've decided to sue them.

B. Not bad. I'll graduate next summer.

C. Thanks! This loan will really help.

D. Pretty good, thanks. We are starting to turn a profit.

選項：A. 嗯，我們決定要控告他們。　　B. 還不錯。我會在明年夏天畢業。

　　　C. 謝謝！這筆貸款會提供很大的幫助。　D. 很不錯，謝謝。我們將要開始獲利。

D 12. What would you like on your burger?

A. Just a few slices, thanks. B. Please pass the salt and pepper.

C. Pretty good! I like its flavor. D. A little mustard, but hold the ketchup.

問題：你的漢堡上想要加點什麼？

選項：A. 幾片就好，謝謝。　　　　　　B. 請把鹽和胡椒遞過來。

　　　C. 很棒！我喜歡它的調味。　　　　D. 一點芥末醬，但不要番茄醬。

D 13. You're truly the smartest person I've ever met.

A. No big deal! 　　B. Oh, it's OK! 　　C. How rude you are! 　D. Well, I'm flattered!

問題：你真是我見過最聰明的人了。

選項：A. 沒什麼大不了的！　　　　　　B. 喔，沒關係啦！

　　　C. 你真是太粗魯了！　　　　　　D. 嗯，過獎了！

C 14. My boss gave me a raise.

A. Sure! I'll help you apply. B. Never mind! You'll get another one.

C. Great! You deserve it! D. Oh dear! I shouldn't have told you.

問題：我老闆幫我加薪。

選項：A. 沒問題！我會幫你申請。　　　　B. 別在意！你會得到另一個。

　　　C. 太棒了！這是你應得的！　　　　D. 天啊！我不該告訴你的。

B 15. The strawberry cake you made tastes awesome!

A. It's obviously fake. B. Thanks for the compliment.

C. Sorry, but that's not my problem. D. I'm trying to lose weight.

問題：你做的草莓蛋糕吃起來真棒！

選項：A. 它很明顯是假的。　　　　　　B. 謝謝誇獎。

　　　C. 抱歉，那不是我的問題。　　　　D. 我正試著減肥。

第三部份：簡短對話

D 16. M: These family photos are great. Is that your sister?

W: Yes. And those cute little boys are her sons, Paul and Simon.

M: I didn't know you have twins in your family.

W: I do, and I enjoy playing with them together.

Q: Who are the kids in the photograph?

A. The brother's sons. B. The woman's twin sons.

C. The man's sisters. D. The woman's nephews.

男：這些家族相片好棒。那是你的姊姊嗎？

女：是的。而那些可愛的小男孩是她的兒子，Paul 和 Simon。

男：我不知道你的家族中有雙胞胎。

女：我有，而且我喜歡跟他們一起玩。

問題：照片裡的小孩們是誰？

選項：A. 哥哥的兒子們。　　　　　　　B. 女子的雙胞胎兒子。

　　　C. 男子的姊姊們。　　　　　　　D. 女子的外甥們。

D 17. W: Could we have the check, please?

M: Certainly.

W: Oh, and we'd like a cheesecake to go.

M: No problem.

Q: What is the woman doing?

　　A. She is feeding her pet.　　　　　B. She is asking to see the manager.

　　C. She is ordering a drink.　　　　　D. She is paying for the meal.

女：可以幫我們結帳嗎？

男：當然。

女：另外，我們想要外帶一份起司蛋糕。

男：沒問題。

問題：女子正在做什麼？

選項：A. 她正在餵她的寵物。　　　　　B. 她正在要求見經理一面。

　　　C. 她正在點一杯飲料。　　　　　D. 她正在買單。

B 18. M: May I help you, ma'am?

W: Yes. Was this bread made today?

M: Yes. In fact, I baked these loaves of bread myself this morning.

W: Great! I'd like to buy two loaves of bread.

Q: Where is this conversation taking place?

　　A. At a gas station.　　　　　　　B. At a bakery.

　　C. In an ice cream shop.　　　　　D. At a fish market.

男：有什麼需要我幫忙的地方嗎，女士？

女：有的。請問這麵包是今天做的嗎？

男：是的。實際上，這幾條麵包都是我今天早上親自烤的。

女：太棒了！我想要買兩條麵包。

問題：這個對話的發生地點是在？

選項：A. 加油站。　　　B. 麵包店。　　　　C. 冰淇淋店。　　　　D. 魚市場。

D 19. W: What do you usually do during the lunch break?

M: Eat lunch, of course!

W: I mean after lunch. I don't usually see you taking a nap like everyone else in the office.

M: I prefer to read a few chapters of a novel, or sometimes I'll just take a walk somewhere.

W: Don't you feel tired in the afternoon?

M: Not really. Well, a little I guess. I find that if I do sleep at lunchtime, I wake up feeling like I could keep sleeping for another hour or two!

W: I know that feeling well.

Q: What does the man usually do during his lunch hour?

    A. Take a nap.   B. Learn a language.   C. Walk his dog.   D. Read a novel.

女：你午餐時間通常都在做什麼？

男：當然是吃午餐啊！

女：我是說午餐過後。我看你不常像其他人一樣在辦公室裡睡午覺。

男：我喜歡看幾章小說，或是我有時候會散步到別的地方。

女：你下午不覺得累嗎？

男：也不是。嗯，是有一點吧。我發現如果我真的在午休睡覺的話，我起來時會覺得我還可以再繼續睡一兩個小時！

女：我很了解那種感覺。

問題：男子通常在他的午餐時間做什麼？

選項：A. 睡午覺。   B. 學習語言。   C. 溜狗。   D. 讀本小說。

B 20. M: How's your mother now?

W: She's fine. She's out of hospital, but it will still take another month before she can start walking again.

M: Will she be able to walk like she could before?

W: Oh, yes! She will have to do special exercises to strengthen her leg muscles.

Q: What does the woman say about her mother?

    A. She is still in the hospital.

    B. She will make a full recovery.

    C. She'll never be able to move her legs again.

    D. She needs to use a wheelchair from now on.

男：你的母親還好嗎？

女：她很好。她已經出院了，但還得再過一個月才能再開始走路。

男：她還能像以往那樣正常走路嗎？

女：喔，可以！不過她得做一些特殊的運動，好讓她加強腿部的肌肉。

問題：關於她的母親，女子做何表示？

選項：A. 她還在醫院。   B. 她會完全康復。

      C. 她的腿之後再也動不了了。   D. 她從此之後都得用輪椅代步。

D 21. W: How long will it take to reach the airport?

M: In this heavy traffic, it will probably be an hour.

W: An hour? But we have to check in at 4:30.

M: Well, there's nothing I can do about it.

Q: What do we learn from this conversation?

    A. There has been an accident.   B. The man is not a good driver.

    C. The woman has missed her plane.   D. They might miss their flight.

女：到機場要多久？

男：依現在交通堵塞的狀況，大概要一小時。

女：一小時？但我們必須在四點三十分辦理登機手續。

男：嗯，這也是沒辦法的事。

問題：從這段對話中我們得知什麼？

選項：A. 有車禍發生。　　　　　　　　B. 男子的駕駛技術不好。

　　　C. 女子已經錯過了她的班機。　　D. 他們可能會錯過他們的班機。

A 22. M: Are you ready to order?

W: Not yet, I can't decide what to eat.

M: Today's special is great.

W: I know, but I am on a diet and that is too greasy for me.

Q: Why doesn't the woman order today's special?

A. The woman is trying to lose weight.　B. The woman is trying to gain weight.

C. The meal is too spicy for her.　　　D. The waiter is too busy to take orders.

男：你準備要點餐了嗎？

女：還沒，我無法決定要吃什麼。

男：今日特餐很不錯。

女：我知道，不過我正在節食，而那對我來說太油膩了。

問題：為什麼女子不點今日特餐？

選項：A. 她正試著減肥。　　　　　　　B. 她正試著增加體重。

　　　C. 餐點對她來說太辣了。　　　　D. 服務生太忙了以致無法點餐。

A 23. W: I came across those old photos in the drawer.

M: Look! That's me when I was five.

W: How time flies!

M: You can say that again.

Q: How do they feel when looking at the old photos?

A. They both feel time passes fast.

B. They both enjoy being grown-ups.

C. Both of them would like to be children again.

D. The woman likes the man better when he was young.

女：我在抽屜裡找到這些舊照片。

男：看！那是我五歲時的照片。

女：時間過得真快！

男：你說得沒錯。

問題：他們在看舊照片時的感覺為何？

選項：A. 他們兩人都覺得時間過得很快。　B. 他們都喜歡當成人。

　　　C. 他們兩人都希望能再變成孩子。　D. 女子比較喜歡男子年輕的時候。

B 24. For question number 24, please look at the shopping list.

W: Hello, Dad. I've got your list. I'm doing the shopping at the supermarket, but I've got some questions.

M: What do you want to know?

W: I've got some cookies for Jim's school snacks, but I don't know what type of milk to buy.

M: Get skim milk since your younger sister is on a diet.

W: Right, skim milk. Now, should I get Coke or juice?

M: Get both. We'll have juice for breakfast and Coke with dinner tonight.

W: Speaking of dinner...you want beef with baked potatoes, right?

M: Yes, that's right. And don't forget the beans and carrots. I want them for tonight's salad.

Q: How many items on the shopping list are for the speakers' dinner?

    A. 4.   B. 5.   C. 6.   D. 7.

購物清單
1. 餅乾
2. 牛奶
3. 可樂／果汁
4. 牛肉
5. 馬鈴薯
6. 豆子
7. 胡蘿蔔

第二十四題，請看購物清單。

女：喂，爸。我拿到你的清單了。我正在超市購物，但我有些問題。

男：你想知道什麼？

女：我已經買了餅乾作為 Jim 上學吃的點心，但我不知道要買哪一種牛奶。

男：買脫脂牛奶，因為你妹妹在節食。

女：好的，脫脂牛奶。現在，我應該要買可樂還是果汁？

男：兩個都買。我們早餐會喝果汁，今晚晚餐喝可樂。

女：說到晚餐……你要牛肉配烤馬鈴薯，對吧？

男：是的，沒錯。還有別忘了豆子和胡蘿蔔。我要用它們做今晚的沙拉。

問題：購物清單上有幾項物品是為說話者們的晚餐準備的？

選項：A. 四項。   B. 五項。   C. 六項。   D. 七項。

解 析　由對話可知購物清單上作為晚餐的物品有可樂、牛肉、馬鈴薯、豆子和胡蘿蔔，總共有五項，故答案選 B。

C 25. For question number 25, please look at the pie chart.

M: Nowadays, what do teenagers do when they have free time?

W: A recent survey found that over half of those teenagers use their smartphones or tablets when they are free.

M: It's to be expected.

W: Nearly one-quarter of them prefer to only watch TV.

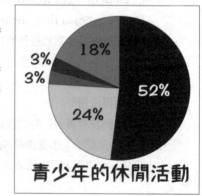

M: It seems that fewer and fewer teenagers read or do exercise in their leisure time.

W: Exactly. Only 3% read and another 3% do exercise.

M: It is clear that using mobile devices is extremely common among young people.

Q: What percentage of the teenagers surveyed watch TV in their leisure time?

    A. 3%.   B. 18%.   C. 24%.   D. 52%.

第二十五題，請看圓餅圖。

男：青少年現今有空閒時會做什麼？

女：最近有一份調查顯示超過一半的青少年會在空閒時使用他們的智慧型手機或平板電腦。

男：這在意料之中。

女：他們有將近四分之一的人偏好只看電視。

男：似乎越來越少青少年在閒暇時閱讀或做運動。

女：沒錯。只有 3% 的人閱讀，另外 3% 的人運動。

男：這清楚顯示年輕人中使用行動裝置是極其普遍的。

問題：受調查的青少年中有多少百分比的人在閒暇時會看電視？

選項：A. 3%。   B. 18%。   C. 24%。   D. 52%。

解析　由對話可知將近四分之一的人偏好看電視，換句話說是將近 25%；而根據圓餅圖，最接近的數字是 24%，故答案選 C。

第四部份：簡短談話

C 26. Venice Coffee Shop is currently closed. The owner has purchased the second floor of this building and will make it become a bookstore. Come to our grand opening on July 10th and receive 50% off all books and coffee. Our shop will be renamed Venice Books and Coffee. We hope you come and enjoy here. We not only have great books, but add new items to our menu.

Q: What is the owner going to do?

    A. Open a new branch in July.

    B. Celebrate the 10th anniversary of the store.

    C. Combine a bookstore with a coffee shop.

    D. Try to design a brand-new menu.

威尼斯咖啡店目前關閉中。老闆已買下這棟建築物的二樓，且將它改變為書店。歡迎蒞臨我們在七月十日的盛大開幕儀式，所有書籍及咖啡飲料屆時一律半價。我們的店將更名為威尼斯書與咖啡。我們希望你蒞臨且喜歡這裡。我們不僅販售好書，也在菜單內加入新品項。

問題：老闆將要做什麼？

選項：A. 七月時開新分店。   B. 慶祝店家開業十週年。

      C. 結合書店與咖啡店。   D. 試著設計全新的菜單。

D 27. After careful consideration, members of the community committee have voted to plant new trees in the park across the street from our apartment buildings. We want to make our living environment more pleasant for people who live here. However, some people have complained that pet owners have left pet waste on the ground in the park. We ask that when the residents take their pets to the park, they have to bring bags to pick up pet waste. If we find anyone who breaks this rule, he or she will be fined by the community committee. On the other hand, we are raising funds to build a new playground in the park. If you would like to help with this project, please contact Thomas.

Q: What is the most likely reason that a resident would contact Thomas?

    A. To plant new trees in the park.

    B. To complain about neighbors' pets.

    C. To ask for help to take care of their children.

    D. To donate money to build a new playground.

在審慎考慮之後，社區委員會成員表決同意在我們公寓大樓對街的公園種植新的樹木。我們想要讓這裡的住戶生活環境更加令人愉快。然而，有些人抱怨寵物主人將寵物排泄物遺留在公園地上。我們要求，住戶帶寵物到公園時，他們必須攜帶撿拾寵物排泄物的袋子。我們若發現任何人破壞這項規定，社區委員會將對他或她處以罰款。另一方面，為了在公園裡蓋一座新的遊戲場，我們正在募款。如果你想要協助該計畫的話，請與 Thomas 聯繫。

問題：住戶與 Thomas 聯繫最有可能的原因是什麼？

選項：A. 在公園裡種植新樹木。   B. 抱怨鄰居的寵物。

       C. 為照顧孩子而求助。   D. 捐款興建新遊戲場。

B 28. Special report. A ship crashed into a rocky shore today, releasing millions of liters of oil into the sea. Apparently the captain got lost in foggy conditions this morning and then the accident happened. All of the crew were saved. However, this is a disaster for the environment as the oil has polluted many kilometers of shoreline. Thousands of sea birds have already been trapped by the oil. To make matters worse, the beauty of the beaches has been destroyed, and this will affect the local tourism industry.

Q: What caused this accident?

    A. Local people.   B. Foggy weather.   C. The tourism industry.   D. Oil leak.

特別報導。今天一艘船撞上岩岸，數百萬公升的石油流入海中。顯然，船長今天早上在大霧中迷航後，事故就發生了。所有船員皆已獲救。然而，對環境而言，這是一場浩劫，因為石油汙染了數公里的海岸。數以千計的海鳥被困在油汙中。更糟的是，海灘的美景遭受摧毀，這將會重創觀光產業。

問題：什麼導致意外？

選項：A. 當地人。   B. 起霧的天氣。   C. 觀光產業。   D. 漏油。

C 29. Are you feeling tired every day? Does your productivity suffer from exhaustion? Now, there's a natural way to gain energy. Avoid the caffeine from coffee and sugar from unhealthy energy drinks. Take one QRT tablet every morning, and you will feel energetic without side effects. QRT is made from natural ingredients, including vitamin B, vitamin C, and minerals. Enjoy the benefits of QRT and tell your friends!

Q: What kind of product is being promoted?

    A. A healthier coffee with no caffeine.   B. A new type of exercise program.

    C. A natural health product for energy.   D. A cream for smoother skin.

你每天都覺得累嗎？疲勞拖累你的生產力嗎？現在，有一種獲得能量的天然方法。避免攝取咖啡中的咖啡因和不健康能量飲料中的糖分。每天早上服用一顆 QRT 錠，你會感到精力充沛，而且沒有副作用。QRT 是由天然成分製成，其中包括維他命 B、維他命 C 及礦物質。享用 QRT 的好處，然後分享給你的朋友！

問題：在推銷什麼產品？

選項：A. 較健康的無咖啡因咖啡。   B. 新型運動課程。

    C. 天然健康的能量產品。   D. 使肌膚更為平滑的乳液。

A 30. Ladies and gentlemen, I am pleased to welcome you to the opening of the 15th film festival. Before the opening ceremony starts, I would like to introduce Jennifer Smith, who is an excellent movie director. Were it not for her help, we couldn't hold this amazing festival here. Jennifer has devoted herself to the movie industry for more than 20 years. She shot many great movies here. The whole town has benefited from these movies and has become a new tourist attraction. Now let's give her a warm welcome.

Q: Who is being introduced in the statement?

    A. A movie director.   B. A hit movie.

    C. An annual festival.   D. A resident of this town.

各位女士、先生，誠摯歡迎各位蒞臨第十五屆電影節的開幕典禮。典禮開始之前，我要介紹一名優秀導演，就是 Jennifer Smith。若非她的協助，我們無法在此舉辦這場盛會。Jennifer 投身電影事業二十多年，她在這裡拍攝許多好電影。全鎮因這些電影而受惠，也因而成為新的觀光景點。現在，就讓我們一起熱烈歡迎她。

問題：這段敘述介紹了誰？

選項：A. 一位電影導演。   B. 一部賣座電影。

    C. 一個年度節慶。   D. 鎮上的一位居民。

B 31. Please be seated for our lecture. Before the Internet, people listened to the latest news and music on the radio. Radio was one of the ways people connected to what was happening in their area. However, radio listeners could not listen to music or news broadcast from far away because the radio waves could not travel very far. Today, everything has changed. Thanks to the Internet, we can listen to music popular in other countries. We can learn the news that is important to people in other parts of the world. Thanks to modern technology, people can expose themselves to different cultures all over the world.

Q: Why can't we use the traditional radio to listen to radio stations worldwide?

    A. We can't understand foreign languages.

    B. The radio waves can't travel very far.

    C. The traditional radios don't have enough power.

    D. Radio stations from other countries require a fee to listen.

請就座聽講。在網路時代之前，人們用廣播收聽最新消息及音樂。廣播是人們得知當地發生事件的方式之一。然而，廣播的聽眾聽不到自遠方播放的音樂或新聞，那是因為無線電波無法長途傳送。今天，一切都改變了。多虧了網路，我們可以聽到其他國家的流行音樂。我們可以得知發生在世界其他地區、攸關人類的重要新聞。托現代科技的福，人們可以接觸到世界各地的不同文化。

問題：為什麼我們無法使用傳統收音機收聽世界各地的電臺？

選項：A. 我們無法了解外國語言。　　　　　B. 無線電波無法傳播到很遠的地方。

　　　C. 傳統收音機電力不足。　　　　　D. 外國的電臺要求收聽費用。

D 32. WANTED! We need a kind and patient social worker to care for the elderly residents in our community. Experience is required. This job offers 35 hours per week at NT$250 per hour. There are 10 days of paid leave. The social worker will spend quality time with the residents and make sure they have the help they need. So come join us and be a part of our large family!

Q: Which of the following is Not mentioned in the job advertisement?

　　A. Work experience.　　　　　　B. Wage.

　　C. Personality traits.　　　　　　D. Medical skills.

誠徵！我們需要一名既體貼又有耐心的社工人員照護我們社區的年長居民。須經驗。每週工作三十五小時，時薪新臺幣 250 元。包含十天的給薪假。社工人員要與這些居民相處愉快，確認他們都得到需要的幫助。所以，快來加入我們的行列，成為這大家庭的一分子吧！

問題：下列何者沒有在這則招聘廣告中提及？

選項：A. 工作經驗。　　B. 薪資。　　　　C. 人格特質。　　　　D. 醫療技術。

C 33. Now! There is a special offer on the latest line of smartphones. If you buy a new smartphone in our shop, you can get your next smartphone without paying extra fee. With this special offer, our customers don't have to worry about their smartphones being out-of-date after a few years. That's because the next one will be on us.

Q: According to the advertisement, what is the special offer?

　　A. Get free Internet service after signing a three-year service contract.

　　B. Catch a flight, and get the meal for free.

　　C. Buy a new smartphone, and get the next new phone for free.

　　D. Get two sets of designer phones that will never be out of fashion.

現在！有最新款智慧型手機的特惠活動。如果你在我們店裡購買新手機，不需額外花費，你就能得到下一隻智慧型手機。有了這項特惠活動，我們的顧客不必擔心幾年後手機就會過時。因為你的下一隻新手機將算在我們帳上。

問題：根據這則廣告，特惠活動是什麼？

選項：A. 綁約三年即享免費上網服務。

　　　B. 搭飛機，就能獲得免費餐點。

　　　C. 買一隻新智慧型手機，免費獲得下一隻新手機。

　　　D. 獲得兩組永不退流行的名牌手機。

C 34. For question number 34, please look at the poster.

Good morning, everyone. I am here to present you four of our brand new products. Clean Water Straw is designed to turn any water into drinkable water. With Cake Knife, you can cut and pick up a slice of cake easily. If you need to hide something from your family, you may get Mini Safe. Finally, with Baby Mopper, babies can help their moms clean the floor as they crawl around.

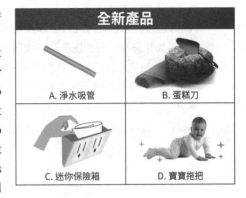

全新產品

A. 淨水吸管　　B. 蛋糕刀

C. 迷你保險箱　　D. 寶寶拖把

Q: Betty is worried that her mother may find her love letters. Which product may interest her most?

第三十四題，請看海報。

大家早安。我在這裡為你們呈現四項我們全新的產品。淨水吸管是設計來把任何水變成可飲用的水。有了蛋糕刀，你可以輕輕鬆鬆切下並拿起一片蛋糕。如果需要藏某物不讓家人發現，你可以買迷你保險箱。最後，有了寶寶拖把，寶寶們到處爬時，就可以幫他們的媽媽清理地板。

問題：Betty 擔心她媽媽可能會發現她的情書。她對哪一項產品可能最有興趣？

解析　由談話可知如果需要藏某物不讓家人發現，可以買迷你保險箱；而根據海報，最像迷你保險箱的是產品三，故答案選 C。

C 35. For question number 35, please look at the poster.

ABC Supermarket is scheduled to open on September 9th and will be hosting a grand opening event with special offers for the first 100 customers. We offer a 20% discount on Matt's Sunflower Oil. If you buy one Fabio's Frozen Pizza, you will get one free. Another must-buy item is Jerry & Ben's Ice Cream. Buy two and get another one 40% off. Green Hill Whole Milk is also a good bargain. You may buy one and get one 50% off.

Q: Lucas would like to have two Fabio's Frozen Pizzas. How much should he pay?

A. $8.   B. $10.

C. $15.   D. $30.

ABC 超市

打8折！

買1件，第2件5折！

折扣商品：
- 麥特葵花油 $20
- 法比歐冷凍披薩 $15
- 傑利&班冰淇淋 $10
- 綠色山丘全脂牛奶 $8

買1送1！

買2件，第3件6折！

第三十五題，請看海報。

ABC 超市計畫在九月九日開幕並會舉行盛大的開幕會，提供特惠給前一百名顧客。麥特葵花油打八折。如果你買一份法比歐冷凍披薩，就會再得到免費一份。另一項必買商品是傑利 & 班冰淇淋。買兩件，第三件打六折。綠色山丘全脂牛奶也很划算。你買一件，第二件五折。

問題：Lucas 想要兩份法比歐冷凍披薩。他應該付多少錢？

選項：A. 8 美元。　　　B. 10 美元。　　　　　C. 15 美元。　　　　　　D. 30 美元。

解析　由談話可知法比歐冷凍披薩買一送一；而根據海報，一份披薩 15 美元，兩份還是 15 美元，故答案選 C。

第一部份：看圖辨義

C 1. For question number 1, please look at picture A.

Question number 1: What is the man doing?

A. He is browsing the menu.　　　　B. He is baking something.

C. He is preparing a meal.　　　　D. He is cleaning out the kitchen.

第一題，請看圖片 A。

第一題：男子在做什麼？

選項：A. 他在瀏覽菜單。　　　　B. 他在烤東西。

　　　C. 他正在準備餐點。　　　　D. 他正在清理廚房。

B 2. For question number 2, please look at picture B.

Question number 2: Why is the little boy upset?

A. His finger hurts.　　　　B. He is getting a shot.

C. The nurse is mad at him.　　　　D. He doesn't want to take the medicine.

第二題，請看圖片 B。

第二題：小男孩為什麼難過？

選項：A. 他的手指受傷。　　　　B. 他正在打針。

　　　C. 護理師對他很生氣。　　　　D. 他不想吃藥。

C 3. For question number 3, please look at picture C.

Question number 3: What is being offered in this special promotion?

A. A vacation at the beach.　　　　B. The low price of just NT$33.

C. A discount on a certain day.　　　　D. A free gift with each purchase.

第三題，請看圖片 C。

第三題：這項特別促銷提供了什麼？

選項：A. 在海邊度假。　　　　B. 只要新臺幣 33 元的低價。

　　　C. 在特定的一天打折。　　　　D. 凡購買就贈送免費禮物。

C 4. For questions number 4 and 5, please look at picture D.

Question number 4: Who might be interested in this poster?

A. People who want a new bike.　　　　B. People who like mountain climbing.

C. People who have joined a cycling club.　　　　D. People who thumb a ride.

第四題及第五題，請看圖片 D。

第四題：誰可能對這張海報感興趣？

選項：A. 想要新腳踏車的人。　　　　B. 喜歡爬山的人。

　　　C. 參加腳踏車社團的人。　　　　D. 想要搭便車的人。

B 5. Question number 5: Please look at picture D again. How long will the event last?

A. Exactly 20 days.　　B. For 3 days.　　　　C. A week.　　　　D. A month.

第五題：請再看一次圖片 D。這項活動將持續幾天？

選項：A. 剛好二十天。　B. 三天。　　　　C. 一週。　　　　D. 一個月。

C 6. Do you think this shirt suits me?

A. Yes, it's one of my favorite jeans.

B. I prefer the other pair, to be honest.

C. Not bad, but the sleeves are a bit too long.

D. You can only take three items into the fitting room.

問題：你覺得這件襯衫適合我嗎？

選項：A. 是的，它是其中一件我最喜歡的牛仔褲。

B. 老實說，我比較喜歡另一雙。

C. 還不錯，但袖子有點太長了。

D. 你只能帶三件進試衣間。

C 7. Hello. Are you here on vacation?

A. No, I'm downstairs in the lobby.　　　B. No, I'm just suffering from jet lag.

C. No, I'm an exchange student.　　　D. No, I had called in advance.

問題：哈囉。你是來度假的嗎？

選項：A. 不是，我在樓下大廳。　　　B. 不是，我還受時差所苦。

C. 不是，我是交換學生。　　　D. 不是，我有先打電話。

B 8. I'd like to check these books out, please.

A. It's on the best-seller list.　　　B. May I have your library card?

C. Please return the books to the library.　　　D. May I have your room number, please?

問題：我想要借這些書，麻煩你。

選項：A. 它在暢銷書榜上。　　　B. 可以給我你的圖書館借閱證嗎？

C. 請把書還給圖書館。　　　D. 可以給我你的房號嗎？

A 9. Would you prefer to raise a cat or a dog?

A. Neither! They make me sneeze.

B. I take him for a walk once a day after dinner.

C. The vet gave her all the necessary shots.

D. I think training them would be the hardest part.

問題：你比較想要養一隻貓還是狗？

選項：A. 兩者皆不！牠們讓我打噴嚏。　　　B. 我每天晚餐後帶他散步一次。

C. 獸醫給她打了所有必要的針。　　　D. 我認為訓練牠們會是最困難的部份。

D 10. Why should we hire you?

A. I've been unemployed for over a year.　　　B. I want to negotiate for a higher salary.

C. I have brought my résumé.　　　D. I have previous experience of this work.

問題：為什麼我們要聘用你？

選項：A. 我已經失業超過一年了。　　　B. 我想要為提高薪資進行協商。

C. 我帶來了我的履歷。　　　D. 我有相關的工作經驗。

B 11. Are you ready to order?

    A. A table for four, please.

    B. I'd like a seafood pasta.

    C. A single room for October 8th.

    D. I'd like to book a seat in business class, please.

    問題：你要點餐了嗎？

    選項：A. 請給我四人座的餐桌。   B. 我想要一份海鮮義大利麵。

           C. 一間單人房，十月八日要住。   D. 請幫我訂一個商務艙的位子。

D 12. Did you have a part-time job when you were in college?

    A. Yes, I want to be a lawyer.

    B. Yes, I've applied for a job in marketing.

    C. Yes, I graduated from New York University.

    D. Yes, I babysat for my neighbor's children.

    問題：你讀大學時曾打工嗎？

    選項：A. 是的，我想成為一名律師。   B. 是的，我已經應徵了一份在行銷部的工作。

           C. 是的，我畢業於紐約大學。   D. 是的，我曾當保姆幫鄰居看小孩。

C 13. Don't you think Andrew is a handsome man?

    A. Yes, he certainly does.   B. Yes, she's very attractive.

    C. Yes, but he's not my type.   D. Yes, I'm so proud of you.

    問題：你不覺得 Andrew 是帥哥嗎？

    選項：A. 對呀，他肯定這樣。   B. 對呀，她非常迷人。

           C. 對呀，但他不是我喜歡的類型。   D. 對呀，我為你感到驕傲。

C 14. Mary? I'm Jennifer! We went to school together.

    A. I'm Mary. Pleased to meet you, Jennifer.

    B. That sounds incredible, Jennifer. I can't wait.

    C. Jennifer! I almost didn't recognize you!

    D. So, Jennifer, are you ready for the big exam today?

    問題：Mary？我是 Jennifer！我們以前一起去上學。

    選項：A. 我是 Mary。很高興認識你，Jennifer。

           B. 那聽起來太棒了，Jennifer。我等不及了。

           C. Jennifer！我差點沒認出你來！

           D. 所以，Jennifer，你準備好今天的大考了嗎？

A 15. What do you think about my new tie?

    A. I think it really suits you.   B. I'm already dressed for work.

    C. I usually wear a dark suit to work.   D. The other pair of shoes looks better.

    問題：你覺得我的新領帶如何？

    選項：A. 我覺得它真的很適合你。   B. 我已經穿好衣服要去上班了。

           C. 我通常都穿深色套裝去上班。   D. 另一雙鞋比較好看。

B 16. M: I heard that you had spent your summer doing something unique?

W: Yes. I spent the summer on my brother's farm.

M: So, how was life there?

W: I milked the cows, fed the chickens, and did a lot of other things.

M: Sounds like you were having fun there.

W: I did, but I had to get up early every day.

Q: What does the woman think about the life on the farm?

　　A. Easy but rewarding.　　　　　　　B. Enjoyable but challenging.

　　C. Difficult and boring.　　　　　　 D. Luxurious and comfortable.

男：我聽說你今年夏天做了些不同的事？

女：是的。我在我兄弟的農場度過了夏天。

男：那麼，農場的生活如何？

女：我擠牛奶、餵雞和做了許多其他的事情。

男：聽起來你在那邊玩得開心。

女：我的確如此，但我每天都要很早就起床。

問題：女子對農場生活的想法為何？

選項：A. 輕鬆但有意義的。　　　　　　B. 有趣但具挑戰性的。

　　　 C. 困難且無聊的。　　　　　　　D. 奢侈且舒適的。

C 17. W: Oh my God, Matthew! What happened?

M: Someone punched me in the face and ran off.

W: What? For no reason? That's crazy.

M: Tell me about it. I was just waiting at the bus stop then. Ouch, it really hurts.

W: Should I call an ambulance?

M: I can take care of myself. And, I had called the police.

W: OK. Let me get you an ice pack.

Q: Why does the woman want to call an ambulance?

　　A. There is a car accident.　　　　　B. She needs an ice pack.

　　C. The man was attacked.　　　　　 D. She is going crazy.

女：我的老天，Matthew！發生什麼事了？

男：有個人一拳揍在我臉上然後跑走了。

女：什麼？沒有任何原因嗎？這太瘋狂了。

男：可不是嗎。我那時只是在站牌等公車。噢，真的好痛。

女：我要叫救護車嗎？

男：我能照顧我自己。另外，我已經報案了。

女：好的。讓我去幫你拿冰敷袋。

問題：女子為什麼想要叫救護車？

選項：A. 有一起交通事故。　　　　　　　B. 她需要冰敷袋。
　　　C. 男子被攻擊了。　　　　　　　　D. 她快要瘋了。

C 18. M: Where's Charles? He was supposed to be here at 3 and it's already half past.

W: Where did you tell him we would meet?

M: Right here at the entrance of the bowling alley.

W: Have you tried calling him?

M: I just did, but he didn't answer. I've texted him twice as well.

W: Try Amanda's phone. I bet he's with her.

Q: How many times did the man try to contact Charles?

　　A. Once.　　　　　B. Twice.　　　　　C. Three times.　　　　　D. Four times.

男：Charles 人呢？他應該三點就要到了，現在都超過三點半了。

女：你告訴他我們會在哪裡碰面呢？

男：就在這保齡球館的門口。

女：你有試著打電話給他嗎？

男：我打了，但他沒接。我也傳兩次簡訊給他了。

女：試試看 Amanda 的電話。他八成和 Amanda 在一起。

問題：男子試著連絡 Charles 幾次？

選項：A. 一次。　　　B. 兩次。　　　C. 三次。　　　D. 四次。

B 19. W: Got any ideas for our vacation? I want to do something different this year.

M: I've always wanted to go hiking in New Zealand. What do you think?

W: Ha! Ha! Send me a postcard!

M: OK. Here's a new idea. Something we've never done before. Stay right here at home!

W: That does sound like fun. We can stay home and watch movies.

M: Right, we won't have to put up with rude waiters, crazy taxi drivers, and expensive hotel bills!

Q: Where will the speakers spend their holiday?

　　A. In New Zealand.　　　　　　　　B. In their own house.

　　C. They haven't decided yet.　　　　D. They will spend the vacation apart.

女：對於我們的假期有什麼想法嗎？今年我想做些不一樣的事。

男：我一直都很想到紐西蘭去登山。你覺得呢？

女：哈！哈！寄張明信片給我！

男：好吧。我有個新想法。我們從沒這樣做過。就是待在家裡！

女：這聽起來蠻有趣的。我們能待在家裡、看看電影。

男：對呀，我們不必忍受無禮的服務生、瘋狂的計程車司機還有昂貴的飯店費用！

問題：說話者們會在哪裡度過他們的假期？

選項：A. 在紐西蘭。　　　　　　　　　B. 他們自己家中。

　　　C. 他們還沒決定。　　　　　　　D. 他們會各自度過這個假期。

B 20. M: Mom, where is my school uniform?

W: Isn't there one in your dresser?

M: No. I can't find one anywhere.

W: Oh, I just did the laundry last night. There may be one hanging to dry on the balcony.

Q: Where might the boy find his school uniform?

A. In the dresser.   B. On the balcony.

C. In the dryer.   D. In the washing machine.

男：媽媽，我的學校制服在哪裡？

女：你的衣櫥裡不是有一件嗎？

男：沒有。我到處都找不到。

女：喔，我昨晚才洗衣服。可能有一件在陽臺上晾著。

問題：男孩可能在哪裡找到他的學校制服？

選項：A. 在衣櫥裡。   B. 在陽臺上。   C. 在烘衣機裡。   D. 在洗衣機裡。

A 21. W: My son is really into comic books at the moment. I'm concerned that his good grades might slip.

M: Are you thinking of taking them away from him?

W: Maybe I'll limit them to the weekends only.

M: I'm not sure that's a good idea. It seems like he already knows how to balance between his schoolwork and his love of comic books.

W: I guess you're right. Let's see how things go.

Q: What do we know about the woman's son?

A. Right now, his grades are fine.

B. He can't keep up with his schoolwork.

C. His mother has taken away all his comic books.

D. He mostly reads comic books on Saturdays and Sundays.

女：我兒子現在很喜歡看漫畫。我擔心他優異的成績可能會下滑。

男：你有考慮不讓他看漫畫嗎？

女：或許我會限制只有週末才能看。

男：我不確定這是不是好方法。他似乎知道如何平衡學校功課及他對漫畫的喜愛。

女：我想你是對的。再觀察看看好了。

問題：關於女子的兒子我們得知什麼？

選項：A. 現在他的成績很好。   B. 他無法維持學校功課。

      C. 他母親不讓他看漫畫。   D. 他大多在週六、週日看漫畫。

C 22. M: Let's have Italian food tonight.

W: OK, but remember I can't eat seafood.

M: Why's that?

W: Don't you remember? It makes me itch.

M: Oh, that's right. I had forgotten it makes you sick.

Q: What will the speakers most likely have for dinner?

    A. Shrimp pasta.   B. Mapo tofu.   C. Mushroom pizza.   D. Fried rice.

男：我們今晚吃義大利料理吧。

女：好啊，但記得我不能吃海鮮。

男：為什麼？

女：你忘了嗎？它讓我發癢。

男：喔，對耶。我都忘了它會讓你不舒服。

問題：說話者們晚餐最有可能會吃什麼？

選項：A. 鮮蝦義大利麵。   B. 麻婆豆腐。

        C. 蘑菇披薩。   D. 炒飯。

D 23. W: Excuse me, sir! No photography is allowed inside the train station.

    M: But I was just taking a few shots of the architecture. This is such a wonderful old building.

    W: I'm sorry, but that's the rule. It's for security reasons.

    M: I see. I'll put it away.

    Q: Why can't the man take pictures?

        A. He isn't a photographer.   B. The woman was offended.

        C. The police recognized him.   D. It is a regulation.

女：先生，不好意思！火車站裡不能拍照。

男：但我只是拍幾張這建築的照片。這真是個漂亮的老建築。

女：我很抱歉，但這是規定。這是基於安全理由。

男：了解。我會收起來的。

問題：為什麼男子不能拍照？

選項：A. 他不是一位攝影師。   B. 女子被冒犯了。

        C. 警方認出他來了。   D. 這是一個規定。

B 24. For question number 24, please look at the pie chart.

    M: Among romance, fantasy, comedy, and horror movies, which do you girls like seeing the most?

    W: Fantasy and romance are the most popular types.

    M: These two types are also enjoyed by most boys. What's the third most favorite type for you girls?

    W: It's comedy. This type of movie always makes people laugh and has a happy ending.

    M: How about horror movies?

    W: It is by far the least popular. Last year, I saw a horror movie with my friends, and it gave me nightmares that night.

女生最喜愛的電影類型

    Q: What percentage of girls like comedy movies the most?

    A. 7%.   B. 20%.   C. 35%.   D. 38%.

第二十四題，請看圓餅圖。

男：在愛情片、奇幻片、喜劇片和恐怖片之中，你們女生最喜歡看哪一種？

女：奇幻片和愛情片是最熱門的類型。

男：大部份男生也喜歡這兩類。你們女生最喜歡的第三名類型是什麼？

女：是喜劇片。這種電影總是讓人們發笑且結局皆大歡喜。

男：那恐怖片呢？

女：這是最不受歡迎的。去年，我和朋友看了一部恐怖片，它讓我那晚做了惡夢。

問題：有多少百分比的女生喜歡喜劇片？

選項：A. 7%。　　　　B. 20%。　　　　　C. 35%。　　　　　　D. 38%。

解析　由對話可知喜劇片是女生喜愛的電影類型中的第三名；而根據圓餅圖，占比第三多的是 20%，故答案選 B。

C 25. For question number 25, please look at the menu.

W: What would you like to order?

M: I would like to get a double cheeseburger.

W: Do you want any fries?

M: Large fries, please.

W: Can I get you anything to drink?

M: Sure, a medium Coke.

W: Is that everything?

M: That'll be all. Thanks.

Q: How much will the man pay for his order?

　　A. $9.　　　　　　B. $10.

　　C. $11.　　　　　　D. $12.

菜 單	漢堡	
	牛肉堡 ·········	$6
	起司堡 ·········	$4
	雙層起司堡 ·········	$6
	薯條	
	小份 ·········	$1
	中份 ·········	$2
	大份 ·········	$3
	可樂	
	小杯 ·········	$1
	中杯 ·········	$2
	大杯 ·········	$3

第二十五題，請看菜單。

女：你想要點什麼呢？

男：我想要雙層起司堡。

女：你要薯條嗎？

男：請給我大份的薯條。

女：要喝任何飲料嗎？

男：當然，中杯可樂。

女：就這些嗎？

男：就這些。謝謝。

問題：男子要為他點的東西付多少錢？

選項：A. 9 美元。　　　　B. 10 美元。　　　　C. 11 美元。　　　　D. 12 美元。

解析　由對話可知男子點了雙層起司堡、大份的薯條和中杯可樂；而根據菜單，價錢分別是 6 美元、3 美元、2 美元，所以一共是 11 美元，故答案選 C。

第四部份：簡短談話

B 26. Welcome to the local news. We have a heartwarming story today. A group of five students heard some puppies barking from the riverbank yesterday. The students caught the attention of a truck driver who was passing by, and he lent a hand to rescue the puppies. The driver used his tools to save the puppies. The puppies were cleaned at the school. They are now waiting to be adopted.

Q: Who most likely is the speaker?

    A. A truck driver.   B. A newscaster.   C. A student.   D. An adopter.

歡迎來到地方新聞。今天有一則溫馨的報導。昨天，五名學生聽見河岸傳來一些小狗的叫聲。學生們引起一位路過卡車司機的注意，他伸出援手拯救了小狗。該名司機使用自己的工具將小狗救了上來。小狗在學校清洗乾淨了。現在正等待被領養。

問題：說話者最有可能是誰？

選項：A. 卡車司機。   B. 新聞播報員。   C. 學生。   D. 領養者。

A 27. When I was a little girl, my parents always reminded me that it is very important to have good manners. I had to say "Please" and "Thank you" and needed to ask permission to leave the table at mealtimes. It seems that things are quite different nowadays. Many of the children I know never say "Please" and rarely ever say "Thank you." They eat with their mouth full and are also rude to their parents. However, I still think having good manners is important regardless of your generation.

Q: What does the speaker emphasize about being polite?

    A. It is important to every generation.

    B. Only kids have to be aware of that.

    C. Actions speak louder than words.

    D. Parents should always say "Please" and "Thank you" to their children.

在我還是個小女孩的時候，我父母總是不斷提醒我，有禮貌非常重要。我需要說「請」和「謝謝」，而且用餐時，也要請求准許才能離開餐桌。時至今日，狀況似乎已大不相同。我認識的許多小孩從來都不說「請」，也鮮少會說「謝謝」。他們吃飯時會把嘴巴塞滿，對他們的父母也很沒禮貌。然而，我還是認為，無論你是哪一代的人，禮貌都還是一樣重要。

問題：關於有禮貌這件事作者強調什麼？

選項：A. 它對每個世代都很重要。   B. 只有小孩們需要注意。

      C. 坐而言不如起而行。   D. 父母都應該對孩子說「請」和「謝謝」。

B 28. Do you want to share some interesting videos with your friends and family on the Internet? Come and share your video on our website. You can do that with the following instructions. First, make sure that the video file is in an acceptable format, and it can't exceed 500MB in size. Second, click on the "Upload Now" button. Once the file is uploading, do not leave the web page until the upload is complete. When the upload is complete, your video can be viewed online.

Q: What is the purpose of this advertisement?

    A. To share an interesting video.   B. To promote a video website.

    C. To teach you how to make a video.   D. To sell a useful file cabinet.

你想在網路上跟親朋好友分享一些有趣的影片嗎？快到我們的網站分享你的影片。你可以按照下列的步驟。首先，確定影片檔案的格式可被接受，且檔案大小不能超過 500MB。第二步，點選「現在上傳」鍵。影片一旦開始上傳，請勿在上傳完成前離開網頁。上傳完成後，你的影片就能在線上被觀賞了。

問題：這則廣告的目的是什麼？

選項：A. 分享一段有趣的影片。   B. 推廣一個影音網站。

       C. 教你如何製作影片。   D. 販賣一個好用的檔案櫃。

D 29. Are you interested in eating a healthy diet and living a lifestyle that is kind to animals and to the environment? Then visit our website, *Vegetable Planet*! We provide all kinds of up-to-date information written by experts in health, nutrition, and environmental sciences. But that's not all. There are also hundreds of amazing meat-free recipes to try, and they are all available for free. Visit *Vegetable Planet* today!

Q: Who is most likely to visit this website?

    A. An award-winning chef.   B. An athlete.

    C. A science major.   D. A vegetarian.

你對健康飲食以及對動物和環境都友善的生活方式感興趣嗎？那麼來看看我們的網站「蔬菜行星」吧！我們提供各式各樣的最新資訊，這些資訊都是由健康、營養及環境科學方面的專家們所執筆。但這還不是全部。我們還有數百種超棒的無肉食譜可供你嘗試，完全免費。今天就來「蔬菜行星」逛逛吧！

問題：誰最有可能造訪這個網站？

選項：A. 得獎的主廚。 B. 運動員。   C. 主修科學的學生。   D. 素食者。

C 30. Thank you all for coming today and helping us raise money for the cancer charity. Your generous donations will be put to good use, helping children fight cancer. Your good deeds have not only warmed their hearts but have also given them a chance to overcome their illness. Most importantly, when they are older, I am sure they will be inspired by your kindness to help other people, just like what you have done.

Q: What is the goal of the speaker?

    A. To make children be nicer to each other.

    B. To help the hospital make money.

    C. To assist children with cancer.

    D. To build new children's hospitals.

感謝你們今天蒞臨和幫助我們為癌症慈善團體募款。你們慷慨的捐獻將會善用在幫助孩童對抗癌症。你的善舉不僅溫暖他們的心，還給他們一個戰勝疾病的機會。最重要的是，當他們長大後，我保證他們也會受到你的愛心的啟發而去幫助別人，就像你所做的一樣。

問題：說話者的目標是什麼？

選項：A. 讓孩子們對彼此更好。　　　　　B. 幫助醫院賺錢。

　　　　C. 協助有癌症的孩子。　　　　　D. 蓋新的兒童醫院。

C 31. Good evening, everyone! Welcome to *The Talk Show*. My guests tonight are Kevin and Rose who starred in the movie *Hunters*. The movie is about an entire town of people being hunted by the walking dead. It has been a big hit over the past few months. If you haven't seen *Hunters*, go watch it now! The movie has won several awards.

Q: What is the audience watching?

　　A. They are watching an award ceremony.

　　B. They are watching *Hunters*.

　　C. They are watching *The Talk Show*.

　　D. They are watching Kevin's new movie.

晚安，各位！歡迎來到《脫口秀》。今天晚上的來賓是主演電影《獵人》的 Kevin 及 Rose。這部電影描述整座城鎮的人被喪屍獵捕的故事。過去幾個月來，它的人氣一直居高不下。你若還沒看過《獵人》的話，現在就去看！這部電影已經贏得好幾個獎項。

問題：觀眾正在觀看什麼？

選項：A. 他們正在觀看頒獎典禮。　　　　B. 他們正在觀看《獵人》。

　　　　C. 他們正在觀看《脫口秀》。　　　D. 他們正在觀看 Kevin 的新電影。

A 32. Thank you for inviting me here today to talk about the problem of homelessness. I basically lived under a bridge for 8 years. At the time I was hooked on drugs and was flat broke. I couldn't pay the rent and ended up getting kicked out of my apartment, which made it impossible for me to get a job. Later on in my talk, I'll share some ideas about how to get homeless people off the streets and back into society.

Q: Why did the speaker become homeless?

　　A. He couldn't afford the rent.　　　　B. He sold drugs.

　　C. Someone stole his property.　　　　D. He lost his job.

謝謝你們今天邀請我到這裡來討論關於遊民的問題。基本上我曾住在橋下八年。那時我身染毒癮又完全破產。我無法支付房租最後被趕出我的公寓，而這也使我無法找到工作。稍後在演講中，我會跟大家分享幾個如何使遊民遠離街頭並且回歸社會的方法。

問題：為什麼說話者變成遊民？

選項：A. 他付不起房租。　　　　　　　　B. 他販毒。

　　　　C. 有人竊取他的財產。　　　　　D. 他失去工作。

B 33. The flowers are in bloom, the birds are singing, and you can smell spring in the air! Imagine that you can see a pretty garden every morning. It is wonderful, isn't it? Now, you can create one in your house without spending a lot of money. This month in *DIY Magazine*, you can learn not only how to build your own beautiful garden, but also the tips on decorating a garden. *DIY Magazine* is for people who love to do things by themselves. Get yourself a copy in bookstores everywhere.

Q: What is offered by this month's *DIY Magazine*?

    A. Knowing how to run your own grocery store.

    B. Learning how to build a beautiful garden.

    C. Finding a place to grow flowers.

    D. Gaining your confidence in doing things by yourself.

百花盛開，鳥兒歌唱，你可以嗅到春天的氣息！想像你每天早上都能看到一個漂亮的花園。真是太棒了，不是嗎？現在，不必花大錢你就能在家裡建造一個這樣的花園。這個月的《自己動手做雜誌》中，你不僅能學到如何打造你個人的美麗花園，也能學到裝飾花園的祕訣。《自己動手做雜誌》要獻給那些喜愛自己動手做東西的人。快到各地書局去買一本吧。

問題：本月《自己動手做雜誌》提供什麼內容？

選項：A. 知道怎麼經營自己的雜貨店。   B. 學習如何蓋一座漂亮的花園。

        C. 找到種花的地方。   D. 增加由自己動手做的信心。

B 34. For question number 34, please look at the poster.

Drama Club will put on a fantastic play, *Who Killed John?*, this Friday. The play begins with the wedding of Gloria and Tony. Oscar is sad because his father, John, who was the former CEO, died, and his mother has married the new CEO. He suspects Tony might have killed his father. As Oscar tries to take revenge on Tony, he kills Bill accidentally. Meanwhile, his lover, Mary, goes mad. In the end, he finds the murderer of his father turns out to be Gloria, not Tony.

Q: In the play, which character killed the former CEO?

    A. The new CEO.   B. Oscar's mother.

    C. Oscar's lover.   D. Oscar's best friend.

第三十四題，請看海報。

本週五戲劇社團將主演一齣精采好戲《誰殺了 John？》。這齣戲以 Gloria 和 Tony 的婚禮開場。Oscar 很傷心，因為他的父親，John，也就是前任總裁，過世了，他的媽媽則嫁給了新任總裁。他懷疑 Tony 可能殺了他的父親。當 Oscar 試圖向 Tony 報復時，他意外地殺死了 Bill。與此同時，他的戀人 Mary 瘋了。最後，他發現殺了他父親的凶手原來是 Gloria，而不是 Tony。

問題：在這齣戲中，哪一個人物殺了前任總裁？

選項：A. 新任總裁。   B. Oscar 的媽媽。   C. Oscar 的戀人。   D. Oscar 的至交。

解析   由談話可知凶手是 Gloria；而根據海報內容，Gloria 是 Oscar 的媽媽，故答案選 B。

A 35. For question number 35, please look at the shuttle bus route map.

Our free shuttle bus service is available to all the guests of Holiday Hotel. We offer three routes. Route B operates on weekdays, while Routes A and C operate on weekends. All the three routes run from 8 a.m. to 9 p.m. If you want to go to any place along Route B on weekends, you may take the other two routes instead and get off at a nearby stop.

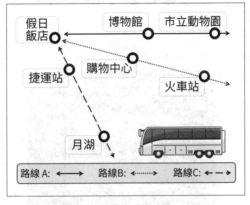

Q: Two hotel guests want to go to the shopping mall this Sunday. At which stop should they get off?

    A. Museum.   B. Shopping Mall.   C. MRT Station.   D. Railway Station.

第三十五題，請看接駁公車路線圖。

我們的免費接駁公車服務供給所有假日飯店的客人使用。我們提供三條路線。路線 B 在平日運行，而路線 A 和 C 在週末運行。所有三條路線都是從上午八點運行到晚上九點。如果你在週末要去路線 B 沿線地點，你可以搭乘另外兩條路線作為代替並在靠近的車站下車。

問題：兩位飯店房客想在本週日去購物中心。他們應該在哪一站下車？

選項：A. 博物館站。   B. 購物中心站。   C. 捷運站。   D. 火車站。

解析 由接駁公車路線圖可知購物中心站屬於路線 B；而根據談話，週末要去路線 B 沿線地點，可搭乘另外兩條路線作為代替並在靠近的車站下車，最靠近購物中心站的是路線 A 的博物館站，故答案選 A。

全民英檢單字通（二版）

三民英語編輯小組　彙編

單字書隨行，英檢輕鬆贏！

- 內容完全符合財團法人語言訓練測驗中心公布之全民英檢中級參考字表。
- 隨字列出同反義字、片語、例句，相關資料一網打盡。
- 口袋大小隨身攜帶，讓你走到哪、背到哪，每天累積字彙實力。

全民英檢新制上路，應試SO EASY！

◆ 完全符合新制全民英檢中級聽力測驗，讓你掌握最新題型。

◆ 全書共8回，情境、用字、語法等皆符合全民英檢中級程度。

◆ 提供試題範例分析，精闢解說各題型解題技巧與出題方向。

◆ 解析採用活動式的夾冊設計，讓你輕鬆對照題目，方便閱讀。

◆ 隨書附電子朗讀音檔，由專業外籍錄音員錄製。讓你培養語感、提升應試熟悉度。

三民網路書店
www.sanmin.com.tw